and piano mu  lie
stopped and le
"You are ed
serious again.

Garrett thought he'd misheard her for a moment.
"Pardon?"

"I said you are really quite lucky."

He had not misheard. "How is that?"

"If you were a woman and you acted with such
disregard toward society"—she slanted him a sideways
and disapproving glance—"as you have, there would be
no second chances for you. A lady could never act as a
rake and be forgiven." She slipped his jacket off and
handed it back to him. He looked down at the jacket,
not sure what she expected him to do with it.

"Take it. I am fine now. I will enter through the
back, and you may use the front door. It is best nobody
knows we spent so much time together, alone."

He took the jacket, not bothering to slip it back on.
He just stood there dumbfounded, watching her. "Why
would a lady wish to play the part of a rake?" he
couldn't help asking. Was she referring to *herself*?

The girlish sparkle disappeared from her eyes, and
a bleak longing replaced it.

A Lady's Prerogative

by

Annabelle Anders

Lord Love a Lady Series, Book 2

A Lady's Prerogative

COPYRIGHT © 2018 by Annabelle Anders

Cover Art by *Debbie Taylor*

The Wild Rose Press, Inc.
PO Box 708
Adams Basin, NY 14410-0708
Visit us at www.thewildrosepress.com

Publishing History
First Tea Rose Edition, 2018
Print ISBN 978-1-5092-2069-4
Digital ISBN 978-1-5092-2070-0

Lord Love a Lady Series, Book 2
Published in the United States of America

Dedication

To my husband,
who reads my work (under duress)
but provides suggestions and encouragement.
And to my mom,
who is my best beta reader and cheerleader!

Chapter One

May 1824

Less than twenty-four hours ago, Lady Natalie Spencer had been an engaged lady—a future duchess. Today she was the object of London's latest scandal. And on this particular morning, the esteemed daughter of the Earl of Ravensdale was like any other girl, awaiting her father's punishment and the lecture he was sure to dole out.

For yesterday, only one week before the wedding, she'd broken off her engagement to the Duke of Cortland. Despite the extenuating circumstances, she was a jilt. It was time to face the music. Her parents had demanded her presence in the study first thing this morning. After handpicking and then practically courting the duke himself, her father was none too happy.

Natalie's maid, Mrs. Tinsdale, helped her dress for the occasion with care, admonishing her to not appear overly pleased *nor* terribly distraught. The day dress they settled on was well cut but unimaginative, fashioned from a dull lavender muslin. It was a gown a lady might wear if she were in half-mourning. Natalie's blonde hair was pulled back from her face, braided tightly, and wound about her head. With the accentuated paleness of her face and the circles under her eyes, Natalie felt her appearance was appropriate for the solemn mood the occasion demanded. Over and over, Tinsdale urged Natalie to try to be demure. "For your own sake, dearie," she said.

And so Natalie sat straight backed, with her feet flat on the floor and her knees pressed together. Twisting her hands in her lap, she took a deep breath when Lord and Lady Ravensdale stepped in and quietly closed the door behind them.

Her father's presence filled the room. He did not sit but stood behind his imposing desk, hands clasped behind his back. Her mother dropped into the chair adjacent to Natalie's. Thank heaven her mother was not the vaporish sort! Her father did not require further aggravation.

Following Natalie's emotional outburst the previous day, his lordship had promised she *would* be held accountable this morning. Her mother shrugged and smiled tentatively in encouragement. Her father cast his eyes downwards and scowled.

"Well, my girl," her father began, using his very serious voice (the one he used when he wished to inflict the greatest amount of guilt on one of his children). "I am none too pleased at the disgrace you've brought upon your family. What in God's name were you thinking? You promised yourself to the duke! I expect a daughter of mine to keep her promises." With a quick glance at her mother, he asked, "Has notice of the broken engagement been sent to all the papers?"

In her normal calm and efficient manner, Mama responded, "First thing this morning, dear."

Lord Ravensdale nodded before turning his attention back to his daughter. "We will remove you from society for what remains of the Season and then confine you at Raven's Park for the summer. There will be no house parties for you, young lady. No traveling. No suitors and no balls—not even country assemblies."

"But Papa—"

Her mother broke in to reassure her, "But it is believed, Natalie, by Aunt Eleanor and me, that if you remain above reproach this summer, you may participate in the Little Season this autumn. Then, assuming you behave properly of course, you may take up your position, once again, in society next spring. With your dowry, there will be no shortage of suitors, darling. I have no concerns on that point."

Hearing mention of the dowry, her father winced. "Cortland won't sue for breach of contract. A saving grace, for certain." Lord Ravensdale's voice was less cajoling than his wife's. "But you must regain the approval of the *ton* if we're ever to land you a husband half as suitable as the duke." An expression akin to physical pain crossed her father's features. He was undeniably very sorry to have lost the Duke of Cortland as a son-in-law. "A perfect match broken—such a shame." And then recalling his previous train of thought he continued, "Otherwise, I could not care less what those old biddies think."

"Broderick." Her mother shot the earl a warning look.

Her father pinched the bridge of his nose. "What I would like to know, daughter, is why you consented in the first place. I had always thought you were a young lady who knew her own mind." Before she could begin to answer, he went right on speaking. "Your indecisiveness has wasted a great deal of time and money for the duke, the solicitors, myself, and your mother. In addition to all of that, you have tarnished your reputation and the good name of this family. I chose a man who would treat you well, a man I could trust. By jilting him, you've made me look a fool! What were you thinking, girl?" In the midst of his tirade, he began pacing. And then, clenching his jaw, he ceased moving and fell silent.

Natalie stared at her father innocently. She did not feel guilty for her decision, only the timing of it.

"Do you wish for me to answer your questions, Father, or are they rhetorical?"

His eyes narrowed. "I would have an answer," he said curtly. Her tone had obviously not pleased him.

Summoning a meeker countenance, Natalie schooled her features and stared solemnly at the colorful rug upon the floor. "I accepted the duke's proposal, Father, because I did not wish to disappoint *you*." She raised her gaze to his face and pouted. "At the time, it all felt very sensible. Father chooses a governess; I mind my governess. Father says I am to have my come out; I make my entrance in society. Father chooses me a husband; I marry the husband. But a marriage is not the same thing, is it?" She held her eyes wide as she pleaded with her father. "It is not! And the wedding date was getting closer and closer and I…" She swallowed a not entirely feigned sob. "I did not want to disappoint you, but I could not go through with it. Marriage is for life. I want to love my husband, just as you love Mother." She looked over at her mother. "And just as Mother loves you."

She could hardly blame her father for feeling thwarted. She *had* consented, after all, when the duke

4

proposed—despite her reservations.

Like a child, she'd been more concerned with pleasing her papa than considering her future as the Duchess of Cortland. The farce of her engagement had proceeded far too long. Any longer and she might have jilted him at the altar. *That would not have gone over well.*

And then she thought of Lilly. "Would you have me marry a man who is in love with another woman, Papa?" Natalie dared ask. She was not the only one at fault. Why must she take all the blame?

Her father's voice thundered. "He is a man of honor. We had already signed the contracts. It would not have been an issue." He did not appreciate it when his children challenged his decisions—especially if said child was his only daughter.

Natalie took a breath to argue further, but her mother put out a hand and interjected.

"What the duke would or would not have done is not our concern. Our concern is restoring Natalie's reputation and moving beyond this scandal." Her mother's voice had a calming effect on the earl, but Natalie's eyes still glared defiantly.

After an uncomfortable silence, her father cleared his throat. "Very well." But he continued his tirade. "We shall leave for Raven's Park immediately following Joseph's nuptials. At least all the money I've put out for the ceremony and reception will not go to waste." Late last night, it had been decided that Natalie's brother, recently engaged himself, would utilize the church on the date Natalie and the duke were to have been married.

"Is that all then, Father?" Natalie stood, ready to

escape, hoping the interview was concluded.

"It is not. Sit back down. I've a few rules you will follow until we leave London." Not giving in to the urge to sigh loudly, Natalie dropped back into her seat and made herself comfortable. *Demure, be demure.*

Her father and mother then listed a litany of requirements to be adhered to in order to minimize her social fallout.

She was to remain in the townhouse unseen for the entire week while they awaited Joseph's wedding, the wedding that was to have been her own.

She was not to go shopping.

She was not to go to Gunter's with her friends.

She was not to receive any visitors.

Nor write any letters.

In no uncertain terms, she was to be kept out of the public eye until they departed for London.

Surely she could not stay locked inside for the entire week! As her father's little princess, Natalie usually was able to soften her father up when he was angry. And she needed some sort of freedom for goodness sake! That being said, it took her a considerable amount of beseeching for him to relent. Eventually, he gave her permission to take one thirty-minute walk per day, in Hyde Park, with her chaperone, in the morning hours only.

She was not to stop.

She was not to converse with anyone.

She was not to extend the thirty minutes to thirty-two minutes or even to thirty-one minutes. If she did not follow these rules exactly, she would lose this privilege as well.

With that settled, Natalie sought one more

concession. "May I attend the wedding?" Despite her extreme reluctance to be in the church on that particular day, she could not imagine missing Joseph's wedding.

Her father looked to his wife for her opinion.

"The ceremony, I think," Mother said, "but not the breakfast."

They all sat without speaking for several moments, the rhythmic ticking of the ancient long-case clock the only sound in the room. Containing her desire to escape for as long as possible, Natalie waited two whole minutes before speaking. "May I be excused now, Papa?"

With narrowed eyes, her father pointed one finger at her. "You had better not disobey me! I will have your complete obedience, Natalie. And lest you find yourself tempted, remember your aunt Mary lives in Scotland and I am not opposed to sending you up there for a year or two, if necessary."

Of course he would never do such a thing!

"Yes, Papa." Natalie rushed around the desk to kiss her father's weathered cheek and then dashed from the study. Relief swept through her to be finished with such disagreeable business. She would obey her father's silly rules, and before she knew it, all this rubbish would be far behind her. She simply needed to avoid trouble until after Joseph's wedding. That ought not to be so hard. The Season *was* winding down, after all. How difficult could it be?

****

The newly titled Earl of Hawthorne braced himself as three familiar gentlemen strolled toward him along the walk. They were men with whom he'd broken bread, wagered cards, and practiced fisticuffs at

Gentleman Jackson's. As they neared him, their conversation halted and their countenances transformed from pleasure to distaste. All six eyes focused on some unknown distant object behind him. The only sound was their booted heels and wooden canes tapping along the pavement as they passed. This wasn't the first time he'd received the cut today.

Walking aimlessly upon leaving his new office at Whitehall, Garrett Castleton resisted the urge to turn around and call the three of them out. Instead he clenched his fists and increased his pace. News of his father's crimes had spread quickly, and men he'd considered friends now treated him as though he had the plague. It ought not to bother him.

Although the morning air was cool, he reached up and tugged at his cravat. Resentment festered in his chest. To avoid any further unpleasant encounters, Garrett crossed the street to Hyde Park and headed down one of its less populated paths. The leaves rustled in the trees as a gentle gust stirred the air. Any breeze this time of year in London was welcome.

Unfortunately, solitude was not to be his for long. For the fragrant waft of nature carried with it the distinctive scent of ladies' perfume. Oh, wonderful, Lady Natalie Spencer—diamond of the first water—was just ahead. Careful to avoid soiling her slippers, she daintily picked her way toward him with a maid in tow. Just what he needed, another snub by one of London's elite.

He slowed his pace and scrutinized her, not bothering to move to one side or the other. By no stretch of the imagination was he feeling amicable in that moment.

She looked pale and fragile, wearing an icy blue confection of a dress. Of course, she carried the ridiculous ruffles and lace elegantly, not a bit of it hindering her practiced grace. Atop blonde tresses, she wore a jaunty hat, decorated with, of all things, two ladybugs and a butterfly. Ladies of the *ton* never failed to surprise him in their frivolousness.

Apparently sensing his presence, she glanced up. Garrett watched her lashes flutter and noted her blue eyes widen before shifting away.

He halted, opened his stance, and planted his boots on each side of the path. The trail was narrow here. She would be forced to acknowledge his presence if she wished to pass. In no mood to play the gallant, he removed his hat and bowed mockingly.

"My lady." His gaze travelled the length of her. He did nothing to hide his appraisal. In fact, he allowed it to linger over her tiny waist, bodice, and exposed décolletage. A flush spread across her creamy skin.

Hesitating for only a moment, with downcast eyes, the lady dipped into a flawless curtsey. "My lord…" She still had not looked directly at him. "I'll thank you for permitting my maid and me to pass." Garrett's eyes fixed upon a loose curl dangling teasingly over one silken shoulder. His mind conjured up thoughts of how her skin might taste, how it would feel beneath his lips. In another world, she would be his for the taking.

But not in this one.

Although acquainted with the girl's father and brothers, he'd never been allowed an introduction to the delicate flower herself. "We've not been introduced, my lady. The Earl of Hawthorne at your service." His tone made a mockery of his words. Standing before her, he was aggravated to note he suddenly felt coarse and brutish. How could he not? She embodied all of that which polite society esteemed.

She bit her lip and looked about, as though seeking escape. He could have sworn her sapphire eyes flashed. "You'll excuse me please, my lord. I haven't time to converse." For the first time, he noticed she clutched a timepiece tightly. She glanced at it and frowned.

Goaded by her cool demeanor, Garrett reached out and snagged her fingers in his. Unwilling to release her, he pried opened her palm to reveal the gold watch. She held herself rigid. Did he frighten her, or was she merely too proud to tug against his grip? With an irresistible urge to shock her sensibilities, he raised her hand to his lips. Turning it over, he pressed his open mouth upon the silk of her glove and then slowly slid his tongue along the sleek fabric.

The silk was scented with something floral, but the material itself tasted sweet. Cruel satisfaction infused his cold heart when he felt her tremble. "A lady such as yourself should never be hurried. Won't you allow me to escort you to your destination?"

She glanced up with a shudder. Her expression nearly crushed him.

She was horrified!

Shaking her head from side to side, she practically cringed. "Oh, no! You mustn't, my lord. My father...I cannot possibly...No one must see me speaking to you!" and then pulling her hand from his, she grasped her maid from behind and pushed her way past. As she did so, the tight space of the path forced her to brush her entire person against him.

"I'm so very sorry, my lord," she mumbled into his

coat as she passed. For such a feminine creature, she'd shown surprising strength. As his hands instinctively grasped her hips, he was momentarily, and most inconveniently, tempted by the womanly curves pressed against him. But Lady Natalie Spencer's response was chilling. He would detain her no longer. For but a moment he wished she weren't *one of them.*

But only for a moment.

And then, she disappeared as quickly as she'd come.

More than even before, he burned to depart London and all it represented. Even if that meant returning to Maple Hall.

He had one last appointment today, and then he would leave and perhaps never return. He only wished he could dispense with his father's dubious legacy so easily.

****

Sharing a pint of ale with one of his oldest friends, Garrett suppressed a twinge of guilt. Stone Spencer, ironically enough, was an elder brother to the lady he'd practically accosted not an hour ago, in the park.

Having just returned to London, Stone had suggested sharing a quick drink at this place, an anonymous pub, just outside Mayfair. He would have known that Garrett wasn't welcome at White's. Even Brooks' would balk if Garrett were to present himself.

Shame prodded Garrett as his old schoolmate ordered another round of drinks. Along with everyone else, Stone could have easily severed ties with Garrett. But he did not. In fact, he admonished some of those who had. And he worried for Garrett, God save him. The last thing Garrett wanted was pity.

"When you retrieve your mother's trunks, you must stay at Raven's Park for at least a fortnight," Stone insisted. "*My* mother will expect nothing less." The season was wrapping up, and much of London society was preparing to remove themselves to various country estates for the warmer months. Raven's Park was one of the finest.

Although tempted, Garrett had misgivings. In spite of his and Stone's lengthy friendship, and a few business transactions with the earl, Garrett had always done his best to keep himself separate from the Spencer clan. He was an outsider.

As he'd come to realize how perverse his own father was, he'd increasingly avoided invitations which would put him close to "normal" families such as Stone's. Hearing Stone's stories and adolescent complaints had taunted him enough.

To accept their hospitality now might feel something like…charity.

He'd also belatedly recalled the daughter had recently broken her engagement to a duke. The last thing the family would wish for at this time would be to associate with one such as himself.

Ravensdale, perhaps, as they'd done business together in the past. But the mother was a high stickler, and Lady Natalie—although she looked like an angel—had proven again today that she considered herself superior.

Even before the scandal with his father, she'd given Garrett the cut direct on several occasions. And now she'd jilted a duke—the Duke of Cortland, no less!

The thought of Ravensdale's ire directed at the spoiled miss gave Garrett a small measure of gratification. He must have been livid, for the union between Cortland and Lady Natalie would have been a dynastic one. Garrett couldn't help shaking his head in wonder at the chit's impudence. Ravensdale might lock her away for years, under the circumstances. He wondered that she'd appeared in public at all.

But none of that concerned him.

"Maple Hall's reduced to a pile of rubble, Stone. I can't take a holiday now."

His friend persisted. "Maple Hall isn't going anywhere. Stop in there first, if you must, but then come to Raven's Park and stay for a spell. I refuse to take no for an answer. You must collect your belongings regardless. Might as well take a holiday, allow yourself some time to rest—to grieve. I'm certain Mother won't be entertaining, what with Natalie's little scandal. We'll get in some fishing, perhaps some hunting, and in the village, other amusements." Stone waggled his eyebrows, mocking Garrett's serious countenance.

"I will not mourn him," Garrett said.

At which point Stone became serious again. "Nonetheless, you will come?"

Garrett felt his resolve weakening. Stone was relentless when he chose to be. "Very well. I do need to address the conditions at Maple Hall first, so it will be close to a fortnight before I arrive. I have your word you'll notify me if your parents object to the idea?"

"Absolutely."

Garrett shook his head again, exasperated. He hoped this visit wasn't a mistake.

Chapter Two

The morning of Joseph's wedding, Tinsdale chose for Natalie a pale-yellow dress embellished with an abundance of frothy tulle and delicate lace. It was an abomination!

Glancing away from her image in the looking glass, Natalie glared at her maid and insisted the dress be removed from her person at once. This would not do. She wanted to look…sophisticated. The dress Tinsdale had selected made her look naïve and pretentious. *What was Tinny thinking?*

"But you look so pretty, dearie." Tinsdale frowned as she brushed at the gown and fluffed the skirts.

"Tinny, I look like a wedding cake. You of all people know I wish to draw as little attention to myself as possible." Even without the abominable dress, she would be subject to unkind scrutiny and vicious gossip. *This was to have been* her *wedding, for goodness' sake!* In that instant, Natalie knew which dress she would wear. She had purchased a particular gown as part of her trousseau. It was made for a married woman.

She located it herself and presented it to Tinny. "I shall not be an object of pity," she asserted. "But we must hurry. Papa doesn't like to wait, and I've no wish to anger him more than I already have."

Not an inch of lace adorned the new ensemble. Made up of autumn browns and reds, the French gown was sophisticated and sleek. It did not flounce. Rather, it swirled. The tones were muted, and Natalie was satisfied with the effect in the mirror as Tinsdale buttoned long gloves just past her elbows. Looking from side to side, she examined her hair in the mirror and then dismissed Tinsdale. After the maid departed, Natalie added a touch of paint to her lips and then dabbed at them with a handkerchief.

She felt like a different woman. It had been an entire week since she'd appeared in society, and she'd spoken to no one outside her family except for that dreadful man! She shivered at the memory of his nearness, his heat when she'd swept past him. There had been an anger burning behind his eyes, and despite his feigned kindness, he'd seemed dangerous indeed! For the remainder of that day, she'd thought of little else but the encounter. And he'd had the temerity to offer her his escort! Papa would have had an apoplexy!

Shaking her head, Natalie pushed the memory aside.

Today, she needed all the confidence she could muster. With one final glance, she took a deep breath and went to join her family.

And then a thought hit her.

What a very different morning this would have been if she had not jilted the duke. The mere idea was enough to make her shudder.

****

As sister to the groom, Natalie sat behind her parents in the second pew on the right side of the church. She was not alone. Her three other brothers, Darlington, Stone, and Peter, sat protectively beside her.

The Earl and Countess of Ravensdale had been blessed with four sons and one daughter. Natalie was the youngest, and Joseph the brother closest to her in age. And today he would marry. He would leave his family and cleave unto his wife. Natalie swallowed the lump which had formed in her throat and felt her eyes well with unshed tears.

Watching the bride walk down the aisle, Natalie had the oddest feeling, as though she were attending her own wedding in another person's body.

The bride carried *Natalie's* flowers, *Natalie's* ribbons decorated the pews, and the music vibrating from the large organ at the back of the church played the hymns *Natalie* had chosen. Not one detail of her meticulous planning was discarded.

But Natalie had even more cause for discomfort. Her ex-fiancé and his new wife sat in the pew just across the aisle. In an ironic twist of fate spun by the universe specifically to embarrass Natalie, the bride, Glenda Beauchamp, was niece to the Duchess of Cortland. Although recently married, the duke and duchess had not yet left for their own honeymoon. Of course, they would not. Lilly, the duchess, was like a mother to Glenda. She would not miss the girl's wedding.

Natalie watched as Lilly raised her hand to her eye to capture a stray tear. The duke noticed as well and with a tender look, discreetly placed a handkerchief in his wife's hand. The smile she bestowed upon him was full of love.

And then the duchess glanced toward Natalie. She was one of the only guests to not look away when Natalie met her eyes. Her watery smile, instead, held an abundance of gratitude. Natalie felt her own expression soften and tipped her head ever so slightly in acknowledgement. She'd done the right thing. Of course, she had!

Her former betrothed, Michael Redmond, the Duke of Cortland, was not unattractive or unkind in any way. She esteemed him. She even respected him.

But there had been no *passion,* no *romance* between them whatsoever. And as their wedding date neared, this deficiency grew to matter more than everything else.

Not to mention he was in love with another woman, Lilly Beauchamp.

And thank heaven for Lilly! Although Natalie's mother said she ought to be angry with the woman her former fiancé loved, Natalie was not. In fact, she would forever be grateful to her. For seeing the duke and Lilly, so very much in love, had infused Natalie with the courage to cry off. Cortland might never have ended their engagement, left to do so on his own. She had done him a great favor. She'd done them both a great favor!

No doubt other women would not have released the duke. They would have seen the chance to become a duchess as the opportunity of a lifetime. But Natalie did not.

She would never regret it; of that, she was certain.

She turned to watch the proceedings at the altar.

She would not cry. She *could* not cry. Too many people watched her. They would think she regretted her decision. It took all her self-control to keep her chin up and a polite smile on her lips. She was Lady Natalie Spencer. She needed no one's pity.

"By the power invested in me, I now pronounce Mr. Joseph Spencer and Miss Glenda Beauchamp, by the joining of hands and the giving and receiving of rings as witnessed by God, to be man and wife…" The bishop raised his hands in prayer over the couple as he ended the ceremony, and Joseph, bending forward, placed a chaste kiss on his bride's lips.

Natalie's mother sniffed and pressed a handkerchief to her mouth. Natalie's father, of course, was stoic and controlled. Or so he seemed. He loved all his children and was likely filled with both sadness and joy seeing Joseph marry. In the moment before Joseph and Glenda turned to face the congregation, Natalie watched as her father's jaw clenched. He was not unaffected.

And then the bride and groom were leaving the church, and it was all over. Not allowing Natalie to mingle with the rest of the congregation following the newly married couple outside, Peter—ever the protective brother—took her by the arm and escorted her through a side door and into a waiting carriage.

She would not attend the breakfast.

Tinsdale was dressed for travel and readied to depart without delay for Raven's Park. Settling into the cushioned seat, Natalie was grateful her mother had not allowed her to attend the breakfast. As the travelling coach pulled into traffic, she allowed her tears to fall.

She felt both happy and sad for Joseph. She was happy for Lilly and the duke. And she was frightened for herself. Would she ever find love? Natalie collapsed into Tinsdale's familiar warmth and allowed her old nanny to comfort her.

"There, there, luv," Tinsdale cooed. "Let's get you

home. Everything will work out. You trust your old nurse now. You'll feel much better when we get home."

****

After two days of travel, being at home had, in fact, brought Natalie some small comfort. At least here, she could go outside whenever she wished. She could spend hours at a time taking nature walks outdoors—alone—without a maid trailing her.

But even that was not enough to shake her doldrums.

So, upon sensing a lowering of her father's watch, on this particular morning, Natalie took it upon herself to venture off the estate and go into the village alone.

Rising earlier than all but the servants, Natalie set out on foot, determined to enjoy the beautiful day. She'd known these people as far back as she could remember and welcomed the familiarity of the village as she greeted the milliner, the baker, and the dressmaker. But ultimately, she still just felt...flat. Everything, everyone else, it seemed, was exactly the same as always.

It was she who had changed.

Despondent, Natalie headed home. Perhaps tomorrow she would take some baskets around to the poor. Her mother swore helping others was the best way to lift one's own spirits. She wished she'd had the foresight to think of this today. For already, restlessness nipped at her heels once again.

Natalie's agitation increased even further when she stepped into the foyer of the large country manor. Mr. Winston, the ever-present butler, stood at the door to assist her, the same as he'd done a million times before. He waited patiently as she removed her bonnet and then unbuttoned and peeled off her gloves.

Looking up to thank him, Natalie noticed a small nick along the butler's jaw. "Still letting Marcus practice on you, Winston?" she asked. Winston did not deserve her ire. He'd done nothing to cause it.

Mr. Winston nodded. "Indeed, my lady. He is improving, though." Pointing to the cut, he added, "This one is from two days ago. I'm hoping it's the last."

Marcus was a favorite amongst the servants. At seventeen, the illegitimate son of her father's valet hoped to become a gentleman's gentleman himself someday. He'd yet to master the fine art of shaving though.

Natalie unconsciously touched her own face. A cut with a razor must be painful indeed! Her smile brightened momentarily. "You are too kind, Winston, far too kind."

The sound of rapid footsteps descending the large curving staircase interrupted her musing. Neither her mother, her father, nor any servant clipped down the stairs in such a carefree fashion. She gawked upwards and let out a happy squeal. Stone!

He and Darlington had been traveling throughout all of England this spring, and they'd barely arrived back in London in time to attend Joseph's wedding. She, of course, had not been able to stay to visit with them. They must have arrived home while she was out.

She was *so* happy to see him! His dear, sardonic smile told her he understood exactly what she was going through. In possession of considerably more charm than her other brothers, Stone had the uncanny ability to turn her mood without uttering a single word.

His easy-going personality made him an excellent counterbalance for Roman, the eldest and their father's heir.

She ran up the steps and threw herself into his arms. "Oh, Stone! I am so happy to see you!" Her brother grasped the balustrade so the exuberance of her welcome didn't send them both tumbling. Laughing, he returned her embrace affectionately with his free arm.

Natalie spoke into his shirt front. "You certainly took your time in London. You are staying for a while, aren't you? I've been so miserable!" She hadn't spoken with him in ages, so she had no difficulty summoning a few tears to garner sympathy. What a pitiful creature she was turning into! "With Joseph gone, I have been so bored. Papa is being a tyrant."

Stone tilted her chin up and frowned.

"Ah, Nat, it can't be all that bad." He stepped back and looked her over in mock judgment. "You are still in one piece. All of your parts appear to be in working order."

She summoned a tremulous smile, and his blue eyes sparkled back at her. He could be merciless in his teasing.

"But, Stone, Mama's guests are ancient! I'm stuck here all summer with none of my friends, and I have absolutely no one to talk to! You cannot imagine how utterly wretched Father has been."

Stone dropped his arm around her shoulders and led her down the majestic staircase. "I thought Monfort was here," he said with a quick glance in her direction. "I was surprised to hear they were hosting a party at all. Nobody tells me anything."

Natalie would hardly consider it a "party." Her

mother's guests were all at least twice her age, if not three times! The Duke of Monfort was somewhere near his late thirties, but might as well have been seventy, for all his irritability and lack of humor. "Monfort doesn't count."

Stone emitted a low chuckle. "So you are not heartbroken then, over the loss of Cortland? Just suffering from the consequences, eh?" Pulling her toward the back of the house, he stopped for a moment to regard her affectionately. "And feeling sorry for yourself, too, I'll bet." At Natalie's rueful nod, he guided them down another stairway to the kitchen. "I must locate some trunks a friend left here for safekeeping a few years ago. Tell me everything while we track them to ground."

"Have you asked Mrs. Winston where they might be?" Natalie was intrigued. "What's in them? Whose trunks are they?" She was ready to jump on any undertaking, no matter how minor, if Stone was involved. His mere presence lifted her disposition.

With a hint of condescension, Stone answered her barrage of questions. "I am in search of Mrs. Winston this very minute, as *of course* she will know where they are stored. As for what is *inside* of the trunks, you will have to ask Lord Hawthorne. He merely told me they were important to him, and he did not trust them in his father's care. With good cause, apparently. Seeing that the old man torched Maple Hall."

"*That man* isn't coming here, is he?" She wrinkled her nose in distaste, remembering his demeanor in the park, and on several occasions before that. She didn't care so much what his father had done. The new earl had established his own rakish reputation with no trouble at all, thank you very much. And yet...she shivered at the memory of his nearness...

Stone continued to drag her along without answering. When he caught sight of the sturdy woman who kept house at Raven's Park, he greeted her warmly. Within the same household, a butler marrying the housekeeper was highly unusual, but Natalie's father, having come into the earldom later in life, kept an open mind regarding such matters. He wasn't nearly as traditional as many of England's noblemen.

Mrs. Winston curtsied in Stone's direction and then brushed her hands together efficiently. She never failed to be in the middle of some task or another. "What may I do for you, Mr. Stone? Did you wish me to have Cook add something special to the menu this evening?"

"Whatever she prepares will be heavenly, I'm sure," Stone assured her. "But for now, I need assistance in locating Lord Hawthorne's trunks." He gave her a description of the items he'd stored for his old school friend and the approximate date when they'd arrived. Before he finished talking, Mrs. Winston was nodding. "They are on the third floor, I believe, in the farthest of the servant's quarters not currently being used. Last room facing the back."

Stone thanked her and headed for the servants' stairway. Natalie followed him anxiously.

"Is he not something of a rake, Stone? After this nasty business with his father, ought you to continue associating with him?" Natalie persisted, taking up the conversation where they'd left off. She'd not told anyone how Lord Hawthorne had stopped her in Hyde Park the other morning. Whenever she recalled the encounter, her conscience niggled at her.

Notwithstanding Garrett Castleton's suggestive behavior, the brief meeting had left her ashamed of her own.

Stone stopped and turned to look down at her. His light brown hair was mussed, but his features looked earnest. He seemed to consider his words carefully before speaking. "Not all families are like ours. We have caring parents, aunts, and uncles. We have each other, Natalie. Not only did Garrett lack a mother growing up, but his father was a madman. You can't imagine…" Stone's jaw set, and his eyes narrowed. "My friend did not have a normal childhood."

Remembering how Lord Hawthorne had taken hold of her hand and refused to step aside for her, Natalie bristled. "But the earl acquired his own reputation! He must be nearing thirty. He wasn't *forced* by his father to become such a rogue. He's made these choices as an adult!"

Stone sighed in exasperation and resumed climbing. After they'd ascended a few more steps, he spoke again. "Lord Hawthorne is a good man, and Father agrees. You, my dear Nat, must stop giving so much attention to what so-called polite society says about him. What are they saying about you, my dear sister? That you are a flirt? A jilt? Not woman enough to keep Cortland happy? Is any of it true?"

"Of course not!" Natalie nearly exploded in her denial. How cruel for Stone to rehash such gossip!

"I know that. But just as *you* wish some benefit of the doubt, I ask you to do the same for my friend." He paused, again searching for the right words. "Try to be sympathetic, Nat. Garrett Castleton could have only wished his father dead sooner."

Still reeling from her brother's words, it took a moment for Natalie to contemplate what Stone asked of her. Could she possibly consider the meeting in the park objectively?

She'd known the earl's identity at once, having surreptitiously watched the former viscount from afar on a few occasions. Of similar height to Cortland, but leaner, he exuded a hint of danger. His face was narrow, his chin strong, but his sable eyes could be downright offensive. By flicking them up and down her person, he'd aroused a curious sensation deep inside her.

More than once, he'd stared at her with what seemed like vulgar familiarity. Having been warned to steer clear of him by other respectable ladies, she'd avoided him. Society only received a man such as Castleton due to rank and wealth. He'd never made any attempt to gain society's approval as a gentleman. Could he be anything other than the man she'd already determined him to be? The thought unnerved her.

"Consider the possibility, little Nat, that the man was, in fact, *rebelling* against his father. You wouldn't have any notion of what's that like, now would you?"

She ignored his insinuation. "Please, Stone, do not call me that. It sounds as though you are referring to some sort of a bug." Little gnat, indeed. Her brothers tortured her with that nickname since they were children. Apparently, it was to follow her into adulthood.

Natalie arrived at the landing short of breath and picked up her original train of thought. "So you are saying he flouted the rules of society to get back at his father?" When she'd been forced to greet him in the park, he had been disheveled, his black hair hanging in his face, his eyes bloodshot and shadowed. But there had been something else…If she had she not been forbidden to speak with anyone and had she not been running late, she *would* have been friendly. She would have!

Stone grinned. "You *are* an annoying little bug sometimes," he said, ignoring her question.

"Do be serious." She lifted her chin haughtily. Surely Stone would not invite a menace into their midst? And yet, if she was not to avoid the man, then what exactly was she to do with him?

"He's not had an easy time of it, Nat. Won't you trust me? I wouldn't invite him into our home if he was capable of half the things he's rumored to have done."

"So, he is coming here?" Natalie resisted the urge to bite one of her fingernails as they arrived at the last door. Stone pulled it open and walked into the shadowed room. Curtains blocked all but a few slivers of sunlight, and heavy cloths draped over the furnishings. He pulled a few of the coverings back in a careless manner before discovering what he looked for. There appeared to be a variety of different-sized crates, along with a few trunks.

Ignoring her question again, Stone explained the crates. "The Hawthorne seat, Maple Hall, is in ruins, but the dower house is intact. He's coming to retrieve these and will store them there now that he is Hawthorne." Shuffling about and folding some of the large sheets of canvas, he inspected the condition of the crates. "He was concerned his father would destroy his mother's effects, given the chance. Wise decision. If left in his father's care, they would have burned with everything else."

"He is coming to Raven's Park to retrieve them, then?" Natalie stood with her hands on her hips, regarding her brother in exasperation.

Stone looked up, giving her his full attention once again. "Indeed. He will arrive sometime this week." He put a foot up on one of the trunks and leaned an arm upon his knee. "And, *for me*, will you try to remember he isn't the same person as the old earl? I convinced him to take a short holiday here. I'll keep him out of your way, hunting and fishing and whatnot. But if you run into the man, will you please not give him the cut? Treat him as an esteemed guest in our home?"

Natalie leaned thoughtfully against the doorframe. "Father knows? Father finds his presence here acceptable?" This information gave her considerable pause.

Stone nodded. "Of course. It was at his behest I invited him. Father understands Hawthorne is his own man."

"Well then." Natalie pursed her lips in thought. "In that case, I will be my normal delightful self. But if he says anything unfitting, I shall not hesitate to go to Father."

Stone rolled his eyes heavenward. "I'll keep him well out of your way"—he paused with a grin and then added mischievously—"little Nat."

Chapter Three

After several depressing days going through the charred remains at Maple Hall, Garrett was grateful to leave it behind.

Stone had predicted rightly. The estate's dilapidated condition nearly overwhelmed him. After inspecting that which was still intact and beginning repairs to what was left of the stables, Garrett was more than ready for a reprieve. Although he refused to grieve his father's death, he lamented the condition of his birthright.

The damage from the fire was expected; the godawful tenant conditions were not. Good, hard-working men were living in dilapidated shacks with their families.

Garrett wished the hatred he felt for his father could have died along with the man himself. Anger, he was finding, could be exhausting.

As Rumble, his longtime steed, climbed the last rise, the large Edwardian manor situated in a protected valley beckoned. For several miles, he'd been passing through well-tended fields separated by stone fences and well-groomed hedges. Now though, the patchwork of tidy holdings gave way to a landscaped park, which provided the perfect setting for Ravensdale's stately mansion. The whitewashed limestone of the exterior created a pleasant contrast for the greenery surrounding it. Vines of ivy grew over the façade of the mansion, which was surrounded by copses of trees and lush lawns. The woodlands appeared untamed at first, but if examined carefully one realized this was not the case. For the thick forest was artfully trimmed to allow access to the large lake it encircled. Despite the estate's size, it was pretty and homey. In comparison to Maple Hall, Raven's Park was indeed a little slice of heaven.

Following the drive leading to the entrance, Garrett braced himself despite Stone's reassurances. Would they turn him away? Would Lady Ravensdale rescind her son's invitation? As quickly as the thought arose, it faded when Stone stepped out of the mansion and ambled down the marble steps to the drive. A groomsman appeared as Garrett brought Rumble to a halt and dismounted. Handing over the reins, Garrett then patted his horse on his hindquarters somewhat reluctantly. He normally took responsibility for the care of his own mount, but knowing the Spencer men as he did, Garrett was confident the lad would give Rumble a thorough rubdown and a clean stall. The Earl of Ravensdale would not employ lazy or inept stable hands.

"You've made good time. Decided to travel ahead of the baggage coach?" Stone grasped Garrett's hand and patted his shoulder in a friendly greeting. His friend's eyes sparkled with an honest and warm welcome.

It had been a long time since he'd met with a welcome anywhere.

"I did." Garrett pondered the grand house. "You are certain my presence will not cause discord?" The effects of disgrace could be contagious. Scandal was infectious, and no one immune. "I do not wish to cause—"

Before Garrett could complete his sentence, Stone was shaking his head. "All is fine, Castleton…er, Hawthorne now, I guess."

Garrett grimaced. "Horrid name to go by."

"Time will change that." Stone sounded matter-of-fact as he led him toward the door. "Make it yours. That's what my father said he did when he inherited." He led Garrett inside as the butler held the door wide for them. "I imagine you'd like to wash up. I'll show you to your chamber, and then you can join me downstairs for a late nuncheon. My mother will have something appetizing set out in the dining room."

"Lodging in the main house isn't necessary. I'm more than happy to bunk in the bachelors' quarters." Garrett hoped to avoid the family as much as possible. In fact, he'd counted on it. And as for Lady Natalie, he intended to evade her completely.

"Well, old chap, there's something you never learned about mothers. They get these crazy ideas about looking to your well-being. Like it or not, mine believes you need cossetting and has insisted you be welcomed into the fold." They climbed two flights of stairs before Stone turned left along a richly carpeted corridor. Garrett followed reluctantly. "Besides, the bachelor cottage is in need of repair. Trust me, this will surpass the comfort of those lodgings by far." He opened the door to a well-kept room with masculine décor.

"With Joseph marrying a few weeks ago, his room is not in use. Mother's had it readied specifically for you. She'd have my hide if I put you anywhere else." Glancing at his fob watch, Stone backed out of the room. "I'll leave you for now. Ring if you need anything and then come down when you're ready. Nuncheon is an extended casual affair, so no need to rush."

Garrett tossed his saddlebag on the bed and turned to Stone. "None of this is necessary, you know. I've no need for any of this."

Stone put out his hands, as though to stop him from saying anything further. Staring down at the carpet, he took a moment to think before looking back up at Garrett. "I want you to know there *are* people who can separate you from your father. It will take time, but all will be well. Allow matters to rest."

Appreciating the sentiments, but doubting Stone's optimism, Garrett thanked his loyal friend with a nod. "I'll see you downstairs then. Is your fishing hole well stocked? Been looking forward to that all week."

Stone nodded solemnly. "Downstairs then."

Garrett cleaned up using the cold water by the wash basin, took a swig of the whiskey he carried with him, and then decided he might as well begin his "holiday." If Lady Ravensdale found it necessary to house him in Joseph's chamber, there must be other guests. Good Lord, the woman was probably hosting some sort of house party. Most assuredly, Stone would not have mentioned it. Had he done so, Garrett would have refused the invitation outright.

Wonderful.

As he entered the corridor, an adjacent door opened as well.

Of course. Who else would it be?

Although, admittedly, he'd acted rudely toward her in the park, her outright disgust at his offered escort festered. He'd dealt with blatant disdain from many a spoiled debutante and not cared one fig, but the scorn he'd seen in Lady Natalie Spencer's eyes that day still rankled. And feeling rankled drew the worst out of him.

Unfortunately, now a guest in her parents' home, Garrett would show very poor taste indeed to act upon his feelings.

Which, where Lady Natalie was concerned, were mixed.

Damned if she didn't look ravishing and regal in a pale-yellow dress. Just the right amount of color to enhance her creamy skin and golden hair. Just the right amount of lace to disguise her frosty superiority. As she heard his door close and turned to see who had joined her in the corridor, Garrett braced himself. Would she acknowledge him?

This time she did not look away. This time her gaze held his.

This time *she smiled*.

Surely, hell had frozen over.

"My lord, welcome to Raven's Park." Her voice rang softly in the corridor. A slight blush rose on her cheeks before she dropped into a delicate curtsey. Not only was he surprised by her smile, but an enormous tug of unwanted attraction ambushed him.

Garrett bowed in return. He'd not made it a practice to be charming to society chits. He was in unfamiliar territory.

"My lady." His words were followed by an awkward pause. Her greeting had startled him. He'd expected disdain or rudeness or, at the very least, aloofness. More than a little suspicious, he nonetheless offered his arm. "May I escort you downstairs to the dining room? I presume that is your destination?" He did not smile in return. Would she run from him again?

He ought to have opted for a nap.

Natalie had known he'd arrived. Stone had informed her a few minutes earlier. What a different turn of circumstances this was from their last meeting. A quiver scuttled down her spine despite the warmth of the afternoon.

Lord Hawthorne's demeanor was distinctly different today, as he offered her his arm. He did not speak sarcastically. He seemed, she thought, rather wary instead.

Although the man must have washed, for his hair was still damp, he remained in his traveling clothes. This was obvious as a considerable amount of dust clung to both his jacket and fitted tan breeches. Despite the condition of his clothing, his scent was not unattractive. She caught a whiff of soap and sandalwood, and—well—man.

Feeling petite, she noted he was lean but well-muscled and quite tall. She hesitated a moment before taking his arm.

"I hope my brother informed you nuncheon is casual. Cold meats, cheese, breads, and fruits are the standard fare. You need only ring if you have want of anything. My mother, of course, hopes you feel very much at home while you're here." Natalie addressed him cordially as she would any of Stone's friends. After pondering her brother's advice regarding the new earl, she'd decided to give him a second chance.

She'd so often found herself vexed by his demeanor, she failed to remember him being—hmm, not really handsome, that was not the right word—

arresting fit better. For he wasn't classically proportioned. His chin was hard, and his nose appeared to have been broken a time or two. His eyes gave nothing away. They weren't cold, rather too hot, exuding sensuality and tension. His arm felt firm and warm where her hand lay along the sleeve of his jacket. Such proximity inspired an inward shiver as he escorted her toward the grand staircase. It reminded her of the shock she'd felt when he'd taken her hand in the park. And what he'd done with his mouth…

"You'll have to tell me where we are going, or I will have us wandering in circles." He was trying to be pleasant. How bizarre! She looked up to see his expression. Of course, he was not smiling. Grimacing perhaps…

"My lord, would I be correct to assume your valet is expected later today with your baggage coach?"

The earl slowed the pace of their steps and turned to look at her. "I haven't employed a valet for years. A waste, if you ask me. Damned ridiculous if a man can't dress himself." His expression betrayed his annoyance that a mere girl would take it upon herself to harangue him about his attire. Natalie did not allow him to alter her intent.

"I will speak with my mother. We'll assign one of the servants to valet for you," she suggested confidently. She already had a candidate in mind. Marcus would kill to valet for somebody, anybody.

"My dear lady"—his voice conveyed acute irritation—"I shall hardly require the services of a valet for a few weeks of hunting and fishing. I am here for a quiet holiday and some sport, nothing more."

Halting their progress, Natalie removed her hand

from his arm and turned to face him. She steepled her hands in front of her lips and looked skywards seeking the right words to get her point across. Men! They really could be foolish in the extreme!

"My lord, are you aware my mother is hosting a house party?"

He raised one dark eyebrow. "And this concerns me how? I've no plans to participate. I requested to bunk in the bachelors' lodgings, but the countess insists I reside here instead. I do not expect, nor wish, to be included in any events."

Natalie drew in a deep breath. His bluster did not intimidate her. In fact, she found his scowl rather endearing. But oh, how this man needed her assistance!

"My dear Lord Hawthorne, whether you wish it or not, you are being presented with a unique opportunity—especially for a *gentleman* in your...er...present circumstances." Without thinking, she placed one of her hands over his. Yes, he was an earl, and yes, he possessed a certain rugged appeal, but his circumstances *were* somewhat pathetic. "My mother is very good friends with the highest sticklers in the *ton.* And under this roof, for the next two weeks, several of them are my parents' honored guests." She squeezed his hand with a sense of urgency. She didn't know why it mattered, but for some reason it did. Perhaps if she were to focus on another person's troubles, she could forget her own for a while. She put her words together carefully; this rake would not take kindly to pity.

"My parents are showing these people that they trust you in their home, amongst their family and guests. For heaven's sake, your room is on the same floor as their only daughter's! This is an opportunity for you to impress upon these people that you are not your father. This is a chance for you to have doors opened to you that have been closed for years. Doors that may never open for you again due to present scandals."

Her tirade, an attempt to persuade the earl to put forth his best efforts, seemed to anger him instead. He pulled his hand away and stepped backward.

"Dammit!" He snapped his head to the side as though to gather himself, or perhaps because he was too disgusted to even look at her. "My apologies, my lady, but if I am expected to—You cannot have the slightest idea as to how repugnant your suggestion is. I did not come here for this." His eyes looked pained, but his expression revealed barely controlled fury. "I shouldn't have come at all. I will collect my belongings and return to my estate."

Natalie's eyes went wide. Obviously, she had gone too far. Stone would never forgive her if his friend left because of something she'd said. And after she'd promised to be on her best behavior no less! "Oh, no, I'm not saying you are *required* to put forth some sort of effort on your behalf! I'm merely saying it is an *opportunity* for you. What you wish to do with it, of course, is up to you."

She watched his face as her words settled into the charged atmosphere. Dark circles were etched under his eyes, and for just a moment, she felt sorry to berate him so. He could not *really* turn around and leave. To do so would offend both Stone and her parents. And really, the man was in no position to offend anyone who befriended him right now. "I beg you to reconsider. You are most welcome to spend your time however you wish." She winced before adding, "Stone will have my head if you leave because of something I've said."

Natalie held her breath and awaited his response. A full thirty seconds must have passed before he relented.

"There will be no valet"—he spoke between clenched teeth—"as I have no need."

Natalie watched his profile. The tensely corded muscles of his neck and his broad shoulders gave away the tension within him. He gave her the sense of a wild animal, trapped but not defeated. His voice was firm as he spoke again.

"I will not give in to this occasion by licking anybody's boots." He looked at her crossly. "Nor by having a servant polish my own."

Natalie fluttered her lashes and tilted her head to the side. "So you will stay then?" At her obvious ploy, he seemed to relax and then rolled his eyes heavenwards.

"Are you going to show me where this damned nuncheon is being served or not?"

Natalie could not help but laugh in relief. *This* was the rogue she had been expecting. Relieved she hadn't scared him away, she took his arm and gestured toward the back of the house. "Right this way, my lord, right this way. If you prefer to carry on as an uncouth brute, then so be it. But later, when you realize how wrong you are, don't say I didn't warn you."

Chapter Four

With a languid stretch, Garrett leaned forward and rested the fishing pole on a carefully selected rock. He and Stone had been sitting by the lake for over an hour. They'd each caught a few good-sized fish but released them, for future sport. Under some very large oaks, they sat partly in sunshine and partly in shade. The strain of the past month began to ease away as he leaned against a smooth boulder.

Stone's voice broke the lazy silence. "I cannot believe Joseph, the youngest of us boys, was the first to get himself leg-shackled." He chuckled. "He's even beaten Natalie to the altar."

Agreeing with his friend's sentiment toward marriage, Garrett grinned. "Perhaps all the Spencer brothers will wed before her. You and Darlington have dodged the matchmaking mamas easily enough, though. How did you manage to escape the responsibilities of the Season?" Garrett could hardly fathom that Lady Ravensdale had allowed her two oldest sons to forgo the marriage mart so easily.

"Not much choice in the matter." Stone's eyes turned serious. "We're having labor issues at our few estates up north. Father required our presence there. The Corn Laws have done nothing but create dissension." He grimaced. "Things are going to have to change here in England if we wish to avoid taking the same course as France. Many workers have already taken flight to America. What choice do they have when they cannot afford to feed their families? It's a difficult role we play. We are landlords and yet also sympathizers. There is only so much one family can do."

Garrett knew Lord Ravensdale opposed protectionism. The earl had not been born into wealth and position but inherited his title after establishing a lucrative career as a barrister. The man had not forgotten the challenges of laboring for one's living.

Stone groaned. "Unfortunately, I don't see the situation righting itself anytime soon." He glanced sideways at Garrett. "How are matters at Maple Hall?"

"It's odd." Garrett rubbed his chin. "Until last week, it had been over ten years since I was last there, and yet, even with the manor burned to the ground, it feels like home. At the risk of waxing poetic, I believe I have something of a connection with the land itself." An old memory stirred to life. "My grandfather's old steward, Mr. Pinyon, most certainly is responsible." Idly chewing on a stem of grass, Garrett stared across the water. The last time he'd gone fishing was before his father sent Mr. Pinyon away.

"He taught you estate management?" Stone asked.

"More than that." Garrett pulled his knees up and rested his arms upon them. "He made me feel as though I belonged. He introduced me to people—taught me that one person alone does not own the estate. The land, the crops, the workers, and the tenants—they are all a part of it, dependent upon one another to produce and sustain their families."

"That poor man can't have lasted very long with

your father."

"He didn't." Garrett had long ago buried such memories. "I trailed after him every chance I could. And then when I returned from school one holiday, I discovered Father had sent him packing." Garrett had been devastated.

"There must be some satisfaction now," Stone finally said, "in that the management of the estate falls to you." The two men fell silent again. Garrett contemplated the twinkling reflections created on the water as a breeze stirred the hot air.

"I can only hope the bastard didn't wait too long to die," Garrett murmured. The task at Maple Hall was a herculean one. "Many fences need mending now, both literally and figuratively."

Stone set his pole aside and sent Garrett a pointed stare. "Are you through gadding about, then? Are you done living life to spite your father?"

Garrett considered taking offence with his friend's statement. But this was Stone talking, after all. They'd never dissembled with each other, so why be offended?

And yes, the time for change was upon him. As the new earl, with hundreds relying upon the estate for their livelihood, he could no longer deny his birthright.

"To some extent." And then he let out a cynical bark of laughter. "Your sister believes my reputation can be restored and that this damned house party is the place to do so." He looked sideways at Stone. "You did not tell me half of London would be here when you invited me. Not well done of you, my friend, not well done at all."

Stone merely chuckled. "Well, I've just returned myself. Had I known of all this hullabaloo I would have planned to meet you elsewhere. And I suppose I could have carted your crates and trunks to Maple Hall myself…" Pulling a pastry out of the basket Mrs. Winston sent along with them, Stone took a bite and then a long drink from his flask. "Natalie said that, eh? Be careful, she may make you into one of her projects. She's bored silly and will do anything for a diversion."

Garrett shook his head, mentally recalling the lady in question. "I can hardly comprehend her jilting the Duke of Cortland. Your father must have been livid."

"He very nearly had her under house arrest in London, from what I understand. Now that she's here, she is forbidden to attend any house parties or assemblies. We'll see how long she stays out of trouble. I think she's less content than my parents would believe. She had more than one reason, I am certain, for breaking off her engagement, but she doesn't talk about it. Simply says she didn't love him." He laughed. "Women."

Garrett pondered this. Why does any young woman throw a man over? It ought to be plain as day—she wants something else, or some*one* else. "Lady Natalie and your parents were more than kind to me during nuncheon," Garrett said. "They made it obvious they expected the same behavior from their guests."

"I saw that. Perhaps Natalie is on to something."

Dammit. The chit may just have been right.

Upon entering the dining room with her, seeing some of the all-too-familiar faces he had left London to avoid, Garrett had braced himself for unpleasantness. His first thought was that Stone had betrayed him. His second was to turn on his heel and arrange for his departure. But Lady Natalie had stood beside him with her hand tucked neatly into his arm.

"Father," she had said brightly, "look who I found! Lord Hawthorne graciously offered his escort when we met in the corridor upstairs. Mother has prepared Joseph's chamber for him. With all the guest rooms occupied, I thought that very clever of her."

The Earl of Ravensdale had risen from his seat and approached Garrett with an outstretched hand.

"Welcome, Hawthorne. Josephine and I were both delighted to hear you were joining our little house party. My beautiful countess has planned several activities, but I hope we can find time to discuss business as well." The earl's eyes had been friendly and his handshake hearty. The countess also came forward to greet him personally and yet very publicly.

After seeing their esteemed host and hostess receive Garrett so graciously, the other guests were given no choice but to welcome him as well. And, although reserved, none had condescended to him in any way.

Even Lady Eleanor Sheffield did not shun him outright. It had been her niece Garrett's father kidnapped and then attempted to murder. If anyone were to object to his presence, this lady in particular had every reason to do so. But she had not. She had watched Garrett closely. She was curious, likely, and with ample justification, guarded.

The nuncheon had not been the ordeal he expected, and by the end of the meal, he realized he'd been extended equal courtesy to every other guest. Not one failed to meet his eyes.

By God, it seemed he was going to have to take advantage of his time here after all.

Garrett stared out at the lake, not really seeing it but, instead, remembering the moment Lady Natalie smiled at him in the corridor outside his bedchamber. In the past, he'd watched her smile or laugh from across a crowded room, but he'd never experienced the full force of her charm directed at him. When she did just that, earlier this afternoon, he'd found himself momentarily—and nauseatingly—smitten.

Lady Natalie was perhaps the most beautiful of all the debutantes to grace the *ton* for the past two seasons. She was tall, but not too tall, with long elegant limbs. Classically beautiful, delicate, and symmetrical features graced her flawless complexion. Her blue eyes sparkled behind long lush eyelashes. Her hair, like golden sunshine. She was perfect in every way.

Perhaps that was why, in the past, he'd done his best to irritate her. She was untouchable by the likes of him, but he'd wanted her notice, nonetheless. Hell, he'd *demanded* it that day in the park.

And yet today, she'd taken his arm and allowed him to walk with her. And she championed him when they entered the dining room. She must have known he would not be comfortable wading in by himself. Or perhaps…

Perhaps she had simply wanted to save them all from the embarrassment of his turning around and leaving.

Under the warmth of the sun, he ought to have enjoyed the rarity of doing nothing but wait for a fish to take his bait, but he was ill at ease. Trusting such a quick change in regard and attitude from these people was difficult. More so, from Lady Natalie.

Her words continued to prod him. *This is an*

opportunity for you to impress upon these people that you are not your father. Should he take it? Even if he did not completely trust it, he would be a stubborn fool to not take full advantage of the goodwill these people were extending.

So, it seemed, he would not have a fortnight of relaxation and escape. Instead, he had work to do. The type of work he'd avoided for years. Ah well...It was time.

****

The very enthusiastic manservant waiting in Garrett's room later that evening should not have surprised him.

A quick look around told him the servant had already unpacked and brushed out the few items of clothing Garrett thought would suffice. He did not recognize, however, the evening dress laid out for a formal dinner.

"Lady Ravensdale instructed me to valet for you, my lord." The young man bowed. "I am Marcus. She also instructed me to utilize any of Mr. Joseph's wardrobe left behind, since you were unaware of the house party." Perhaps sensing Garrett's disposition, his new valet hesitantly gestured to the ensemble laid out upon the bed. "I hope these will be acceptable, sir...my lord," he corrected himself.

Garrett closed his eyes and took a deep breath. *This is an opportunity for you to impress upon these people that you are not your father.* The time had come.

"Marcus, eh? Let us hope young Joseph has grown since the last time the two of us met. He must have been no older than twelve or so, at the time—a skinny lad, a full foot and a half shorter than myself."

Marcus smiled in relief. "Oh, he has, my lord. I believe even your size of shoes is similar. It is fortuitous, is it not? I have taken the liberty of preparing a bath. It is behind the privacy screen, sir, and when you are ready, I can take care of your beard if you please."

Rubbing the whiskers on his chin, Garrett laughed. "And have you any experience with this sort of thing, Marcus? Shaving and whatnot?" His valet could not have practiced upon himself. The young man had not yet graduated from soft peach fuzz to actual whiskers.

"Oh, yes, sir. My father is the earl's valet. I've been training for this sort of thing my whole life!" In his earnestness, the servant looked to be barely seventeen. Ah, so acting as a valet was a promotion of sorts.

Garrett stepped behind the screen and began undressing, tossing his discarded clothing onto the divider. Marcus, showing a mindfulness of Garrett's privacy, carefully removed the items so he could tend to them. "And who have you been practicing on, Marcus?" Garrett asked once he'd relaxed into the tub.

"To be frank, my lord, anybody I can get my hands on. My pa, of course, and Mr. Winston, the butler. On occasion, I get a hold of some of the footmen. More and more of them let me shave them now that Pa and Mr. Winston are sporting fewer nicks." The young man's voice rose and fell as he entered and exited the adjacent closet.

"But that's nothing, my lord." Garrett was startled as the young man peeked around the screen to address him in the tub. "Wait until you see how I can tie a cravat!"

Chapter Five

Lady Ravensdale did not forgo elegance and expense when she hosted a summer house party, and this evening's dinner was no exception.

Gathering promptly in the drawing room for drinks and conversation, the aristocratic guests mingled while waiting for supper to be announced. A conservative group of lords, the men wore formal attire, mostly black and white. The ladies were much more colorful, donning bright gowns along with feathers and plumes in their elegantly styled coiffures. The more ripened the lady, the more embellished the plumes.

Lady Natalie, the youngest person present, wore a simple sky-blue gown with puffed sleeves, a high waist, and embroidered flowers which complemented the lace along her modest décolletage. It draped neatly to the floor, hiding her satin slippers. Her hair, which held a loose natural curl on its own, was drawn up with one silver clip. A few golden tendrils framed her face perfectly. Her scowl, however, ruined the entire effect.

Her mother had visited her chamber earlier and informed her that the Duke of Monfort would escort her into the dining hall for supper. Being a duke, Monfort would be seated to the right of her father, and Natalie was to be seated on his other side. The earl had apparently not relinquished his hopes of Natalie becoming a duchess. Blast and botheration! When she'd broken her engagement to Cortland, Papa had promised he would allow her to find her own husband and marry for love. Or so she had thought…

Not that Monfort was an unattractive man. He wasn't. In fact, some women might find him appealing, undeterred by his cold manner. Along with his elegant looks, he *was* a duke. That's all it took to attract some women.

But not her!

She wanted somebody whose heart she could touch.

Unbidden, Garrett Castleton came to mind. He was as much an opposite of the duke as there could possibly be. His black eyes burned with a fiery intensity, whereas Monfort's silver ones could freeze a person's very soul. Both men boasted black hair, but Hawthorne's was unruly, while Monfort's hair was without flaw—controlled, like the man.

Looking around the drawing room, she wondered if Hawthorne would be in attendance tonight. He'd been furious with her for advising him on how to conduct himself while in the company of her mother's guests. In addition, he'd further shown his disdain by ignoring her throughout the entirety of the afternoon meal. This, in spite of the fact she'd taken her own seat next to his. And yet…

And yet, he'd exhibited a pleasantness of manner toward her parents' guests, which could not have been comfortable for him. As the conversation flowed, Natalie had gradually relaxed. She'd been nervous for him. For some reason, she didn't know why, she hoped he would take her advice. He was her brother's *friend*, after all.

Smoothing the skirt of her dress, quite pleased with herself, Natalie let a self-satisfied smile cross her lips. Lord Hawthorne had not sent Marcus packing. Instead, with no argument whatsoever, he'd accepted the young man as his temporary valet. Marcus reported to her, in fact, that he'd found the earl to be quite agreeable, cooperative, and unassuming.

As though she'd conjured him up with her thoughts, Lord Hawthorne magically appeared in the doorway. Natalie's breath caught.

Dressed to the nines, his respectable appearance added a new dimension to her opinion of him. He was freshly shaven, accentuating his strong jaw and hollowed cheeks. His hair, although still thick and longer than that of the other gentlemen present, was styled with a small portion of pomade. Glancing at his hands, she realized his nails had even been manicured. *Oh, well done, Marcus.* When her eyes moved back to his face, she was embarrassed to see he had noticed her assessment of his appearance. He walked over to where she stood and leaned casually against the wall beside them. Crossing one ankle in front of his other foot, he pressed the toe of his polished boot into the carpet.

"Do I pass muster then, my lady?" he asked, his black eyes hooded.

Such the rogue! Those damn eyes of his—along with the gravelly tone of his voice—sent shivers skating across her skin. He spoke as though he knew all her secrets. As though he knew the cravings she had when she lay alone in her bed…She tried to breathe deeply and concentrate on an appropriate response while a swarm of butterflies danced within her.

"Why would you not?" She attempted to muster

her dignity. "You are my parents' guest, my brother's friend." She opened her fan and waved it to cool the flush she felt creeping up her neck.

The earl looked her up and down in open appreciation. His perusal was thorough but not as sinister as it had always seemed in the past. "Perhaps you have forgotten that you must not be seen with me? Or am I no longer considered the pariah I was in London?" In spite of his cool charm, an edge laced his words, for both of them remembered their meeting in Hyde Park.

She dropped her fan and glared at him. "Perhaps a lady can change her mind."

"A lady's prerogative, eh?" His bitter tone stung. "So, away from the *ton*, away from your friends, you will lower your standards to converse with a reprobate such as myself?" His voice was even, but the look on his face conveyed that she was not yet forgiven.

Luckily, they were set apart from the other guests. She had no wish for this conversation to be overheard. *For his sake.* Well, she admitted to herself, her own reputation wasn't without tarnish either. "Lord Hawthorne, you have done nothing to earn my regard throughout all of our…acquaintance. Why would you expect that I should have given it to you?"

"I was not given an opportunity." His voice was still sharp, but there was something vulnerable behind his gaze.

"You were never presented to me."

He raised one eyebrow. "You cannot have been unaware that introductions to you were critically screened; that only the most exalted of persons were allowed in your presence."

She looked down. He spoke the truth. If not her mother, then some other chaperone had *always* been at her side to vet unworthy introductions. Upon his words, she was no longer certain how she felt about this. She'd merely followed the governing rules of polite society. But she *had* known, in fact, that he'd sought out an introduction to her.

"Of course I was." Natalie squirmed at the truth in his words. Then she looked up with accusation in her eyes. "But you knew what you were doing. You *knew* you would not be presented to any respectable ladies." Fire came into her eyes. "I didn't make up the rules, you know! I have only done my best to follow them!"

Her voice stirred something in him. Pity? Protectiveness? Desire? Garrett tried to shrug it off as he considered her words. She didn't realize how much the last statement, *I have only done my best to follow them*, revealed her vulnerability. For she *hadn't* followed all the rules. She'd broken off a betrothal to a duke. Even worse, she'd managed to lose the regard of said duke to another woman. He watched her closely and then, coming to a decision, pulled himself away from the wall and stood up straight before her. "No, *you* are right. Perhaps we can—" He swallowed, a tad uncomfortable. "Perhaps we can begin anew?"

As he looked down at her, she appeared for all intents to be the innocent girl society expected. And yet, there was something about her that he could not put his finger on. Was he imagining the coiled tension that seemed to roll off her in waves?

She stretched out her hand, palm down, and dipped into a perfectly executed curtsey. "Lord Hawthorne, it is a pleasure to make your acquaintance."

Feeling strangely gifted, he bowed over it.

"The pleasure is mine, my lady." As they rose, Natalie's mother approached them with the Duke of Monfort at her side. Before turning to her mother, Natalie held his gaze steadily for a moment longer than should have been appropriate.

Lady Ravensdale stepped between them, effectively blocking those blue eyes of hers from his sight. "My dear, Monfort is prepared to escort you into the dining room. We will go in momentarily." And then turning back to address Garrett, she placed her hand on his arm and steered him in the opposite direction. "My lord, might I impose upon you to escort my dearest friend, Lady Sheffield, into dinner?"

Feeling the noose being slipped around his neck, Garrett allowed the countess to lead him across the room. He ought to kill Stone for this. "But of course."

Not only was Garrett to escort Lady Sheffield into the dining hall, he'd been seated next to the woman as well. He wondered that Lady Ravensdale hadn't considered the events of the past spring while making her seating arrangements. She ought to have placed him as far as possible from the poor woman. That being said, he was not ill at ease for long.

Dressed with less flamboyance than the other *grandes dames* in attendance, Lady Sheffield made up for it with numerous rings on each of her hands. She wore one purple feather in her silver upswept hair along with matching necklace and earbobs. She was not a large woman but exuded a strong presence.

"Aren't I the lucky one?" she teased, as old ladies are wont to do on occasion, "being sat next to such a handsome rogue as you, my lord?" Glancing toward

Lady Natalie, she laughed. "That poor girl." Her eyes twinkled as she spoke. "The earl is fooling himself if he thinks he'll net Monfort for her. Not that my goddaughter would take him." Like most women of his acquaintance, Lady Sheffield was a matchmaking busybody. Garrett agreed with her sentiments, however.

"I don't think Monfort would allow himself to be 'netted' by anyone," Garrett said in a wry tone. "From what I've heard, he keeps to himself these days."

"He does at that," Lady Sheffield said before turning back toward Garrett. "But enough talk of that poor man. Tell me what brings the new Earl of Hawthorne to Raven's Park? You are an associate of Lord Ravensdale, I understand? And a good friend of Stone's?"

Garrett nodded. "Both, my lady."

"I know it's not proper to talk of business, but I am intrigued by your acumen. What is it, exactly, my lord, that you do?"

Garrett paused to think for a moment before answering. It pleased him to discover that he would not, after all, be subject to banal conversations for the entirety of the meal. The woman seemed to be genuinely interested.

"Importing and exporting. Certain goods we cannot match here in England—cheese, brandy, and certain types of fabric. A strong demand for many British made products has yet been unmet abroad. I endeavor to meet the needs at both ends." Garrett was proud of his accomplishments, but he answered her softly, not wanting to draw attention to himself.

Lady Sheffield spent the rest of the dinner asking thoughtful questions about his life and accomplishments. Which products did he export? Did he lose many shipments at sea? Were pirates a problem for him? Where had he, himself travelled? She did not discuss herself, the *ton*, or any of the latest gossip.

As the last course arrived, Garrett realized that Lady Sheffield was, in all actuality, in a very sticky social situation herself. After all, it had been her niece who had married Lady Natalie's—her goddaughter's—former betrothed. Likely, she tempered her pleasure for her niece in deference to the Spencers' pride. He found himself regarding the older woman with genuine respect for her courage and steady composure.

And occasionally, Garrett found himself glancing toward the other end of the long table, where Lady Natalie sat.

Next to the Duke of Monfort.

So this was how the winds blew. The earl must have already decided to replace one duke with another. But Monfort? Why would Ravensdale bark up that particular tree? Monfort had expressed no interest whatsoever in remarrying. His first wife, along with their two children, had died in a tragic accident three years earlier. They had been skating upon a lake which appeared frozen solid. The duke was watching them from the front steps of the manor several hundred yards away. The ice made a loud clapping sound and cracked beneath the duchess. The children ran toward her.

He had been unable to save any of them.

Word was that the duke's heart froze that day, along with his family.

Monfort *was not* a good match for Lady Natalie. Garrett watched her painstaking attempts to converse with the man. The duke appeared unmoved by her efforts, answering her in curt, one-word pronouncements. When he did condescend to direct conversation her way, he did so in a patronizing manner. What the *hell* was Ravensdale thinking? His daughter deserved much better than that!

And then Lady Natalie's gaze drifted down the length of the table. Garrett caught her gaze and held it, mesmerized. Not until blue eyes shuttered and broke the connection did he realized Lady Sheffield had been watching him. A mischievous smile danced across the older woman's lips.

Chapter Six

Relief swept through Natalie when her mother finally stood, signaling the ladies to remove themselves to the drawing room. Natalie was happy to abandon the duke, and all the others, to their port. God save her from her father and his dukes!

In an effort to appease her parents, Natalie had maintained a stilted conversation with Monfort throughout each carefully prepared course. Talking with the Duke of Monfort, however, had been an utter waste of time and energy. It was akin to wading through a thick Irish bog.

Nonetheless, she had made a valiant effort. Guilt still plagued her for the embarrassment she'd brought upon her father. And for ruining his plans. He'd *so* wanted the Duke of Cortland for a son-in-law. For her papa's sake, she'd forced herself to make an honest attempt at being pleasant.

But enough was enough! At her mother's signal, Natalie bolted out of her chair to make her escape through the large open doors.

Passing Hawthorne, uncomfortably aware of his presence, she tried not to look at him but failed miserably. She had caught him watching her with that smoldering stare of his more than once during dinner. Recalling it, she met his eyes as she passed and found herself with an insane impulse to reach out and touch him. What on earth was the matter with her? Clasping both hands behind her back, she followed the other ladies out of the room.

She did not, however, follow them into the drawing room. Instead, she slipped downstairs and out through the front door.

In the country, far from the smog of London, stars sparkled and the moon shone brightly. The sense of freedom beckoned her.

In spite of Stone and Roman's return, in spite of the excitement she felt around Lord Hawthorne, she continued to feel sorry for herself. She wandered onto one of the paths that circled the lake and attempted to process this restlessness that had taken root inside of her. She did not know how to make it go away.

A broken engagement ought not to force a lady to withdraw from society in shame. Most especially when the former groom, a duke no less, was free to gallivant off with his lover—now his duchess—on the honeymoon trip that she, Natalie, had planned. Frustration gnawed at her as she entered the wooded path.

Her imposed exile gave her far too much time to spend in her own company. It allowed her too much time to think, to doubt, and to yearn. For what, she knew not. Natalie grabbed at a branch that dared dangle in her path and ruthlessly twisted it until it snapped from the tree.

She did not regret her decision to break off her betrothal. She did not! For she'd freed Cortland so he could marry his true love. How could there be any regret in that? Had Natalie and the duke gone ahead with their wedding as originally planned, both would have grown to resent each other something fierce. *That* situation would have been more regrettable by far.

Natalie wanted a husband. She wanted children. But she wanted to actually *love* her husband. And she wanted a husband to love her in return.

She wrinkled her face as she deliberated.

How did one know love without experiencing intimacy with a person, with a man? During her two Seasons in London, mingling with the *ton*, she often witnessed husbands and wives who not only appeared to be indifferent to one another, but displayed outright disgust in each other's company. There were but a few exceptions to this standard. Which vexed her to no end. How did one go about finding "true love."

Not by following the rules, that was for certain. She'd been a good girl. She'd followed all the strictures of society and look where that had landed her.

What a boon it would be if a lady could try her hand at being a rake. She laughed out loud at the thought.

No longer betrothed, she would have enjoyed celebrating her freedom with some flirting. *Ha, like that is going to happen.* Living as a virtual prisoner, there was no chance for that.

Logically, she knew society's stipulations protected young women like herself. All these ridiculous rules—arranged companions, chaperones, even the dragons at Almacks—existed to safeguard both her person and her reputation. And her family was relentless in all of this. She ought not to resent them so much. She *loved* them.

So why the self-pity? Why the anger? Why the…loneliness? For yes, surrounded by her family as she was, a hollow emptiness echoed within her. She had thought she would be the happiest girl alive once freed from her commitment, but such emotion proved elusive. If she had not broken off her betrothal, this very moment, she would be traveling as the Duchess of Cortland all throughout the continent. Heavens, as a married woman, she could even possibly be with child!

At this thought, she scrunched her nose in some distaste. Although Cortland was good-looking, she'd not ever really felt—well—like doing *that* with him. She had some idea of what occurred between a husband and wife to make children, but she found it unappealing to imagine experiencing such intimacy with Michael Redmond, the Duke of Cortland.

"Are you escaping another duke this evening?" Lord Hawthorne's deep voice leapt out of the darkness.

"Did you follow me?" she shivered. For perhaps she *could* imagine doing what it took to make children with this man.

"Would you believe me if I denied it?" He took her arm and turned her to continue walking along the path. "Would you believe me if I told you I am here merely because I needed a break from proper conversation and the smell of cigars?" He tucked her hand into his arm and then nonchalantly strolled beside her. Surprised and curious, she glanced over to look up at his profile. He had long, thick lashes. Distracted by the intensity of his eyes, and the strong definition of his jaw and cheeks, she'd not noticed them before.

And then her gaze dropped to his mouth. Unnerving awareness tugged at her when she remembered how he'd brushed his tongue along her glove that day, slowly, wickedly. She'd been scandalized, of course, but also…intrigued.

"We should not be out here, alone, together." Her own thoughts flustered her. "Is it your wish to compromise me? Are you imagining I would then be forced into marriage with you?" She was feeling prickly but continued traversing along the cultivated wilderness walk beside him. As they walked deeper into the trees, the shadows grew darker.

"And that would be so disagreeable," he said, "marriage to the Earl of Hawthorne?" He spoke of his title with disdain, as though he, himself, found it unpalatable.

She did not respond. They took several steps in silence.

"I thought we declared a truce," she said after a few tense moments. She lifted her other hand to the crook of his arm and grasped hold as they climbed a small rise. "I am sorry for snapping at you. I am irritated with my father.." And then she corrected herself. "Not only my father. I am irritated with my *life*." The darkness made it easier to make such an admission.

He placed his other hand atop hers. "And why is that?"

"Have you not been listening to the gossip, my lord? I allowed a magnificent match to slip through my fingers. I could not keep my fiancé from allowing another woman to steal him away." These spiteful words were not hers. No, they were sentiments she'd read in the papers before leaving town. "And now, I am here." They had arrived atop the hill, leaving the trees behind. She released his arm and stepped away. Gesturing dramatically, she held her arms wide and threw her head back. "Banished to the country, a disgrace to my parents."

Realizing how self-pitying her words sounded, she dropped her arms and looked off into the distance. "She is a friend to me, you know, the new duchess. I am not angry with her, or with him." Natalie knew she should not be outside, at night, alone with this rake. She did not wish to heed her conscience though. Talking with Garrett Castleton was all too easy. She was being careless with her reputation. But as she'd already decided, protecting it had gotten her nowhere. She would rather run, or swim, or fly! She needed to somehow escape her own skin. She didn't care what she did so long as she felt alive again.

She'd told the earl his stay here could be an opportunity for him. That he could find some respectability and perhaps establish a few well-connected alliances for himself. She'd told him he ought to take advantage of the situation for his own benefit.

Well, perhaps she too was being presented with an opportunity. If she truly wanted to know more of intimacy and physical passion, was not a well-practiced rake the perfect person from whom to learn?

Garrett watched the different expressions flit across her face. In truth, he hadn't considered the part *she* had played in his own father's diabolical scheme. Lady Natalie had been but a casualty, a pawn caught in the war his father had declared on Cortland and Ravensdale. Although innocent of any wrongdoing, she was being punished for circumstances completely out of her control. Watching her curl her arms around herself, he removed his jacket and placed it upon her shoulders. He itched to wrap his arms around her as well but would not. He most certainly did not wish to find himself caught in a parson's trap at this time in his life. He had too much work to do.

He was also all too aware that marriage to him would be no prize for any lady.

"And now your father has chosen another duke for you," he said instead.

She looked over her shoulder and laughed at that. Her laughter sounded brittle. "And I shall have to disappoint him once again."

"What do you plan on doing to run the duke off?" he teased.

She turned to face him fully. "I thought I might spill my soup on him."

"If he leads you in to dinner again, you could trip and fall, pulling him to the ground with you."

"And grab one of mother's flower arrangements as well. I could crack the vase upon his head and bury him in water and blossoms."

"That should do it," he said. He was glad to see her smiling again.

Pulling the jacket more closely around her, she glanced back at him. "So, what do you think of Marcus?"

"Very cheeky of you," he said. "To send me a valet who would have been devastated for life had I refused his services."

"He is enthusiastic." They began walking again. The well-maintained wilderness path would take them back to the manor eventually.

"Your family has very…interesting servants. I take it the butler is married to your housekeeper? Is your father's valet married to the cook, by chance?"

"Whipple has never married. Marcus's mother abandoned him when he was seven. I was just a child, myself, at that time, but it created something of a scandal…Not that Whipple fathered a son out of wedlock, but that my parents allowed Whipple to take him in. Marcus is a favorite of the household staff."

Garrett shook his head and laughed. "And this poor boy wants nothing more than to become a gentleman's valet?"

"He does, my lord," Natalie said. "But, alas, is there a gentleman who might be willing to take him on?"

Garrett placed her hand on his arm once again. He assumed they were both using the term *gentleman* loosely. "You don't play fair, my lady."

She chuckled, and they continued around the path. Natalie chided him for not bringing any fish back from the afternoon's expedition. He insisted he'd caught dozens of them, huge beasts too great in size to be carried back to the cook's kitchens. He feigned outrage at her refusal to believe him. They further surprised each other by finding other topics that interested them both, and before they knew it, the manor came back into view. The windows glowed, and piano music drifted out into the night. Natalie stopped and let out a wistful sigh.

"You are very lucky, you know." She sounded serious again.

Garrett thought he'd misheard her for a moment. "Pardon?"

"I said you are really quite lucky."

He had not misheard. "How is that?"

"If you were a woman and you acted with such disregard toward society"—she slanted him a sideways and disapproving glance—"as you have, there would be no second chances for you. A lady could never act as a rake and be forgiven." She slipped his jacket off and handed it back to him. He looked down at the jacket, not sure what she expected him to do with it.

"Take it. I am fine now. I will enter through the back, and you may use the front door. It is best nobody knows we spent so much time together, alone."

He took the jacket, not bothering to slip it back on. He just stood there dumbfounded, watching her. "Why would a lady wish to play the part of a rake?" he couldn't help asking. Was she referring to *herself*?

The girlish sparkle disappeared from her eyes, and a bleak longing replaced it.

"Throughout my engagement, over the course of an entire year, my fiancé bestowed only two kisses upon me." She touched her cheek. "One here." And then she touched her lips. "And once here. And yet, when I caught him looking at the woman who is now his duchess, he beheld her with...hunger! I am certain he kissed *her* more than twice. And with an open mouth, no less." Perhaps she felt safe telling him all this because of the darkness. Perhaps she was restless because of her recent broken engagement. Whatever the reason, an intensity of emotion emanated from her.

And then she stepped forward and put her hand on Garrett's chest. She licked her lips and surprised him by admitting, "I have seen you watch me with a similar expression. You may kiss me, if you wish." Her eyes were bold as they gazed up at him.

Garrett's heart beat rapidly. What on earth was she

saying? Both her hands were on his shoulders now. Of course, he wanted to kiss her. His body roared with hunger. Hell, he'd imagined sharing much more than kisses with her on more than one occasion. And suddenly, she was not so unattainable after all.

But at what cost? She was a young noblewoman set aside to marry a duke. Perhaps not Monfort, but her parents had high hopes for an exceptional match. Garrett ignored the pull of desire coursing through him and continued to hold his jacket between them. He did not trust this. He did not trust *her*.

"What is it that you want, my lady?" he asked. He did not wish to be toyed with.

In an abrupt display of temper, she jerked away and stomped one of her dainty little feet. "Oh, blast and fiddlesticks! You're a rake, for heaven's sake. Must I spell it out for you? I Want. A. Kiss." Her eyes flashed like sapphires. "There, now are you satisfied? You ask me why a woman would ever wish to be a rake, well, I will tell you: To experience life, that's why. Women go from their parents' care to that of their husbands. Always, *always* being protected. Never experiencing anything real. I just want to know…I want to know."

He felt the frustration radiating from her. Or was that his own? When the words stopped flowing, she looked up at him with pleading eyes.

He should turn on his heel and walk back to the house right now. Playing such games with Lady Natalie Spencer would bring him nothing but trouble.

She pulled at him in a most primitive way. In the moonlight, her hair shone like golden silk. The breeze swirled the gown she wore around her person, tantalizing him with hints of her softness and curves.

The look in her eyes, in addition to her words, conveyed how badly she wanted his touch—his kiss. He'd never been a man to deny himself sensual pleasure.

But she was an innocent. She was his host's daughter, his friend's sister.

As he looked at her, a tear, suspended on one of her long lashes, lost its hold and trickled down to the corner of her mouth.

Oh, hell! Now he had caused her to cry. He could not win tonight! His control snapped.

Garrett tossed his jacket onto the path and grabbed her by the elbows. "Do you know what you are asking?" he ground out between clenched teeth. He was angry with her for tempting him, angry with himself for being tempted. Truce be damned! He pulled her close, his face mere inches from hers, and inhaled deeply. The mingled scent of her perfume and soap fed his desire yet more.

He had not asked to come to this damn house party. He had not asked to play the gentleman with the daughter of his host and hostess. He hadn't asked for any of this, and he was damn tired of society's indecipherable games.

There was no more denying himself tonight. He grasped her chin and tilted her head back. His other arm clamped about her tightly.

As his lips claimed hers, passion, fueled by fury and lust, unleashed.

She ought to push him away. She ought to compress her lips into a tight barrier. She ought to twist her face to the side to dodge his assault. She did none of these things.

No, Lady Natalie parted her lips and allowed him full access to the tender skin there. She tasted sweet and warm. Without moving away, he spoke into her mouth. "Is this what you want?" His ran his tongue along her teeth and the roof of her mouth. "And this?" She represented all he could never have. How she had provoked him! He was angry. He was also aroused. Hell and damnation!

Instead of pushing him away as a woman of gentle breeding ought, Lady Natalie clutched him with fierce but delicate hands and arched her body into his. He'd gone from playing the part of an affable gentleman to allowing his baser emotions to take control. Pulling her closer, he pushed his knee into her skirts, between her thighs. A low moan of pleasure escaped her.

She should be frightened.

Her hands grasped at the back of his head, pulling him closer. "Yes," she breathed against his lips. "Yes."

Very familiar with giving and receiving pleasure from willing females, he knew her body was his for the taking. His own rejoiced, but at the same time, his brain sent up an alarm. This was too easy. This was all wrong. Tapping his last vestiges of self-control, Garrett ripped himself away.

Looking bereft, she hugged herself against the shock of the cool night air. As awareness of his rejection struck her, she shivered. Garrett refrained from apologizing.

Retrieving his jacket from the ground, he ran a trembling hand through his hair. His cravat now dangled round his neck. His eyes looked anywhere but at her. Already, guilt dogged him.

"Why did you stop? What did I do wrong?"

He glanced at her coldly. The control that had snapped inside of him moments before was thankfully back in place. "*You* are wrong. Everything about you is wrong!" He gritted his teeth before continuing. "Earlier this afternoon, you implored me to alter my behavior so I could impress your parents' guests with my fine gentility. You even obtained a valet for me. And now, this evening, you're ready to lift your skirts like any Drury Lane doxy? What the hell is your game? Are you *trying* to drive me crazy?"

He would not await an answer. With those parting words, he turned on his heel and strode away from her. He did not look back.

Chapter Seven

Shocked by her own actions, Natalie stood frozen on the path long after Lord Hawthorne's departure. Conflicting sensations ran rampant through her. His abrupt departure was chilling, and yet, inside, Natalie felt warm and flushed from the desire he'd awakened. After several moments, casting off the trance that had captured her, she tentatively touched her fingers to her lips. The normally plump flesh there ought to be burning. It ought to be feverish after his scorching kiss. But her lips felt no different than before. How was that possible?

His departing words cut deeply. If he'd been trying to hurt her, he had succeeded. And she'd deserved every word.

Shame swept through her, both for her wanton actions and her contradictory behavior. But...an overwhelming giddiness came over her nonetheless.

No wonder the mothers and chaperones had kept him away from all the debutantes. The man had practically set fire to her toes!

She would not be devastated by his parting words.

She would not wallow in self-pity from his rejection.

After months of feeling as though her life was fatefully mapped out before her, she thrilled to feel a glimmering of hope in her heart once again. She would not scoff at such a gift.

Light-hearted for the first time in ages, she skipped around back and entered through the servants' entrance, her irritation with being trapped in the country obliterated. What a night!

After climbing the stairs to her room, Natalie's euphoria dissipated as she mulled over Lord Hawthorne's parting words. He had, in fact, been angry when he'd left her. And being thrust away from him so harshly had not been pleasant at all. He'd yelled at her. He'd asked what kind of game she was playing. Was she, in truth, playing games?

He hadn't met her gaze after their kiss. She had seen his eyes though—they had been blazing. He'd looked tormented, almost like a caged animal. *Did I do that to him?* She was not sorry for the kiss, but she did feel bad for making him so explosively angry, especially after getting along so well throughout most of their walk. She had felt as though they were, well, friends. Ought she to apologize?

Her maid, the ever-present and anxious Mrs. Tinsdale, awaited Natalie's return to her room. She even went so far as to scold her, saying a young lady ought not to be gallivanting about the countryside in the dark, no matter it was her own parents' property. The older woman, once nanny to the family, had taken the task as lady's maid to Natalie once all the children had grown. The Spencers were the only family she'd ever known. She'd not given up her original role, however, when it came to caring for Natalie.

"Don't fuss so, Tinsdale. There is nothing wrong with a midnight stroll." Natalie bristled inside. She should not have to answer to her maid, as well as to her parents, her brothers, and all of society! She didn't have the heart to reprimand the woman though. Dearest Tinny didn't deserve Natalie's ire. *Argh!* She felt so…trapped!

Long after Tinsdale left, Natalie lay upon her bed staring at the ceiling. But she did not see the ceiling. No, rather she was recalling intensely black eyes flashing in the moonlight, eyes as black as opals with a few tiny creases at the edges. The creases had appeared when he smiled at her. And he had smiled, yes he had. Before that kiss.

He wasn't dangerous, quite. He was exciting. He represented a world she'd never known. He'd somehow brought her back to life.

And now she'd angered him. She blinked several times at the thought.

She must apologize! Yes, an apology was not only appropriate but imperative. And she mustn't wait until tomorrow. She must apologize tonight!

Buoyed by her decision, Natalie donned her dressing gown and slipped quietly out of her room. Lord Hawthorne was staying in Joseph's old room. As Joseph was nearest to her in age, she'd often snuck into his room late at night for one reason or another. But Joseph was gone. A very different bachelor now occupied his room—one who was not a brother to her—one who was not in good temper with her at the moment.

Pacing outside his door, Natalie very nearly turned around several times to return to her own chamber. Ladies simply did not do this sort of thing. Why, she would be ruined forever if one of her mother's guests caught her behaving so outrageously! But she was not the same girl she'd been all spring. She would take some chances. She would follow her heart.

After looking down both lengths of the corridor to be certain she was not observed, she stepped up to the door and knocked.

She didn't have to wait but a moment.

"Enter," a voice ordered from behind the closed door.

After taking a deep breath, she turned the knob and pushed her way into the masculine abode. Oh Lord, he was not alone.

Marcus was gathering the earl's discarded clothing and preparing to leave his new master for the night. His eyebrows rose in surprise upon seeing Natalie standing at the open door in her dressing gown. "Did you forget that Joseph no longer lives here, my lady?"

Just then Lord Hawthorne appeared from behind the privacy screen. He was barefoot, wearing a deep blue silk dressing gown loosely tied at the waist. The hem barely skimmed the floor. Unbidden, Natalie imagined strong calves rising from those slim masculine feet. As the gown gaped, a deep V of his naked chest stole her attention. The smattering of black hair contrasted with the paleness of his skin.

Natalie tried to remember what Marcus had said. Oh, right, something about this being Joseph's room. "Er, ah, no, Marcus, I have something of import that I must discuss with Lord Hawthorne."

If Marcus could have raised his eyebrows any higher at that moment, Natalie felt certain he would have.

"That will be all, Marcus." Lord Hawthorne dismissed the valet. "Lady Natalie will be returning to her own room very shortly."

Marcus walked toward the door, surreptitiously throwing a speculative glance at Natalie. When he was near enough that he blocked the earl's view of her, she raised one hand to her mouth and made a motion as though locking it with a key. As understanding dawned, Marcus smiled conspiratorially, and then he mimicked her motion.

Accomplices from an early age, she knew he'd not give her secret away. Handy thing, she mused, having a man's valet for a friend.

Marcus closed the door behind Natalie leaving her and Lord Hawthorne—scandalously—alone.

Lord Hawthorne took a seat on one of the cushioned chairs and reclined with a suspicious glower. As he crossed one ankle over his other knee, his dressing gown fell open, revealing a glimpse of one very masculine calf and thigh. Natalie noticed there was less hair above his knee than below it. Would the curling hairs be soft to touch? Her fingers itched to find out.

"Is there something I can do for you, *my lady?*" He pronounced her title with sarcastic emphasis, as though to insinuate she was not *acting* like a lady.

"Um, oh, yes. I was concerned at how we parted." She paused. "I rather thought we were coming to be friends…and I didn't want to go to sleep thinking…Well, I didn't want for you to go to sleep feeling angry with me." She fidgeted with her fingernails. At the end of her poorly rehearsed speech, she peered at him from beneath her lashes. Good Lord, this man was absolutely delicious. However had she thought of him as not-quite-handsome before? With his freshly washed hair, dressed in silk, he made it difficult for her to think straight. She was lucky she'd gotten as many words out as she had.

Garrett stood. He'd behaved unmannerly to remain seated when she entered the room. He should feel guilty about that. Walking across the carpet, he gestured toward the velvet-covered armchair nearest her. "Won't you sit?" He was not going to banish her immediately. He looked thoughtful. Perhaps he wanted to apologize as well.

Smoothing the front of her dressing gown, Natalie sat in the chair he'd indicated. "Thank you." They might well have been in the drawing room with both doors thrown wide open for the formality with which they both spoke.

Garrett returned to his own chair, pulled it closer in front of hers, and sat.

Leaning forward, he draped one arm over a knee and an elbow on the other, resting his chin upon his closed fist. He regarded her with an intensity that made her want to squirm.

"You are right, you know," he conceded softly. "In your opinion that I am lucky to be allowed a second chance." His words surprised her. "I have spent the last decade doing nothing to garner regard amongst society. I have gambled, fought duels, spent time in brothels, and God forbid, made money in business. And when I did attend a *ton* event, I showed no regard for propriety, as you well know."

In a rush, she interrupted his confession. "Why? Why did you do that?" She needed to know. It was as though, within him, there were two different men. For he had not taken advantage of her when given the opportunity earlier tonight.

He grimaced. "Does it matter?"

"It does," she said.

Silence fell so heavy in that moment that the sounds of servants walking overhead suddenly were most apparent. Would he answer her? He looked so very vulnerable. She again felt pulled toward him, as she had in the dining room. But in this moment, she wanted to kneel before him and wrap her arms around his waist.

She sat very straight—feet and knees together—on the elegant high-backed chair.

She didn't move. If she made any move or motion, she feared the intimacy of the moment would be broken and he would snarl something sarcastic.

"I don't know." His voice was low and sounded hoarse. He wasn't looking at her, but at the carpet on the floor between them. He cleared his throat and then looked back at her defiantly. "That's not what we were talking about, anyhow."

She could tell he didn't want to discuss his past. She supposed he thought he didn't need her pity. He was a very proud man.

"I was saying that, upon reflection, I agree that I am lucky. Yes, I have a second chance to be accepted into society—to regain honor and respect for the Hawthorne earldom. And I believe I may do well to take full advantage of this." He leaned forward again, his demeanor ominously serious. He spoke as though he needed to make her understand something very important. "You, my dear lady, are very, very lucky as well."

When she tried to interrupt him, he went right on

talking. "No, do not belittle all you have. I am not referring to this beautiful home and all the material wealth your family is able to bestow upon you. I am talking about your brothers and your parents." He swallowed hard. "You have siblings who would kill anyone who dared ever hurt you, a father and mother who would do *anything* to ensure your happiness. They all love you deeply. Good God, they smile at you. I have even seen your father *hug* you! In public, no less."

Garrett paused a moment. "I beg of you, do not dismiss this." At that, he went silent. A lump had formed in his throat, and he resented it. He rather resented the emotions threatening to overcome him. He far preferred his normal cynical indifference. How had it become so corroded?

"Well, blast." Lady Natalie looked as though she'd tasted something sour.

Garrett sat back, startled. He realized he oughtn't to be startled by anything that came out of this chit's mouth, but he was, nonetheless.

"I beg your pardon?"

"It's just that the irony of the situation is, in truth, rather magnificent. You have what I want, and I have what you want. In order for either of us to obtain what we want, we must sacrifice some of what we already have."

Garrett's mind retraced her words a time or two before understanding what she meant. "Yes, you are somewhat right."

"Why only somewhat?"

"Because you are not going to sacrifice what you have. You are going to honor your parents and forget this crazy notion of playing the 'lady rake.' "

Nonsensical, addlepated female! He did not admit, however that he had no intentions of sacrificing what he'd been doing in the past. He would simply be more discreet about it.

And discretion did not include having the daughter of his host in his bedchamber late at night with both of them in nothing but nightclothes.

Lady Natalie glared at him. "That's a little condescending, wouldn't you agree? How would you feel if I told you something like that? I am not a child, you know."

He regarded her narrowed blue eyes and petulant bottom lip for a moment in silence.

Perhaps, what Lady Natalie needed was a taste of what she wanted. Perhaps that would result in her realizing the wisdom of being more amenable to her father's plans.

Lord Ravensdale ought to appreciate the favor Garrett was going to do for him. He obviously had no idea how much of a powder keg his daughter was.

"What would you like, my lady? To pretend you are not the daughter of an earl?" The taunt caught her full attention. "Would you like"—he paused, enjoying the expressions racing across her perfect features— "another kiss?" He'd meant the offer to scare her, to shake her reckless courage. The acceleration of his own heartbeat surprised him.

Natalie's gaze turned suspicious. She was so very expressive, he could almost read her mind. Oh, yes, she wanted another kiss. But was he asking, or was he mocking her?

"Are you offering?" She lifted her chin and challenged him.

"I am if it will get you out of my room. I'll also have your word that it will put an end to all of this nonsense!" Would her promise be worth anything?

"Very well then," she said quickly—too quickly.

He stared back for a moment and then shook his head, trying not to laugh. Good Lord, she was priceless!

"Don't laugh at me!" she grumbled.

She sounded hurt. He didn't want her to feel hurt. He would give her what she wanted—this one last time. And then he'd have her promise to leave him the hell alone.

"Come here then." He patted his lap.

"You want me to sit *on top of you*? Shouldn't we be standing?" She narrowed her eyes, finally exhibiting some prudent caution. Ah, she wasn't so foolish after all.

But it had been a long day and he was tired. "If you want a kiss from a rake, then you must do as he demands." He patted his lap again. "Come here."

Appearing unusually shy, Natalie rose and inched over to stand in front of him. As she neared, floral perfume teased his senses. Not giving her the opportunity to change her mind, Garrett grabbed hold of her waist and pulled her down to sit across his knees. She dropped her hand onto his shoulder and then slid it around his neck.

The minute her soft bottom landed on his lap, Garrett realized he was making a colossal mistake. Every ounce of blood he possessed headed south, and his own physical response to her was making itself known. Oh, hell.

This was intimate. Far too intimate. The lushness of her body assaulted his senses. He could smell her shampoo, a hint of lavender and citrus. Her long hair flowed silky and sensual on his arms, some even finding his chest. And when her fingers tickled the skin of his neck, his muscles tensed.

Her face was inches from his. "What now?" she asked, all innocence. Her breath was minty. He knew his would smell of whiskey.

He had better make this good if he was going to scare her to such a degree that she stop playing with fire. He turned her face toward his.

He meant to scare her—to slow her down. But as his gaze dropped to her sweet, inviting lips, an unusual tenderness struck him, and his kiss wasn't the onslaught he'd intended.

No, he tasted, gently nipping at the corner of her mouth before claiming it.

The second his lips touched hers, she came to life. Eager for more, in an attempt to be even closer, Natalie twisted her body toward him. As she did so, her hips pressed into his arousal. Garrett winced as he tried to not only control himself but her as well. Was this going to backfire on him? Most likely.

Her tongue danced freely with his, encouraging him to deepen their kiss. The uninhibited enthusiasm of her welcome aroused him in a way the most skilled courtesan could never match. And she responded as though she had been waiting for this moment her entire life.

Needs ignited, and Garrett began to forget himself. Momentarily succumbing to desire, his hand explored her waist, her abdomen, and then the undersides of her breasts. Their seeking mouths mingled mint and whiskey. She trembled, pulled her mouth away, and buried her face in his neck. He gave her a moment to catch her breath. She was gasping.

His own chest rose and fell quickly as well. He traced a path down the side of her neck to her shoulder. Garrett felt his self-control slipping away.

He need not have worried.

In another inspired effort to be closer to him, Natalie made to turn her body to straddle him. Lacking experience in these matters, however, she misjudged the width of the chair, and the point of her knee struck Garrett's person in a most catastrophic location.

Her knee, like a piston, became the deadliest of weapons and slammed into his full arousal with unfortunate accuracy. The red haze of desire he'd been fighting vanished and was replaced with a white-hot flash of agony. Unthinking, Garrett shoved her off his lap onto the carpet and doubled over in excruciating pain.

"What is it? What is the matter?" she asked, crawling over to him. He put a hand out as though to stave her off. Breath hissed between his clenched teeth. His motion was enough to stop her from coming any closer.

"Dear God, what have I done?" she implored.

He took a few deep but labored breaths. "A moment please."

He waited for the pain to recede before addressing his attacker again. But, once able to look back at her, his breath caught. Her lips were swollen from their kiss, and her hair fell disheveled around her face. On her knees, in nightclothes, she looked at him in deep concern. If Lady Natalie Spencer, dressed and pressed for a ball was beautiful, then this Natalie, sultry and awakened, was the most gorgeous woman he'd ever beheld.

Was he going mad?

"What happened?" she asked, sounding impatient. Exasperation replaced her concern.

"You kneed me."

She looked at him in obvious confusion. "Well, I realize I am a bit…wanton, but I don't *need* you. I like you though." She tilted her head and smiled hesitantly.

He raised his brows at her. "Your knee, you struck me with it." He would not spell this out for her. Good Lord, she had brothers; she must have some understanding as to the sensitivity of the male anatomy.

Awareness dawned. "Oh."

He knew precisely what she was going to say next.

"Blast." And the she added. "I'm, er, sorry?"

Garrett grunted. His most vulnerable parts still throbbing.

"Did I…damage you?" she asked.

"For now, yes, thank you very much." He forced himself to stand and tied the belt around his waist more securely. Protecting himself from any sudden move she might make, he somehow managed to present his hand to her so she could stand as well. He didn't think he could suffer any more of her surprises. "And it's off to your own room now. I believe I have kept my part of our bargain. I'd appreciate it if you would keep yours."

She stared at his outstretched hand in consternation and then allowed him to pull her to her feet. With his hand on her back, Garrett steered her toward the door. He did so cautiously, all the while prepared to defend himself from another "attack." Mindful of her reputation, he peeked out to ascertain the corridor was empty and then pushed her into the hall. "Good night then."

She placed her hand on the doorframe, effectively keeping him from closing the door. "You are not angry with me? Are you? Remember, that is why I came here in the first place."

"I am not angry with you, but I will be if you do not leave quietly."

She blinked once, then again, before leaning in and placing a quick kiss on his cheek. "Good night," she whispered. With no further ado, she twirled around and disappeared into her own room.

Wincing, Garrett closed the door behind him and hobbled back to the chair to collapse—not before reaching for the bell pull to summon Marcus, though, for he was going to need some ice.

Chapter Eight

Not one to sleep in, Garrett arose at dawn and went downstairs in search of breakfast. Pleasantly surprised, he met a group of gentlemen guests preparing to embark upon a tour of Ravensdale's estate. They would look over the earl's irrigation system with Ravensdale as their guide. Apparently, this outing had been planned far in advance and was one of the primary reasons some of the gentlemen were in attendance. Eager to escape the house and Lady Natalie, Garrett joined them without hesitation.

Last night, he'd made one mistake after another. He'd be wise to avoid the troublesome minx for the remainder of his stay. If he could not succeed at that, then perhaps he would simply cut his holiday short and return to Maple Hall. But for today, he embraced the reprieve gratefully.

Busy stable workers assisted the gentlemen guests, lugging saddles out of the barn and tightening girths. Ravensdale's estate extended for miles and the expedition would last all day. Garrett refused assistance and saddled Rumble himself.

Forcing himself to be patient, he waited atop his mount watching the kitchen help rush to the stable with packages of rations. Lady Ravensdale stood talking with her husband as his guests took their mounts. Garrett was not surprised to see the couple exchange a brief kiss before the earl bid her farewell. Other gentlemen present were the Duke of Monfort, the Baron of Riverton, the Earl of Blakely, Stone, Darlington—Ravensdale's heir—and another son, Peter. In addition, several other gentlemen had lined up with whom Garrett was not acquainted. As they headed out, Garrett urged his horse away from the manor and away from Lady Natalie.

Stone ambled his mount beside him as they headed across the back field. "I wondered where you'd gone off to after dinner. I'd rather thought the two of us would trek into the village for a few ales last night."

"It was a long day," Garrett answered. He could hardly explain to his friend that he'd been pawing at his sister. And then, not wishing to be rude, he added, "Did you go out alone then?"

"No, stayed back with the old men." Stone laughed. "I wish to assure you again, when I invited you here, I'd no idea my mother had planned such a large house party."

Garrett rode along for a moment without speaking. "No worries. Her guests are reasonable sorts, really. I haven't found reason to cuff any of them yet," he conceded, "and it's always a pleasure to converse with your father."

As though summoned by Garrett's words, Lord Ravensdale cantered up behind them, bringing his horse abreast of the two younger men. He pulled on the reins, and they slowed to a walk. There was too much riding to accomplish that day to push their horses early on.

"Good morning, Hawthorne, pulled yourself from bed early, I see." The older man glanced at Garrett. "I failed to mention the outing to you last night. You disappeared early."

"Not for lack of good company, my lord," Garrett answered.

"Well, I'm glad you have joined us today. My steward's been doing a great deal to maximize the efficiency of our irrigation systems. Have you had a chance to inspect the channels around Maple Hall yet?" he asked.

Garrett shook his head. The condition of the fields left by his father was an embarrassment. "They're in ruins. Aside from the fire, the estate has been so neglected, I have much rebuilding before I can begin improvements." The men rode in silence for a few minutes. "The physical condition of the property is just part of the difficulties, however."

Lord Ravensdale gave a rueful chuckle. "Tenant unrest, I imagine. No doubt the old man left you something of a hornet's nest." The earl adjusted himself in his saddle before continuing, "I've faith in you though. I've seen you turn around some shaky business deals for all involved, myself included. You'll do fine to approach the estate the same way."

As a hedge appeared ahead, the men spurred their mounts and took on the obstacle. Upon clearing it easily, they allowed the horses to walk again.

Garrett contemplated the tenants he'd spoken with. Most of them were willing to work with him contingent upon the investments he'd promised.

He'd heard talk, though, of one particular family in the village who held what might very well be a legitimate grudge. One of the older brothers had been working as a footman for his father and was killed the night of the fire. Evidence showed the man had been shot. Garrett could easily believe the rumors that his old man had pulled the trigger. Although not responsible for his father's actions, and nothing could bring back the man, Garrett felt he owed them some retribution. He needed to approach the matter carefully. Legal issues, as well as emotional ones, must be considered.

Although he would have liked to, he could not discuss any of this with his friends. Certain matters must remain unspoken.

Garrett came out of his musings. The earl had been addressing him. "Pardon?" he asked.

"You'd be surprised how helpful a wife can be. My countess discovers gossip and whatnot that I would never be privy to. A woman can be more approachable, easier to unburden one's secrets to." He looked over at Garrett meaningfully. "You might do well to take on this task *not alone*, but with a good lady at your side." A roguish light gleamed in the man's eyes.

Garrett held the man's stare for but a moment as comprehension dawned. Was the earl implying his own daughter might be a candidate for the position? Such a notion made no sense at all! What about Monfort? What of the shadows looming over the Hawthorne legacy? Surely, no man would want Hawthorne blood running through his grandchildren's veins.

Garrett chose his next words carefully. Shaking his head, he said, "Unfortunately for me, the Season is at an end. Even so, not many marriage-minded mamas are throwing their daughters in my path."

"Lucky for you, I'd say." The earl laughed. "Most chits on the marriage mart are more liability than asset." He rode silently for a moment before adding, "Perhaps the lady you need at your side can be found in the country. Perhaps she's nearer than you think." Looking over, he gave Garrett a sly smile and then spurred his horse into a trot, taking after the gentlemen ahead.

Good Lord, the man *was* suggesting his own daughter.

Stone, watching the look of astonishment on Garrett's face, burst out laughing.

"Did your father just say what I think he said?" Garrett asked his old friend.

Stone tried to bring his mirth under control before he answered. Once composed, he said, "By God, I believe so. But reserve any action on your part, my friend. My sister is not biddable, and it's very likely she'd refuse your suit anyway. I think you've enough troubles without adding to them." Laughing again, Stone shook his head. "She just got herself out of one of my father's schemes, she's not about to allow him to get her into another. What's my father thinking?"

Garrett attempted to look nonchalant. "My sentiments exactly."

****

Natalie did not appear downstairs for breakfast until several hours after the gentlemen had left for their day-long ride. In fact, she arrived just as the footmen began to remove the chafing dishes and pans warming the various breakfast offerings which had been set out. Only Lady Sheffield, Natalie's godmother whom she called Aunt Eleanor, remained, lingering over her coffee as Natalie sat down with a plate of scrambled eggs and bacon.

"You look tired, dear. Did you not sleep well?" Aunt Eleanor asked. Although concern laced her voice, Natalie detected curiosity as well.

"My chamber was a trifle warm. Summer is definitely upon us." Natalie waited to sit as the footman pulled the chair out for her. The weather was always a safe topic, after all. "I don't think I fell asleep until the morning hours." Another footman stepped forward to pour Natalie's favorite blend of coffee into her cup. The rich aromatic liquid perked her up before she'd even taken a sip. She loved coffee. She preferred it even to chocolate in the mornings.

Aunt Eleanor smiled affectionately. "I never thanked you, my dear, for what you did for my niece, my precious Lilly. Not many young women would release a duke as you did. You demonstrated tremendous grace and courage." She blinked rapidly, as though to dispel tears, but had more to say. "I hope you are not…heartbroken? I know you told Lilly you were not, but, oh, you made two people so very happy, and now it is my greatest wish that you find happiness as well."

Natalie inhaled the fragrance of her coffee and took a slow sip. She searched her heart again before answering. She wanted to be truthful. "I was not 'in love' with Cortland. The evidence of his feelings for Lilly became apparent to me when we picnicked at London Hills. They couldn't keep their eyes off one another. I know they did not intend to hurt me. In fact, I believe they'd been fighting their feelings for some time." Natalie studied the delicate roses painted on her cup as she spoke. "In the end, they could not deny their mutual love." She closed her eyes and took another long sip. Looking straight at the older woman, she continued, "I did not wish to marry a man who is in love with somebody else, Aunt. I know there are numerous marriages within the *ton* such as this, but that is something I could never abide."

Again, she studied the steaming liquid in her cup. When Lilly and the duke had returned from their private walk around the lake that day, Lilly had had leaves in her hair.

And the duke's shirttail had been partially untucked from his breeches.

"You are wiser than your years, my dear." Aunt Eleanor shook her head. "As to your astute observation regarding the duke and Lilly, I am impressed. I spent a great deal of time with both of them and was certain they were over past affections." The older lady crossed her utensils on her plate and sat up straight. "Anyhow, I am glad you realized the truth and found the courage to do something about it. And how are you faring now? Trapped in the country with a bunch of folks twice, three times your age?"

Natalie didn't have the opportunity to answer, for just then her mother entered the room. Seeing Natalie, Lady Ravensdale smiled affectionately. "I see you have finally decided to join us today. You haven't slept this late since we left London. You're not ill, are you, dear?" The countess rested her hands on the back of an empty chair and regarded her daughter in concern.

"Oh, I'm fine, Mother." Natalie couldn't truthfully explain why she'd been unable to fall asleep. Kisses like she'd experienced the night before, long, hot, and wet, did something to a girl's ability to sleep. Kisses...and touches...and the feel of his hot breath on her neck... "The nights are turning warm already, and I"—she shrugged—"just couldn't fall asleep." Even to herself she sounded breathless.

Lady Ravensdale blinked a moment as she looked at her daughter. Natalie could almost read her mother's mind. In actuality, the night had been cool. "Well, then. Be that as it might, I wanted to inform you that Lady Riverton received a missive from her daughter, Penelope—Miss Crone—do you remember her? Well, she was planning on spending several weeks at her aunt's home near Bristol—she has a cousin of like age who is still living with her parents. Both the girls are on the shelf, so to speak. Anyhow, Penelope's aunt has injured an ankle or something...I cannot remember exactly. But that's of no matter. Lady Riverton asked if the two young women could join us here instead of returning to Helmsley Manor. I agreed, of course. I thought it would be nice for you to have some ladies here closer to your own age."

Natalie had met Penelope Crone during her first season and found her a stimulating companion. Miss Crone entertained quite scandalous notions as to how females ought to behave and be treated in society. She provoked intriguing conversations, indeed.

Natalie could not recall having met the cousin however. "Who is this cousin, Mother?"

Her mother paused as though counting the years. "Miss Abigail Wright. I believe she is similar in age to Miss Crone. I am not certain. From what I hear, she is something of a bluestocking. In any case, I thought it would be nice for you. You haven't been yourself, and I thought that perhaps..." Tilting her head, she regarded her daughter. "Does that sound agreeable, then?"

Natalie sighed. It *would* be diverting to have some younger ladies about. And Penelope could prove to be entertaining. Her ideas about how a woman ought to manage her own life were revolutionary. Natalie wondered what her mother would think if she realized this. "I'd like that, Mother." Summoning more enthusiasm, she smiled warmly. "You look lovely today, by the way. Did you arise early to send off the expedition?"

When Natalie came out in society two years earlier, she'd realized how lucky she was to have such a youthful-looking mother. Today her mother appeared bright and cheerful in a peach cotton morning gown with a crisp white apron. She'd styled her hair in her usual simple knot, pulled up prettily, with tendrils escaped about her nape.

Lady Ravensdale fluffed her skirts and then smoothed them again. "That's sweet of you, darling. And yes, I woke early to see your father off with all the gentlemen. They are touring the estate's irrigation systems, I believe. I don't expect we'll see them before supper."

Oh. Natalie fought her disappointment. She hadn't thought the expedition would last all day. *Had all the gentlemen ridden out?*

"Did Stone go as well?" she asked.

"Yes, as well as Darly and Peter. Most of the gentlemen, I believe."

Well then. Not that she needed to see the estate, but it was vexing not to have been invited.

Her mother went on talking. "Perhaps we ladies might make a trip into Bath to do some shopping. Just as you suggested, Eleanor." She smiled at her longtime friend. "The weather is gorgeous, and the days have already gotten longer. Would you care to join us, Natalie?"

"I suppose. Have I time to change?" At the very least she could leave the estate. And shopping? Always a satisfying pastime!

Her mother glanced at the clock. "The carriages will be brought around at one, so you have barely an hour. Meanwhile I must locate Lady Riverton to reassure her again of the girls' welcome."

"When will they be arriving?"

"Oh, they don't have far to travel, sometime tomorrow, I imagine." Her mother headed for the door but then turned around quickly. "One hour, Natalie," she reminded. And with that, the countess disappeared as quickly as she arrived.

Setting down her cup, Lady Sheffield spoke first. "Miss Penelope Crone is an…interesting young lady. She is a good friend of Lilly's."

Natalie smiled. "Yes, I know. I don't think Mother knows of her liberal tendencies, nor of her political ideas. She will likely liven things up. Are you acquainted with the cousin?"

Squinting slightly, as though doing so might jog her memory, Aunt Eleanor took a moment to answer. "I do believe I've met her on a few occasions. Miss Abigail something or other. She made her come out the year before Lilly. She was cheerful, but slightly plump. I don't think she took very well. I suppose that would be likely as she is as yet unmarried. Seems to me she was entangled in some sort of scandal…it has been a while…"

"Or she has been spending too much time with Penelope," Natalie suggested.

Lady Sheffield nodded. "Yes, or that." In a change of subject, she tilted her head and surprised Natalie with her candidness by asking, "Your parents aren't setting their sights on Monfort for you, are they?" Lady Sheffield's observational skills were obviously not diminished by age.

Natalie groaned. "Dear God, I hope not. But it does appear they are pushing me in that direction."

The duke's attentions, or lack thereof, suggested to Natalie that she need not be concerned. No woman alive could bring that emotionless man up to scratch. If only her father would desist with his manipulation regarding her personal affairs. Natalie found it disconcerting that she had more faith in her father's ability to bring the man up to scratch than she had in her own.

Lady Sheffield's voice interrupted her absurd train of thought. "A more likely husband, I should think, would be that darned handsome rascal, the new Earl of Hawthorne. He'd be a fine catch." The woman looked pleased with herself. Were all women of the *ton* matchmakers?

Natalie choked on her coffee. Aunt Eleanor was very astute. Keeping her eyes fixed firmly upon her food, Natalie tried not to imagine what it would be like to wake up with Lord Hawthorne beside her. It would not do for her godmother to catch wind of Natalie's inclinations toward…that man!

"You know what they say about reformed rakes…They—"

"Make the best husbands," Natalie finished for her. And then, to curtail the direction of Lady Eleanor's conversation, she continued more seriously, "He is here to collect some belongings Stone has stored for him. From the look and size of the containers, I believe they are paintings or something—large crates and a few trunks." Lowering her voice confidentially, she added, "Didn't trust them with his father, from what I gather."

Lady Eleanor's face broke into a delighted smile. "Oh, I do hope he has preserved some of his mother's paintings! Such a talented lady, she was." She looked as though she wished to say more but took another sip of her coffee instead. Her hand shook ever so slightly.

"You knew his mother?"

Almost as though she were blinking away a tear or two, Aunt Eleanor looked out the window for a moment before answering. "Lady Cordelia was a dear friend of mine, that is, before her marriage." Regaining her composure, she clucked her tongue in disapproval. "That husband of hers took her off to the country, and we never saw her again." She reached for the nearby coffeepot and poured herself another half cup. "Her parents once held a private exhibit in their London home, in lieu of a musicale. Most of the paintings were landscapes. I still remember one I wished I could have taken home with me, an oil painting with all the colors of autumn—not traditionally done. Such an untamed result." She seemed lost in thought. "I do hope young Hawthorne has been able to save them. That would be a great treasure indeed."

After hearing this, Natalie wished she'd not told her mother she would go into Bath for the day, after all. For it would have been the perfect time for her to see if she could take a peek at what Lord Hawthorne had stored on the third floor. She ought to feel guilty for even thinking of invading his privacy, but curiosity often got the best of her. *Oh, blast.*

"Perhaps you could ask him," she said to her aunt

instead. Auntie could very well be a valuable source of information.

But her godmother was on to her. "Hmmm…you are as curious as I am." She looked at Natalie suspiciously. "We shall both be forced to wait, however, as he is out with the other gentlemen." She pushed back her chair and stood, looking around. "What happened to that footman? I suppose we've dallied too late to expect them to wait around for us late risers to finish up in here." Heading for the door, she paused before turning back to Natalie one last time. "Do consider my suggestion, dear. I think Garrett Castleton would be the catch of the year." Her eyes twinkled merrily. "Take the word of an old widowed lady who has seen both the best and the worst of them. I can spot a good man from a mile away." She then laughed and exited the room, not waiting for a reply.

****

The ladies cut a considerable swath through Bath that afternoon. Although not the fashionable scene it had once been, the charming town offered plenty of shopping and walking and taking of tea for the countess's guests to experience. Natalie enjoyed herself more than she'd imagined. She'd done no shopping since breaking her engagement, and that seemed ages ago! She happily seized the opportunity to make up for lost time and did her fair share to keep the Bath merchants flush.

In carriages loaded down with brightly colored packages, they returned to Raven's Park just as the heat of the day burned hottest.

Carriage doors flew open, and liveried footman pulled down steps. Grooms handily unloaded packages, while ladies' maids awaited their mistresses with lavender-scented baths to wash away the grime of the day. Ravensdale and his gentlemen had not yet returned.

The matronly guests took their time bathing, napping, and then dressing again. As the sun set, they at last gathered in the drawing room, still with no sign of the gentlemen. Upon consuming a second glass of wine, Lady Ravensdale suggested they abandon hope of the gentlemen returning in a timely fashion and take supper without them. Tea had been consumed hours ago, and it would be a shame if the efforts in the kitchen were to grow cold. There were a few token protests that the men might feel slighted, but Lady Ravensdale dismissed them. She knew her husband well, she explained to them. It might be well after dark before they returned.

With no assigned seating tonight, the women congregated toward the foot of the table where Lady Ravensdale presided. Being the youngest, Natalie found herself closer to the opposite end, flanked by an empty chair.

Naturally, before the footmen could serve the first course, the sounds of boots and masculine joviality echoed upstairs from the foyer. Barely one minute passed before the earl himself swaggered in and leaned down to whisper something into his wife's ear. By the expression on her mother's face, Natalie guessed he smelled of horses and spirits. The earl and his scotch, although not bosom buddies, were, at times, good friends.

The countess rolled her eyes and then spoke to the table in general. "The gentlemen, it seems, will be joining us after all." Some cavalier and others quite sheepish, the fellows wandered in one by one. Apparently, the meal was to be further delayed.

In one moment Natalie anticipated seeing Lord Hawthorne, only to dread his company in the next. She'd never before acted so crudely with a gentleman! What would she say to him? Would he ignore her? She kept her eyes fixed upon her empty plate as various gentlemen found their seats near her father's end of the long table.

Lord Hawthorne drifted into the dining room with the second wave of gentleman. Taking the empty chair beside Natalie, he sat down and greeted those around her. As more and more of the gentlemen arrived, it could not help but be noticed that not one of them had declined to partake of the earl's scotch. Voices were louder than usual, and some slurred their words. Many of them forgot their manners, placing elbows upon the table and ignoring the carefully folded napkins completely.

Natalie sat still as a statue. Lord Hawthorne had chosen to sit beside *her!*

Chapter Nine

Feeling particularly amenable, Garrett turned to lazily regard Natalie. She was a child in a woman's body, a spoiled debutante. He ought to treat her as one.

Except that he wanted her. And if he were honest with himself, he'd wanted her since the moment he first laid eyes upon her in London nearly two years ago.

But who was Lady Natalie Spencer, really? The spoiled chit who'd spurned him in London, or was she this new minx? Flirtatious and innocent? Likely, she could not answer these questions herself. Her actions were brash and inappropriate for a young unmarried woman of the *ton*. And yet, she did not seem to lack moral fortitude. She merely seemed to be too curious for her own good.

And, although scoffing at the concept earlier that day, Garrett was now unbelievably considering the unfathomable notion of marriage to her. Not only to satisfy his physical needs, but to satisfy her father, and also to help smooth the path of rebuilding the Hawthorne earldom. Was this all incredible luck on his part or a gilded trap? Good God, he *must be* foxed!

"And how did you spend your day, *my lady*?" he asked, perhaps condescendingly. "I understand the ladies were to travel to Bath for the day. Did you purchase a new bonnet, or perhaps a bright new ribbon or two?"

"Both, to be certain," she said, oh, so casually, glancing at him sideways. "You are recovered from your…ah…injury?" She appeared adorable and alluring this evening, shy, even, after last night's debacle. A rosy pink blossomed on her cheeks as she seemed to struggle to meet his eyes. When she did so, she could only hold his gaze for a moment before once again finding her food fascinating.

Garrett winced at the remembered shock and pain of the night before. "We can thank the Almighty that such injuries pass quickly and leave no permanent damage." Or he wouldn't have spent the day riding about on a horse, that was for damn sure.

The afternoon *had* been enjoyable and enlightening. Upon examining the efficiencies Ravensdale's steward had incorporated into the irrigation systems, the earl proffered a large jug of fine scotch. Following a visit to the last tenant's farm, the gentlemen's pace slowed considerably. In fact, they stopped several times on their way to refill flasks from the jug the earl's assistant transported on the back of his nag. By that time, the men were conversing on numerous topics such as horses, cards, gambling, agriculture, philosophy, or women. Garrett found his own thoughts constantly returning to an impetuous young lady. Dared he even consider her father's suggestion? The more scotch he drank, the more confused he'd become.

When Lady Natalie had first appeared in society, Garrett had known her for a woman he could never pursue. She'd represented all he'd spurned for most of his adult life. And why would such a woman even consider him? The financial security he could provide came along with a tarnished title. Lady Natalie needed neither. And so, he'd contented himself with admiring her from afar. And then she'd become engaged to the Duke of Cortland.

But now she was not.

In fact, it seemed she was no longer off limits at all.

Their brief encounters over the past two days had awakened something inside of him. She amused him and yet, somehow managed to affect him sexually. Would he ever want more from her? His immediate instinct to the threat of a leg-shackle had always been to flee. Being tied to one woman for life was, in a word, terrifying.

Garrett had never desired steady companionship from anybody, let alone a woman.

But as today progressed, a voice in his head contemplated the hare-brained idea planted by Ravensdale.

He could have her in his bed every night.

As she had shown the previous night, she yearned to explore her sensual nature. Under the right circumstances, of course, Garrett would be more than pleased to assist her in this endeavor. He would introduce her to all manner of carnal experiences. He'd hastily dismissed visions of the lady beneath him, or possibly riding him, as soon as he'd begun conjuring them. Physical arousal and riding horseback were not conducive to one another.

Her conversation did not bore him.

In fact, he found bantering with her—well, amusing. Although he'd spent a great deal of his life seeking pleasure, he could not recall any woman who entertained him as much with simple conversation. This thought muddled his mind a bit.

Marriage to Lady Natalie would include the full backing of the Earl of Ravensdale.

Although he'd planned upon undertaking the rebuilding of the Hawthorne earldom alone, the road would be smoother with the public endorsement of one of the *ton's* wealthiest members. It was not the wealth that mattered, so much as the power and influence the Spencers carried.

He could have her in his bed every night.

Oh, yes, he'd already considered this fact. He pictured her as she had been last night on her knees, in her nightclothes. He remembered the soft feel of her breast in his hand.

Now, sitting beside her, his senses buzzed. She'd been in his thoughts all day. She was becoming something of a possibility. For now, though, he simply wanted to touch her.

He reached his hand over to her lap and grasped her tiny wrist. She did not startle, as he thought she might, but he felt her breathing quickened. Each of them continued conversing with the people seated around them as though nothing whatsoever were untoward. Her skin felt like the petal of a rose. Her hand, fragile and delicate.

After several minutes, Garrett began rubbing the underside of her wrist. Her pulse raced beneath his thumb.

Natalie was certain the other guests must be aware of the emotions boiling up inside of her! The instant his hand possessed hers, it encompassed all her awareness. Her entire being suddenly focused on the feelings he created with a simple touch, a light caress. The more he held her hand, the more her body felt drawn toward him. Like a physical hunger, his nearness enflamed and, yet, overwhelmed her.

As though underwater, Natalie turned her head and watched Hawthorne converse with Lord Malmsteen. Fully distracted by her own inner turmoil, she comprehended none of their conversation. She then glanced around at the other guests near her. Not one had the slightest clue that the man beside her was seducing her with just the touch of his hand. And yet she felt as though she were turning to liquid, as though her bones were melting.

Did Hawthorne know of the havoc he created inside of her? Of course, he must! Unwilling to sit docilely while her heart raced madly, she shook the slipper from her foot and edged it over to Lord Hawthorne's. Most conveniently, he'd exchanged his boots for buckled shoes this evening. In a daring move, she pressed the arch of her foot onto the top of his ankle. As she did so, both of his eyebrows rose at once. His foot felt hard; his ankle felt hard. She knew from the previous night that his legs were hard all over.

He was not a soft man in any way whatsoever.

Her foot rose slightly when Lord Hawthorne lounged backward and stretched his legs out in her direction. He'd done this intentionally! He was making it so that she could explore his person more thoroughly with the tender sole of her foot. The expression on his face remained impassive.

Feeling the need to participate in the conversation somehow, Natalie met Lord Hawthorne's eyes innocently. "What did you think of my father's irrigation system? Do you not think it clever that he extended the canal to transport loads of coal right through the village? Oftentimes, I am amazed by the feats of man."

Lord Hawthorne appeared surprised by her comment. Perhaps he was as distracted by her touch as she was by his, for he took a moment to absorb her words. Natalie knew her father's estate covered a tremendous amount of land, and the system designed and implemented was quite impressive. She had paid attention, even as a girl, to what sustained her family's wealth.

"It is inspiring." His answer referred to the canal, and yet a zing of awareness shot through her. "Water in Great Britain can be either a blessing or a curse. When managed properly it can, for the most part, be the former. Even so, the powers of nature cannot always be contained."

Like passion. Like whatever was building between the two of them.

Still holding his gaze, Natalie explored his stocking-covered ankle with her foot. "Before my father took over the earldom, many of the fields often flooded. Under his management, the lake was constructed and the channels dug out in order to contain the water." She grimaced and added, "It is most effective—most of the time, anyhow."

"An admirable system," Garrett declared. "An excellent model to be considered." He grazed her palm with the tips of his fingers. "Do you swim in the lake?"

His voice sounded low and gravelly. Heat spread from her chest to her thighs. Were they really discussing water? And swimming?

Natalie swallowed hard before answering. "Yes. There's a beach on the south side. Sand is brought in every two or three years. Father made it a point that we all learn." She removed her foot and ran the V of her toes down the back of his ankle. "He knew of too many needless drownings and did not wish to lose any of his children thusly." But Natalie did not want to discuss her father. "Do you swim, my lord?"

He smiled at her with the sensuality she'd always noticed before. "I manage to stay afloat." Likely he did better than that. "I didn't learn to swim as a boy. I learned after I'd reached my majority—in the ocean while visiting a...friend. My friend's late husband's estate extended along a few miles of both hazardous and swimmable beaches. The process was humbling."

Just then, Lady Natalie's mother stood and invited the ladies to join her in the drawing room. The announcement shattered their private cocoon of intimacy. Natalie reluctantly slid her foot back into her slipper. When she went to withdraw her hand from Hawthorne's grasp, his fingers tightened.

For a moment, a hunger burned in his eyes as she glanced over at him. She stared back boldly before dropping her gaze to their hands. His grip loosened suddenly.

She stood on shaky legs and followed the ladies out.

Chapter Ten

Wandering into the drawing room, Natalie's thoughts remained with Garrett Castleton. There was more to him than she had thought. Was he *truly* a rake? Was he a gentleman at heart? Upon leaving Raven's Park, would he go back to his disreputable ways? And how was it that he appeared more handsome every time she laid eyes upon him?

Examining the handkerchief she'd been embroidering for the past twenty or so minutes, she cursed. Not paying attention had produced disastrous results. The delicate flowers were now a riotous splash of dandelions and weeds with no order whatsoever. Such work could almost be considered artistic if the back of the fabric didn't consist of crazy knots and loops.

She jumped guiltily when her mother addressed her. "I cannot imagine what you have been thinking about that would cause you to lose your concentration." Her mother gestured toward the handkerchief with a disdainful glance. "That fabric, I believe, is irreparable."

The other ladies looked over at the embarrassing results in her lap and clucked their tongues. Aunt Eleanor winked.

The unwanted attention shifted to the entry when the gentlemen appeared, many still cradling their port.

A few drifted out to the terrace and lit cigars, but Lord Ravensdale placed his hand upon the Duke of Monfort's shoulder and steered him toward Natalie's chair.

The duke, ever the stoic, glanced at her blankly as he and her father took their seats upon the adjacent settee. "Good Lord," her father exclaimed, "what on earth are you embroidering there, daughter? Has some newfound style for handkerchiefs come into fashion?" He laughed as Natalie tucked the offensive piece of cloth into the chair behind her.

"I'd like to see any embroidery you produced, Father," she retorted. Parents could be so annoying.

The haughty duke raised one eyebrow at her.

Her father then remembered why he'd come over. "The duke here has invited your mother and me, and you of course, to join him on his estate. I was just telling him how much I thought you would enjoy such an outing. Especially since you've been confined to Raven's Park all summer."

Her father seemed to expect some sort of response, so Natalie forced herself to smile graciously. "Oh…um…that would be…er, lovely." Argh! Had her father already drawn up betrothal contracts?

At last, the duke deigned to speak. "I maintain a first-rate stable and dressage arena upon my estate. Your father says you are an excellent horsewoman. Of course, you shall be most welcome to make use of the facilities." Although his words were welcoming, his eyes were not. Such a cold man!

"How kind of you, Your Grace," she murmured. And then out of nowhere she felt a heightened awareness. The air within the room suddenly charged, much like the air outside before a summer storm.

Lord Hawthorne had entered. Casually propping himself against the back of a loveseat, he unashamedly observed her. He wasn't smiling, but she sensed his amusement. He flicked his gaze toward a large floral arrangement, and his eyes twinkled further. She nearly laughed out loud. He had remembered her desire to deter the duke's suit.

The duke and her father continued their own conversation, Natalie more than happy to stay out of it. A few women gathering around the pianoforte plucked out some tentative notes.

Her mother beckoned. "Come over here, dear, and play for us."

Dutifully, Natalie excused herself and followed her mother's wishes. She actually enjoyed this feminine pursuit. Needing no written music, she placed her fingers on the keys and played notes she heard in her head. She, in no way, fancied herself a great musician, but she did enjoy entertaining others. It was a vanity she could live with and feel no guilt whatsoever.

Settling herself upon on the wooden bench, she began in the upper register with a few convoluted scales and arpeggios from left to right. As her mood lifted, she interspersed personal melodies with songs she'd memorized years ago. She did not play loudly. She played so people could continue conversing around her. She often marveled at the construction of such an instrument. She also marveled at the constraints her various musical instructors had attempted to put upon her playing.

They'd used every means at their disposal to convince her to play written music that was boxed in to specific counts and keys. Such restrictions annoyed her. She believed that, once she understood the instrument and how it worked, she ought to be able to play whatever she wished. Two of her instructors had quit in frustration. After the fourth such instructor resigned, her parents deferred to her inclinations at last and allowed her to play as she wished.

Dismissing such memories, she slowed her music down and then sped it back up at will. Her music was a story, and she the storyteller.

After a few minutes, the hair on the back of her neck seemed to stand on end. Lord Hawthorne had moved to sit behind her. She faltered a few notes and then halted her play altogether. Her music reflected her mood and her feelings. She was not comfortable playing something while thinking about Garrett Castleton. And she could not help but think about him with him watching over her shoulder.

The notes would be too loud, too bold. She looked down at her hands at a loss. Nobody else paid much heed to her playing, so she did not feel compelled to continue. Sliding to the side of the bench, she stood and tamped down the impulse to stretch like a cat. Sometimes her muscles tied up in knots if she played for too long. Lord Hawthorne stood as well.

"Would you care to stroll outside?" he asked. "We shall stay close enough to the house so that you don't need to worry about—being chaperoned and all that nonsense." Eyes that were nearly black twinkled down at her. His playfulness was something new. She *liked* it.

Natalie agreed with a nod. Slipping her hand upon his arm, she allowed him to lead her outside through the terrace doors. Going in the opposite direction from her father's cigar-smoking cronies, they stepped from the marbled patio onto the grass and walked toward a distant folly.

Garrett had attended several recitals, but he'd never heard a young lady play like Lady Natalie. At times her music sounded quiet, reflective, and relaxing, and then it would change, becoming angry, even chaotic. Then again, she would drift into something whimsical or exotic. It had taken several minutes before he realized she was not playing any arrangement ever written. The music came from within her. She created in the moment.

Like the lady herself, the music intrigued but also baffled.

"A chaperone is not only for my protection, you know, my lord." Together they strolled away from the lights pouring through the drawing room windows and french doors. "My brothers, when paying attention to any particular young lady of gentle birth, are adamant about keeping chaperones within a safe distance." She laughed a little before continuing. "When Darly— Darlington, my eldest brother—was one and twenty, he very nearly found himself betrothed to the vicar's daughter. If not for my mother and Aunt Eleanor's watchful eyes, he'd have a full nursery by now. The girl's mother had purposely left them alone in the rectory. Luckily, Mother and Aunt felt a strong urge for spiritual guidance that morning."

"What happened?" Garrett asked, intrigued despite himself. Stories like this normally bored him, but he enjoyed listening to her talk. Her perspective charmed him.

Natalie laughed again. "Well, they never went into

any details where my innocent ears could hear, but…"

"Yes?" Garrett glanced sideways and grinned at her.

"According to Stone, the girl was pretty, and Darly not immune to her…allure. Fortunately for him, Mother noticed this."

The two stopped walking when they reached the trunk of a large tree. Garrett removed his jacket, placed it on the ground, and indicated she sit. Organizing her skirts, Natalie settled upon the jacket, pulled up her knees, and hugged them with both arms. For all her bravado, she looked forlorn. Garrett took a seat behind her and leaned against the tree. With his long legs bent along each side of her, he pulled her back to lean against his chest. This intimacy was inappropriate, but she did not protest or even lose track of her conversation.

"Mother and Aunt Eleanor followed him to the rectory that day." Natalie chuckled and let her head relax against him. "They slipped into the side door after seeing the girl's mother running back to the vicarage. Already suspicious, they assumed rightly that the girl's mama had gone to fetch someone to witness the compromising situation. When the girl's mother returned with a few ladies and burst into the chapel, all four of them were earnestly praying in the front row." She paused for effect. "According to Stone, the daughter's hair was unbound and her dress wrinkled. What could be said, really, with both Mother and Aunt Eleanor sitting between them?"

Garrett laughed, picturing the young viscount sitting with his mother and godmother between him and the ambitious girl. Darlington was lucky to have such devoted womenfolk in his life.

Garrett tipped his head and inhaled the sweet scent in Natalie's hair. When he did so, a few tendrils tickled his lips. He'd wrapped his arms around her waist and could feel each breath she took.

Jolted by an unwelcome memory, Garrett spoke without thinking. "There are women who will use whatever means available to capture a title."

Natalie leaned to the side and looked over her shoulder so she could meet his eyes. "There are men who will use their superior strength to capture a dowry."

This gave Garrett pause. He raised his eyebrows in question and felt his jaw tighten in anger. "Cortland?" he asked incredulously.

"Oh, no. Good Lord, never him." She spoke with derisive laughter, relaxing into him once again. "Anyhow, the scoundrel did not succeed." She sighed. "I was ridiculously naive. It was my first season, and I'd not become betrothed yet." She moved her arms from her knees and placed them atop Garrett's. "He convinced me to walk outside with him. Believe it or not, I took him at his word when he told me a kitten had caught itself in a rosebush." Again, she laughed at herself.

"Of course, there was no kitten." Garrett spread his fingers wide and threaded hers through them. He tucked them into his fists.

"Once we reached the roses, in which of course, there was no kitten, he attempted to kiss me despite the fact that I'd told him 'no' more than once."

Garrett nuzzled his lips at the juncture where her neck sloped into her shoulder.

"I was saved though, as Joseph had followed us. He sent me back inside and settled matters to his satisfaction. I was terrified he would call the cad out."

"He did not?" Garrett asked. "But punished the brute with his fists, I hope?"

Again, Natalie turned her head to look at him. "How did you know that?"

"Your brothers are protective of you." He nuzzled the soft skin on the lobe of her ear with his lips. "They are not all bad, now, are they?"

She didn't answer. Instead, a shiver ran through her body. He responded by pulling her closer. This was madness! When had he become such an utter fool? He ought to remove his hands from her person and lead them back inside, back into the safety of the drawing room surrounded by her mother and father and several of their close acquaintances.

"What?" she asked, her voice barely a whisper.

Garrett chuckled softly this time. "Your brothers, protecting you." Where were they now? They ought to be protecting her from him. His tongue traveled along the peach-like skin at the top part of her ear. He trailed it around the inner edge.

"Oh…" She sighed softly. "Not so bad."

Lady Natalie Spencer was affected by his touch. With his arms around her waist, he felt her breathing quicken. His lips explored the outer shell of her ear in a lazy manner, nipping and licking the tender skin. Pleasure coursed through him when she moaned softly.

"Um…" she murmured. "Uh…Tell me about…the women," she finally managed to get out.

This time it was he who paused. "The women?"

"The ones who have tried to marry you for your

title," she prompted.

"Similar girls to the one who attempted to trap your brother, only…" He stopped playing with her ear.

She tilted her head toward his mouth as though bereft without his lips. But she persisted in her question. "Only?"

"Only I had no womenfolk to ward off the mothers." His voice came out harsher than he'd intended.

"But you are not wed," she said curiously. "You have not married."

"How do you think a gentleman gains a reputation such as mine, sweetheart?" He stilled. His arms loosened around her waist. As though sensing his withdrawal, Natalie grasped on to his hands and wrapped them about her firmly.

"It is ridiculous, is it not?" Annoyance, he thought, shook her voice. "That two people would be forced to marry regardless of their emotions. The notion of being compromised seems a terrific penalty for so innocent a crime—or no crime at all! And the punishment of a lifetime married to whomever one might be trapped by? I am appalled, and yet we are bound by society's rules. Marriage ought not to be a penalty. It ought to be a gift shared between two people—two people who *want* to pledge themselves to one another for life."

Garrett pondered her words. She had obviously given this subject a great deal of thought.

"I am *glad* you did not let yourself be trapped and bound to a woman you did not wish to wed," she continued. "I do not care if that is why you have been labeled a rake."

Moments passed, and then he let out a deep sigh.

"But what of the girl? You do not have sympathy for her?" He was not convinced. He'd been a cad.

"Well…" She paused as though working out a mathematical equation. "You did not ruin her? In truth?"

He nuzzled her again, just below her chin, ever so softly. But he needed to answer her question— somehow it mattered, her opinion of him. "I did not. We kissed open mouthed. We were, um, embracing. When her aunt burst into the room with some cousins, the girl somehow managed to rip the bodice of her dress." He held himself very still, his mouth still resting against her skin.

"She must have been very ambitious indeed." The words escaped her with a hint of awe. "To expose oneself intentionally! I don't blame you for not offering for her. She ought not to have acted with such coldhearted motivation."

"I did compromise her. I did *not* ruin her—contrary to rumors spun in that direction." His chin rested upon her shoulder. "I do not like to be toyed with or manipulated. I suppose I am more sensitive to both, having the Earl of Hawthorne for a father."

"And yet you were discovered and ordered to marry the girl, am I right?" Natalie must have learned interrogation techniques from her father.

Garrett was almost amused at the accuracy of her line of questioning. And yet disgust sounded in his voice. He wouldn't sugarcoat his actions. "I refused. I flat out refused."

They sat silent for a few minutes, staring back at the manor, candlelight shining from within. "And now, would you ever marry a woman you…well…merely to

113

salvage her reputation? Even if you did not find her to be compatible?"

"The women I keep company with pose no threat to my bachelor status. Under normal circumstances." He nearly laughed at the irony of this very moment. "Would you ever marry a man to salvage *your* reputation?"

She shook her head side to side adamantly. "I have just been released from an unwanted engagement. I am in no hurry to place myself in another one."

"You would allow yourself to be ruined in the eyes of society?"

"There are other ways to smooth these things over—ways that do not require two reluctant people to tie themselves together for a lifetime."

Garrett's hands rested just below the thrust of her breasts. He could not help but move one up until he felt the ridge where her stays ended and plump softness began. Drawing light circles, he felt her skin tighten beneath his fingers through the light cover of her dress. His mouth resumed trailing kisses along her chin. He continued thusly, and Natalie turned her head so he could access her neck more easily. Good God, he must be foxed.

Trifling with this lady was beyond reckless. They sat in plain sight of the house. Admittedly, they enjoyed the cover of darkness, but their absence would be noticed soon. Allowing himself one more taste of her skin, he dropped his hands and leaned back against the tree. She turned her head and gazed at him in a leisurely fashion. She, apparently, was quite comfortable and unperturbed at the possibility of their imminent discovery.

"And now you have realized you are once again tempting fate," she goaded him, still not moving. He was beginning to understand that at times, she donned a sophistication she did not own. He'd better watch himself. *She* could not be relied upon to bring any restraint to their…What was this between the two of them? He must not continue this dalliance.

"You ought not to make yourself so…available to me," he said. "I might allow myself to be seduced by your innocence one of these days, and that would put us both in a scrape."

Her eyes flashed in the moonlight as his words sank in. "Ah, well, apparently neither of us knows what it is that we want." She scrambled away and stood abruptly. After brushing the grass from her skirts, she glared at him. "And don't be thinking I'm *available* to you, *my lord*." Her attempt at sounding scornful was ruined when her voice caught. Nonetheless, with a very feminine flourish, she twirled about and marched away. She held her head high as she fled. Garrett watched as she avoided the terrace and disappeared around the side of the house. She would not return to the other guests. She would be in no mood to play charades.

Ah, so, he had hurt her.

Garrett hardened himself against a niggling remorse. Lady Natalie Spencer was an unwanted complication. He lay back upon the grass and stared up at the sky. It would be best to avoid spending any more time alone with her. He wished he could offer her more. He wished he could be the type of man she needed, a romantic white knight in shining armor. Being caught between honor and dishonor was one of the most uncomfortable situations he'd ever experienced.

Chapter Eleven

Natalie wished she'd never laid eyes upon Garrett Castleton!

How could a person, *a man*, make a girl feel beautiful and lovable one minute and then like a pitiful piece of unwanted baggage the next? And then why would that girl allow herself to care what *that man* thought of her after he behaved so despicably? Natalie pulled a handkerchief from her pocket and wiped at a few stupid tears she'd lost control of. And then she stopped. In between her sniffles, she thought she'd heard a small cry from within the trees. After a moment, the sound came again.

Not considering her safety, she, slowly, so as not to make a great deal of noise, stepped into the trees before pausing to follow the sound again. Sure enough, the small cry grew louder. She stepped cautiously on the leaves and pine needles until she heard the sound right in front of her. And then, upon pulling a branch aside, she revealed a tiny creature huddled in the shimmering moonlight.

Was it a bear? No! A puppy! He must be no more than a few months old and lay curled around himself crying pitifully.

Natalie knelt and reached out her hand. A tiny tongue licked at her fingers. "Oh, you poor baby, where's your momma?" She reached her other hand around to grasp the small body of the dog and pull him into her chest. He sported floppy ears, a longer than normal body, and very short legs. He must have been a runt that had somehow managed to escape an ignoble fate.

And he was near starved! Forgetting Hawthorne's insults for the moment, Natalie carried him back to the house and entered through the kitchen door. In the light, she could see the black puppy had tan spots on his spindly neck and paws. Poor baby. His tiny black eyes gazed up at her adoringly. How could anybody abandon such a precious little life? Ah, well, it was their loss. She'd always wanted a dog. She was going to keep him, by Jove.

When she entered the busy kitchen, filled with warmth from the ovens and mingled aromas of both savories and sweet, his ears perked up at attention. Natalie ignored the curious and disapproving glances she received from some of the kitchen help and peeked into a pantry in search of a bowl for some milk. Seeing Cook approach, with a deep scowl on her face, Natalie cuddled the pup close to her.

"Cook, what do we have that I can feed this poor pup? Some horrible person abandoned him in the trees near the house. Can you help me find some cream or milk and a small bowl? The poor dear is near starving." Seeing disapproval on Cook's face, Natalie turned the pitiful pup toward her. "This is Cook, little one. She will help me see you to rights. Cook's a fine one. Cookie just loves animals."

Cook raised her eyebrows doubtfully.

Natalie continued, "Cook, this precious baby is my pet, his name is…well, I haven't thought of one yet."

She lifted the little dog to look into his eyes once again. "What shall I name you? I thought you were a baby bear at first. Should I call you Baby Bear?"

The puppy gave one short high-pitched bark. Natalie took this for approval. "Baby Bear, it is, then."

Shaking her head in resignation, Cook disappeared into the pantry. Natalie cuddled and cooed at Baby Bear until the large woman returned a moment later with a bowl filled with cream.

Taking the bowl, Natalie thanked her and slipped out of the kitchen and up the servant's stairs, making it to her room unobserved by any of her mother's guests. Once there, she placed the pup on the floor with the bowl, and Baby Bear lapped at the cream heartily. Relief settled on her. This surely was a sign of good health. Kneeling on the floor, Natalie leaned back and rested her weight upon her feet as she watched Baby Bear enjoy his meal.

With the dog occupied, she contemplated her encounter with Lord Hawthorne more rationally. He was a known rake. Practically an outcast. But such a handsome one.

And an exasperating one! She hated that he treated her like a woman one moment and a child the next. She didn't expect him to fall in love with her, did she?

Did she?

The question gave her pause as she considered the pink flounces on her window coverings and the lacy pink pillows on her bed. Dolls she'd collected as a young girl lined the top of her dresser. This was the room of her girlhood. Suddenly, it felt wrong.

Did Garrett Castleton consider her too young for him, too juvenile? Could that be why he resisted her?

She'd always been the baby of the family, the only girl amongst four strapping boys—now men. Everybody in her family forever protected her. While engaged to Cortland, she'd been treated, again, like a youthful sister by her betrothed. It had aggravated her to no end.

Could that be her problem? Was she a woman now, living the life of a young girl? Hearing sounds from the door across the hallway, Natalie hopped up and peeked into the corridor. Marcus was exiting Lord Hawthorne's room.

"I need your assistance." She gestured for him to enter her room.

"What have you gotten yourself into, Nat?" Marcus treated her like an older sister much of the time. Despite their different stations, being close in age, they'd often played together as children. Marcus shoved his hands into his pockets and slipped into Natalie's room. Upon catching sight of the puppy, he gawked at her with raised eyebrows.

"I don't know what I need to do for this little mite, but I intend to keep him," Natalie explained before he could say a single word. "Do you know anything about caring for a puppy?"

Marcus stared at Baby Bear and then, exhaling dramatically, ran a hand through his lanky black hair. "Well, Lady Nat, this puppy is going to need to...ah...relieve himself about every two or three hours." He took a few steps around Baby Bear and considered the situation. "Pups don't like to wet where they sleep, so a box and a blanket would be a good start. But you will need to watch him. If he begins sniffing around, you must take him outside right away so he can do his business." Squatting down, he gave the pup a scratch on the top of his little head. "Every time he piddles outside, give him a treat. Are you sure you want to do this? If you don't watch the pup carefully, he'll be going all over your room and making a dreadful stench. Why don't you just take him out to the stable and let the grooms care for him?"

Natalie was already shaking her head. "I want to care for him myself. Would you find me a box, Marcus? And a blanket? I will do as you say and watch Baby Bear carefully." At his doubtful look, she shook her finger at him. "Just you wait and see, Marcus Whipple! I'll have this dog trained in no time."

Laughing, Marcus backed away. "Very well then, I'll get you a box and a blanket." He stepped out of the door. Before departing though, he poked his head back in. "I'll bring you some treats for the little pup, too. It'll be worth it just to see you play nursemaid to a dog." Laughing again, he dashed off to retrieve the required items.

Baby Bear carefully finished the last drops of cream, his adorable pink tongue making sure to find every last drop. When he found no more, he looked up at her soulfully. Baby Bear needed her!

She picked him up and cuddled him close. She could do this. She could!

****

More than a little remorseful over his treatment of Lady Natalie, Garrett remained out of doors, lying in the grass, late into the night. At least she'd abandoned him in a good place for thoughtful reflection.

He'd decided the direction his life would take years ago—accepted himself as a fringe member of the

English aristocracy. He'd entered trade initially to defy his father's archaic beliefs. And now, irony of ironies, the funds he'd amassed would rebuild his father's legacy. No, his *grandfather's* legacy and that of all those before him. His father had squandered the benefits and privilege of holding an earldom. The legacy Garrett embraced was from those who had lived before his sire.

In his youth, Garrett had resisted his claim to nobility. Associating its members with his father, he'd beaten them at cards and leered at their daughters.

And now, with his father out of the picture, and the approval of the Spencers, some of these aristocrats were ironically befriending him. And as confounding as it might seem, he now found himself presented with one of their daughters. The daughter of a man he'd long respected.

The Earl of Ravensdale was everything Garrett's father had not been—hardworking, shrewd in business, and loyal to his wife and family. Lady Natalie had been raised well. She did not exhibit all the spoiled tendencies so many of the aristocracy's marriageable misses did, contrary to his initial impression.

Not that she wasn't just a tad spoiled, and rebellious, and delightfully spontaneous. She was all of these things and more. Against his own inclination, Garrett felt drawn to her.

But did he need a wife? For that was where all this dallying would eventually land him. Lady Natalie Spencer would not be ruined and allowed to languish in the country as a spinster. She had a brawny father and four brothers who would assure her reputation.

Frustrated by his thoughts, Garrett brushed the

grass from his jacket, sauntered down the hill and slipped back into the manor. All the other guests had apparently retired for the evening and the only sounds to be heard were of servants clearing up before taking themselves off to bed. He hoped Marcus hadn't waited for him.

Upon reaching the corridor outside his room, Garrett stopped short. A high keening sound, muffled but unmistakable, drifted into the hallway from Natalie's room. He paused a moment and took a deep breath. He heard crying…

Surely, she was not still upset? Could his words have hurt her to this extent?

Rubbing a hand over his face, Garrett exhaled slowly. Of course. She'd experienced a devastating rejection earlier this summer, and his toying with her merely piled on to her insecurities. He thought to knock on her door to offer comfort, but reason told him this would surely backfire upon both of them.

The weeping, however, went on and on. It was mournful and oh, so pitiful.

Dragging himself from her door, Garrett entered his own chamber instead. He could not go into her room, could he? Surely her maid attended her?

Marcus had laid out his dressing gown and night shirt but thankfully was not awake to wait upon him in person. Relieved, Garrett tended to his own ablutions and climbed into bed. The barely audible crying tormented him mercilessly. He knew, though, that if he were to go to her room, were to attempt to comfort her and be discovered, there would likely be a great deal more cause to weep. And both of them would be crying then.

He wished the effects of the whiskey he'd consumed earlier hadn't worn off. That would have at least allowed a semblance of sleep. Diving under the pillow in an attempt to block the pitiful sounds from next door, Garrett didn't drift off until just before dawn.

Chapter Twelve

When Garrett finally descended the next morning, the sun had long since risen, but his hosts and their guests had yet to vacate the morning room. The countess sat checking items off a list while the earl perused one of London's broadsheets. Garrett had barely sat down with his plate when Lady Sheffield informed him she had planned a large garden party for that afternoon. Guests from all over had been invited. Glancing out the stately windows, Garrett caught glimpses of servants rushing about with flowers, baskets, and linens. Others busied themselves setting up chairs and tables on the lawn. For a moment, he wondered idly if anyone would notice if he were to duck out of the day's entertainment. He would not, though. He had made this blasted decision to be amiable.

And there was this particular lady…

He turned away from the spectacle on the lawn and perused the faces at the table. Although most seats were occupied, Lady Natalie was absent. He refused to recognize the twinge he experienced as guilt or disappointment. He'd acted in her own best interest. Surely, someday she'd be grateful to him. And yet…his food now tasted little better than sawdust.

Just as Garrett thought he was going to have to make some sort of conversation, the clatter of a coach arriving outside halted most of the normal breakfast chatter.

If it had been a service vehicle, it would have driven around back. The ancient contraption could only mean additional guests were arriving. Garrett forced himself not to wince visibly. Although he'd been treated graciously thus far, he couldn't help feeling wary.

Just then the Baroness of Riverton pushed her seat back and rose to her feet quickly. "Oh, it's Penelope and Abigail! I am so glad to see they are arriving safely."

Taking his time, the baron stood up beside his wife. Garrett had conversed briefly with Riverton yesterday. Although a quiet, henpecked man, he was a rather affable sort. "My apologies, Lady Ravensdale. You were aware the girls were coming, weren't you?"

As dawning recollection caught up with the lady of the house, she rose as well. "Oh, yes, Lord Riverton, we discussed it yesterday. With this afternoon's festivities, I forgot about the girls' arrival." Looking around, she added, "I had hoped Natalie would be present to welcome…" Catching a footman's eye, she said, "Leo, would you please have Tinsdale fetch Lady Natalie?" She addressed the servant graciously. The Spencers were uncommon in the courtesy afforded to their servants. It was something Garrett was coming to appreciate about this unusual titled family.

The earl, at his wife's nudging, gave up on his newspaper and with something of a scowl, excused himself from the table to welcome the new arrivals. Garrett remained seated and determined to finish drinking his coffee. As did Lady Sheffield beside him.

They could watch the flurry of activity through the windows.

After observing the other breakfasters either leave to greet the arriving ladies, or perhaps to their own devices, Lady Sheffield turned her attention to Garrett. She had a curious gleam in her eyes and did not look to be uncomfortable in his presence this morning. He was grateful for this.

"I understand you have saved your mother's paintings? It is true?" she asked.

Damned if anybody's business remained private anymore. That being said, it wasn't often anyone mentioned the late Countess of Hawthorne—if ever. "You had an acquaintance with my mother, Lady Sheffield?" he asked. He would not satisfy her curiosity immediately.

Obviously delighted, Lady Sheffield nodded. "We came out the same season. I was fortunate enough to have been invited to view her artwork at your grandparent's townhouse that year." She shook her head mournfully. "My brother, Arthur, attended with me. Shortly after the showing, your father swept her away to the country. *Did* you manage to save her paintings? It would be such a shame if they perished along with your *dreadful* father."

What could he say to this? What *could* one say when a person referred to one's father as dreadful? Even if said father *was*, in fact, dreadful? "I did. They have been safely tucked away upstairs for a few years now." And then, acknowledging her other statement, he continued, "My father *was* a dreadful man. I knew they would be in peril if I left them in his care." Reaching for the pot of coffee, he gestured to her cup. She lifted it, and he poured hot liquid to the rim before refilling his own. "I feared he might destroy the paintings out of spite. They were left specifically to me."

"Your mother was a very sensitive lady, my lord. I never did fathom how her father could allow such a match." A flash of sadness crossed her face, but she covered it. "Oh dear me! Such a long time ago, but looking at you now, it feels as though it were yesterday." And then she smiled at him in a motherly sort of way, the wrinkles at her eyes creasing deeply. "Your mother did manage to produce a handsome son though! And clever, too, I am discovering."

Garrett stared at his coffee, a strange lump forming in his throat. God damn this emotion. "If you'd care to see the paintings, I'd be happy to show them to you. I must inspect the crates before travel anyhow. I plan on doing so tomorrow morning, if you'd care to take a peek." He stared into the dark richness of his coffee, the warm cup cradled in his hands as he made the offer. He hadn't yet looked at the paintings himself. Knowing the contents of the crates, he'd done his best to ignore them. He'd avoided them, in fact.

Lady Sheffield clasped her hands together in childish delight. "Oh, that would be delightful, and Lady Natalie has expressed an interest in them as well. If you wouldn't mind, I will bring her along with me."

Garrett studied her face for indications that she was matchmaking. "If she wishes, I am amenable."

At that very moment, a tired and drawn Lady Natalie entered the room with a scowl. "If she wishes what?" she asked.

Oh, hell, the night had been worse on her than he'd thought.

Garrett stood and pulled out a chair for her gallantly. "I've invited Lady Sheffield to view the paintings left to me by my mother, tomorrow morning. Would you care to join us?" He asked with as much charm as he could muster. He did not like seeing her so defeated. Especially when he was at fault. He would not take all the blame, however. He'd leave some of that to the Duke and Duchess of Cortland.

A spark of interest lit her eyes, along with a fleeting smile. "Oh, that would be lovely, thank you." She followed her gratitude with a dainty little yawn. "I'm so sorry, please forgive me."

Garrett lifted the coffee pot and gestured to her cup. She held it out for him to fill and then added cream and sugar. Forgetting her manners, she relaxed her elbows on the table and took a deep sip of the hot brew.

Garrett studied her. Her eyes were neither red nor swollen. Her hair and dress were as pristine as ever. There was a tiredness to her face, however, no amount of dressing up could cover. As she drank the coffee, she appeared to relax.

"It's all set then," Lady Sheffield said. "We'll examine your mother's works after breakfast tomorrow morning." She looked to Natalie for confirmation.

Natalie looked up after a moment. "Oh, yes, of course." Her mind was elsewhere; Garrett could tell by the distracted tone of her voice.

Lady Sheffield looked from one to the other before standing and excusing herself. "I'll see you both at this garden party then. Enjoy your breakfast, dears." And with that, she left the two of them alone together.

Garrett folded his arms across his chest and observed the contrary woman before him. She puzzled him. "You are well this morning?" he asked.

The minx set her coffee down and met Garrett's unwavering gaze for the first time since entering the room. "Why would I not be? I'm not going to fall into some grand decline merely because *you* decided I am not worthy of your amorous attentions."

Ah, the spark was back. But what of the wailing he'd overheard the previous night? Good God, the crying had gone on forever! He'd not realized women could carry on so. He was also more than a little surprised that Lady Natalie would carry on so. She seemed to be made of sterner stuff.

Setting aside any semblance of formality, Garrett rested his elbows upon the table and leaned toward her. "Sweetheart, it has nothing whatsoever to do with you being *worthy.* Perhaps it is *I* who am not worthy of burdening *you* with my, as you say, amorous attentions."

"If it's all the same to you, I prefer not to be on the receiving end of your...gallantry! The result is the same." A shadow crossed her face. She would brazen through what she'd obviously decided had been rejection. In an obvious attempt to dismiss him, she lifted her cup and turned her attention to the window. Outside, a great deal of hugging and unloading of luggage was going on. "If you'll excuse me, *my lord.* I must assist my mother in welcoming our guests."

She took one last drink of her coffee before slamming, yes, *slamming*, it down on the linen-covered table and standing abruptly.

Garrett watched her swaying hips as she flounced off, leaving nothing but a hint of perfume behind her. What was it about a woman walking away from him that made him want her all the more?

****

Natalie left the breakfast room before she did anything stupid, like giving in to the strange attraction that constantly compelled her to make a fool of herself over Garrett Castleton. She did not feel like being sociable with Miss Crone and her cousin. Baby Bear hadn't allowed her more than thirty minutes of sleep at a time throughout the night. Who knew a pup could be so demanding?

In between hourly trips downstairs and outside, Baby Bear protested vehemently about being separated from his mama—that was what Natalie presumed anyhow. For she'd provided every possible luxury a pup could hope for, including all manner of canine snacks, a warm blanket, and one of her favorite slippers for teething. The poor thing had cried long and often.

The lack of sleep left her exhausted. But not so much that she ever considered giving up on Baby Bear. Just the opposite, in fact. Feeling the need to peek in on the little pup, Natalie had a strong urge to return to her chamber. She did not wish to return to find aromatic droppings. Especially after traipsing outside every few hours to prevent just such an occurrence throughout the night.

But her mother would seek her out if she did not welcome the two ladies. And she was not yet ready to share her new pet with her parents. Her father was not one for allowing animals of any kind within the house, and she must show them that the pup could mind his manners.

She first needed to show herself the same.

If it was even possible.

Twisting her mouth into a weary smile, she joined the welcoming party in the front foyer.

Penelope Crone was easily recognizable with her emerald green eyes and blondish red hair twisted into a tight coil behind her head. She was taller and slimmer than Natalie. Some might consider her sticklike, if inclined to be unkind. She strode forward and offered Natalie a sympathetic smile. "My lady, I am *so pleased* to see you this summer. I have been thinking about you *often* since the Season ended." And then came the sympathetic eyes. "How *are* you?"

Natalie knew the question to be sincere but wished everybody would forget about her broken engagement. Her heart remained fully intact.

Trying not to roll her eyes heavenwards, she responded with equal warmth. "I am well, and you? How was your journey?" Without waiting for an answer, Natalie turned to the lady at Penelope's side. "This must be your cousin?"

Miss Penelope Crone nodded and introduced the other lady. Miss Abigail Wright could not be more different from her cousin in looks. She was barely five feet tall, curvy and soft-looking with dark hair knotted severely behind her head. She wasn't plump. She was…voluptuous. She reminded Natalie of some actresses she'd viewed on occasion. Except that she dressed primly and properly—as did Penelope. Not quite spinsterish but not in the lighthearted manner of young debutantes either. No lace, no flounces, not much color.

Natalie's mother joined them and asked Natalie to show the ladies to their quarters so they might freshen up. As all the regular guest rooms were appropriated already, they were given some of the nicer rooms set aside for servants on the top floor. Lady Ravensdale apologized as Natalie led them away. Two footmen were already carrying their trunks up the long flights of stairs.

Miss Wright climbed the steps beside Natalie, and Penelope followed effortlessly. "I hope our presence is not an inconvenience." Miss Wright's entire manner carried her apology. "Even though your mother assured Aunt Emily it was not. My mother was out of sorts with herself for her inability to overcome her injury so she could chaperone us adequately. We both told her it was not necessary, but being confined to her suite, she felt we would be subject to all manner of indiscretions. She has an extensive imagination."

"A bunch of tripe," Penelope inserted. "Your mama saw the opportunity to put us in the way of a few bachelors and fabricated the most transparent of excuses." Miss Penelope Crone, as Natalie already knew, had long ago dispatched with the notion of minding her tongue when she was of an opinion.

Natalie stopped and stared back at the taller girl. Surely they would not be setting their sights on Lord Hawthorne? The thought gave rise to an ugly feeling inside her. "But there are no bachelors here, really."

At Miss Crone's dubious raised eyebrows and tilted head, Natalie caught on to who those bachelors were. Not Lord Hawthorne. "My brothers?" Her relief was greater than she ought to have experienced. She had no claim to him. Except for a few kisses…

"You have no need to worry, my lady," Miss Wright inserted. "They are perfectly safe—as I am sure you can gather on your own."

Natalie glanced between the two ladies. Contrary to their spinsterish clothing and lack of style, they sparkled with a vibrant energy. Both were far too clever to overlook. In fact, she thought that if either of them, notwithstanding their advanced age, took it into their heads to chase one of her brothers, the outcome would in no way be preordained.

"Nonetheless, I am glad of your company." She turned and began ascending the stairs again. "As much as I enjoy my mother's friends, it will be a pleasure to have the companionship of a few ladies closer to me in age." As she arrived at the landing, she gestured them along. "There is to be a garden party this afternoon; the staff is busy with preparations, but please ask a maid if you have need of anything at all—or if you need directions. The house isn't massive, but it is possible to get turned around if one isn't familiar." Natalie felt guilty for not offering them a tour herself, but she knew Baby Bear might now be awake and restless. To smooth over her lack of hospitality, she added, "I truly am glad to have both of you here."

The two ladies entered the door to the single room with two twin beds and turned back to Natalie. With a quick curtsey, they thanked her, and Natalie made her escape.

She considered bringing the ladies into her confidence regarding the pup but had decided against it. She would wait before determining whether that would be wise. Not all ladies liked puppies.

Meanwhile, she rushed back to her charge.

When Natalie opened the door, Baby Bear looked at her with such adoration, it nearly brought tears to her eyes. She crossed the room and gathered the warm little pup into her arms and was rewarded with a pink tongue attempting to lick every inch of her face. Giggling, she cooed and fussed with the dog before wrapping him in a blanket and making her way down the back stairs. It was going to be more difficult to keep her secret during the daylight hours. Once outside, she slipped into the trees and set Baby Bear down. Grasping the leading string she'd devised from an old ribbon, she allowed the pup to sniff around until he'd decided upon the perfect spot to relieve himself. Following Marcus' instructions, she rewarded the pup with some small pieces of bacon and a brief stroll through the trees. Hopefully, Baby Bear retained something from these efforts.

Sighing with relief upon making an undetected return to her room, Natalie turned the knob, slipped inside, and set the puppy down.

When she straightened, she let out a shriek.

She was not alone.

Tinsdale was laying out a newly laundered dress. At the smirk she wore, Natalie's heart sank. The cat was out of the bag…well, er, the dog, that was.

"I wondered what you were up to, my lady." The older woman used her foot to push the improvised doggy bed toward the center of the room. Within it lay one shredded slipper and a half-empty bowl of cream. "Mongrels tend to bring with them a certain odor. Am I right in assuming your father has no knowledge of this recent acquisition?" The woman, for a mere servant, boasted an extensive vocabulary—and used it— whenever need be to chastise her young charges.

"Oh, Tinny." Natalie pouted, using her former nanny's pet name. She lifted Baby Bear and carried him across the room. "Look at poor little Baby Bear. I found

him all alone and starving in the trees by the house."
Natalie pushed the pup into Tinsdale's arms, knowing
of the woman's maternal feelings—they being her one
great weakness. And who but a cold-hearted soul would
not feel maternal toward little Baby Bear and his
sorrowful eyes?

Tinny had no choice but to grasp the pup close to
her chest. Baby Bear worked his magic by placing some
perfectly timed kisses on the old matron's chin. Not
thirty seconds passed before he had Tinny cooing and
kissing him right back.

Perhaps bringing Tinny in on this wasn't such a
bad thing after all. Natalie would need another
accomplice if she were to entertain guests with her
mother this afternoon. Otherwise, she would have to
make some sort of excuse every hour to take Baby Bear
out to do his business.

Eyeing the dress on the bed, Natalie began her
campaign. Normally, she would outright refuse to wear
such a garment. Pink, for heaven's sake. "Oh, Tinny!"
She held the dress in front of her. "This is simply
perfect! And I love the blush bonnet! I'm so glad you
thought to pull them out today."

Mrs. Tinsdale knew Natalie too well to be fooled.
She sighed in defeat, sat the pup on the floor, and put
her hands on her hips. "And how often does the pup
need to be taken outside?" she asked.

Natalie beamed at her. "Every hour. I take him to
the trees just beyond the old well." As an afterthought,
she added, "And do hold tight to the ribbon, Tinny.
Baby Bear has very predatory instincts when he senses
a squirrel or bird within his sights."

Nodding absently, Tinny pulled out some pale-pink

lacy gloves and indicated Natalie take a seat at the dressing table in front of the looking glass. "You owe me for this, young lady. I'm thinking ringlets are in order."

Natalie grimaced but submitted gracefully.

****

Natalie felt all of sixteen strolling onto the front lawn with a lacy pink parasol and her blond hair caught back into a plethora of tiny ringlets. Mrs. Tinsdale had chosen her retaliation effectively. As much as Natalie tugged and pulled her fingers through the curls, they did not relent. When one curl seemed to only grow tighter, she gave up and decided to ignore them and enjoy the afternoon. With this thought in mind, she glanced around looking for a particular gentleman.

Drat.

Lord Hawthorne was nowhere in sight.

She did catch a glimpse of Misses Crone and Wright and, with a small wave, set a course to join them in the shade they'd found beneath a large oak. It grew near the pond where three small watercraft were set out in a row for the guests to use. The two ladies sat primly in the iron chairs beneath it.

Miss Crone wore a serviceable afternoon gown made up of muted grays and lavender with little adornment. Miss Wright wore an equally serviceable dress, but with a shawl wrapped around herself—odd, since the sun shone high in the sky, and its heat could even be felt in the shade. Natalie felt like an iced wedding cake sitting next to the other two ladies. Tinny was far too fond of lacy pastels.

"Lovely afternoon, is it not?" Natalie greeted the ladies with the usual meteorological comment.

Penelope took one look at her and snorted.

"What on earth are you doing dressed in *pink*, of all colors?" Penelope said. The more she grew into her spinster role, the less she bowed to the rules of polite society.

Natalie could not take offense. Instead, she laughed at her own plight. "My maid thinks I am still six years old, Penelope," she said, ignoring formal address. "But what of you? Couldn't you spare even the barest nod to fashion in your own attire? You are not a matron after all, and," she said with a hint of audacity, "my brothers are not immune to a little lace and finery."

Chuckling, all three ladies took a moment to peruse the faces of the guests in search of said brothers. The young Spencer men were in the process of setting up stakes for a game of horseshoes. With the top buttons of their waistcoats undone and shirt sleeves rolled to their elbows, Natalie could see how other ladies might find them attractive. They were nearly identical until a person took the time to speak with each of them. Darly was verifying the measurements between the stakes, while Stone had one hand in his pockets and looked back at Natalie with an amused smile. He had noticed her ringlets and lace as well. Peter, the spare to the spare, was tossing the horseshoes, testing their weights. He'd always been the quiet one in the family.

And Joseph was on his wedding trip touring the Continent. Surprisingly, Natalie felt a pang at the thought that he would never dwell in their family home again. She'd not taken much time to consider his future absence, since she'd been so caught up in her own travails. Thinking about this now, she let out a sad sigh.

This caused the two ladies to return their attention

to her. Penelope did not hold back. "They do present an abundance of manhood, at that." She said this in a deadpan voice, but humor lit her eyes.

Miss Wright handed her fan over to Penelope. "Dear cousin," she said, feigning concern, "fan yourself, my dear, lest you faint from palpitations."

Natalie could not help herself. She doubled over in laughter.

Chapter Thirteen

After allowing Marcus to fuss over his cravat for a full seventeen minutes, Garrett dismissed the eager valet and braced himself to make his appearance at Lady Ravensdale's garden party. He'd eschewed both the top hat and cane Marcus tried foisting upon him. He wasn't a doddering old man yet, for God's sake.

Feeling overdressed for a summer afternoon, he slipped downstairs and out to the front lawn. Most of the other guests had already arrived, but he wasn't really interested in any of them. No, he found himself searching for one individual in particular. He leaned against the ornate wall lining the drive and perused the various clusters of ladies and gentlemen. They held dainty cakes in gloved hands and drank lemonade from sparkling crystal. Conversation rose and fell as it echoed off the waters of the nearby lake. The moderated tones, however, were interrupted by a delightful burst of feminine giggles.

Lady Natalie, overcome with laughter, dressed in pink and lace, was enough to dispel any reluctance he'd had in attending. Without stopping to think, he purposefully strode toward the group of ladies where they sat near the water.

Garrett's heart lightened as he drew closer. Her earlier despondency had fled, and a bubbling effervescence now overflowed from her. He'd not enjoyed contemplating her misery.

Upon reaching them, he bowed. "My lady, would you be so kind as to present me to your lovely companions?"

Miss Crone actually snorted. Garrett ignored the sarcastic gesture and instead complimented them upon their frocks. They seemed a cheerful group, less restrained and rigid than the countess' other guests.

Lady Natalie's eyes gleamed. "Won't you sit with us, my lord?" She indicated a vacant chair across from her. Before any further conversation, however, Lord Ravensdale ambled toward them with the Duke of Monfort following at a more leisurely pace.

Gesturing toward the empty rowboats, the earl turned in the direction of his sons and with no thought to propriety, shouted, "Come over here, Darlington. We have three ladies in need of coxswains and just two bachelors to comply." Returning his attention to the ladies, he laughed at his own cleverness. "I'm sure you gels might have waited all day for these gallants to put away their games and take you out for a paddle, eh? Gentlemen sometimes need prodding, heh, heh."

Natalie tilted her head back, closed her eyes, and likely was wondering that her father was such a favorite of the *ton*. Garrett supposed it had something to do with the man being an earl—a very wealthy one at that.

Showing no tact whatsoever, the earl persisted. "Natalie, I'm sure Monfort here has a knack with the oars. Hawthorne, you take out dear Miss Wright, and Darlington can row Miss Crone. What a nice picture you all will make, eh?"

Looking resigned, Natalie rose and the duke bowed low before her. "My lady, it would be an honor to take you for a turn on the lake, if you wish it."

She curtsied and smiled politely—too politely. "It would be my pleasure, Your Grace." Garrett turned to Miss Wright and offered his arm, and just arriving to join them, Lord Darlington did the same with Miss Crone. The resigned little group obediently stepped out onto the dock and began arranging themselves onto the various boats.

Monfort claimed a boat first and steadied it for Lady Natalie. Ignoring the duke's outstretched hand, Natalie gasped in dismay. "Oh, I have forgotten my parasol! Miss Wright, you must go with the duke, and I shall follow with Lord Hawthorne." Natalie pulled the lady forward and thrust her toward the duke's craft.

If not for the quick reactions of the duke, Miss Abigail Wright might very well have fallen into the lake.

Garrett chuckled as Natalie dashed back onto shore, presumably to fetch the very essential parasol. Heaven forbid her honeyed English complexion be exposed to the intermittent afternoon sunlight. As the duke pushed off with Miss Wright, Garrett watched Natalie slow to a promenade, open the lacy umbrella, and twirl it flirtatiously on her shoulder. A secret smile danced upon her lips as she glanced at him from beneath her lashes.

In no hurry himself, Garrett took a seat in the third rowboat, reclined on the bench, and enjoyed her performance. He admitted to himself, unashamedly, that he was not displeased with this turn of events.

When she arrived on the jetty once again, he couldn't help but return her impish grin.

"Well, my lady, that was effective. I am most

impressed."

Natalie turned her head and followed the progress of the other two boats as they drifted atop the calm lake waters. "I think the duke might very well enjoy a few moments in the company of Miss Wright. If anybody can find a crack in his demeanor, I think it could be her. She has a marvelous sense of humor!" Her smile took a wicked turn as she then looked down at Garrett. "Do you know how to row us around this lake, or are we to remain tied to the jetty all afternoon?"

Again, Garrett was sitting in this lady's presence! Immediately, he corrected his manners by standing and taking hold of the nearest pillar for balance. With a courtly gesture, he beckoned her to join him on board. "I am at your service, my lady." He reached out his gloved hand and took hold of her fingers. Although she, too, wore gloves, he could feel the delicate bones in her hands as she leaned into his assistance. He did not release her until she sat safe and secure on the boat.

"Do you have any particular destination in mind?" he asked as he untied the lines.

Natalie lounged back on her elbows and pulled one glove off. Dipping lazy fingers in the water, she let her head fall back sleepily, the parasol forgotten on the seat beside her. "We could go around the island," she suggested.

Garrett removed his own gloves and slipped off his jacket while allowing the boat to drift aimlessly for the moment. He rolled his sleeves up before taking the oars and performing smooth slow strokes, drawing them away from the shoreline.

All the while, he considered the options before him.

If ever a gentleman was presented with an opportunity to court a lady, this was it.

Did he wish to court her?

As she leaned her head back, she must have dislodged one of the pins holding her mass of ringlets in place. Several spiraling locks came free and cascaded down to settle on her shoulders and around her décolletage. Instead of reaching for the pin to try to rearrange her coiffure, she shook her head slightly, causing even more strands to come loose.

Catching him watching her, Natalie grimaced. "My maid got carried away," she said dryly.

Sweet Lord in heaven, this gorgeous girl was completely unaware of the seductive effect she had on him. Could she be that naïve? Even decked out in such a profusion of pink lace and chiffon, she ignited a sensual longing within him. Perhaps courting her was not such a very bad idea, all things considered.

"I find your ensemble delightful." He complimented her as a gentleman would but did nothing to disguise a more carnal appreciation from entering his eyes. He then enjoyed her blush.

Exhibiting an unnatural wave of shyness, she pulled herself to sit up straight on the wooden bench and looked down at her lap. "Thank you." The words came out softly. She fidgeted with some of the ridiculous lace on her skirt. "You are looking fine as well." An impish smile formed on her mouth. "You are still allowing Marcus to valet for you?" Her eyes danced with mischief.

Garrett nodded. "I am, and I thank you for recommending him." Realizing the small boat approached a branch protruding from the water, he took a moment to right his direction. "Why don't you acquire a new lady's maid?" he asked, remembering she'd referred to the servant as being responsible for all the pink and lace.

Lady Natalie touched her hair self-consciously and sighed. "My lady's maid is both my former nanny and at times governess. She's left behind neither role." She reached into the water, pulled out a floating twig and used it to draw swirls in the water. "I love Tinny—Mrs. Tinsdale—it's just I would like to find a maid who has been exposed to some fashion, a woman of my own choosing. Perhaps closer to myself in age. I feel as though it is a constant battle between us as to how I ought to present myself." She gestured downward. "Tinny won the battle today."

Garrett stopped rowing and regarded her solemnly. "Why don't you tell your mother this?"

Natalie let out a short laugh. "You and I have discussed the differences in our families before. One of the—*challenges* of being cared for is, these people have the ability to weigh one down with their love. The love of one's family can, at times, be a considerable burden." She smiled ruefully. "Tinny loves me."

"You do not wish to hurt her feelings," Garrett surmised.

"Precisely."

They glided along the lake in silence. Garrett continued contemplating his options. The sun was high and warm. He was glad he'd removed his jacket.

"If you were to marry"—he spoke casually—"you could experience a measure of independence."

"Not all would agree with that opinion," she countered. "In truth, a lady cannot know what her

144

circumstances will be until it is too late to undo them."
She was quite serious-minded about this. "I would hope
my brothers would terminate such an unfortunate
alliance if it were to occur, but the law is on the side of
the man. A woman becomes the property of her
husband. That's why I cannot understand my father's
eagerness to marry me off."

Her father confused Garrett, as well. One day he
seemed to be offering his daughter to Garrett, and the
next he was pushing the girl into the Duke of Monfort's
damned arms. Perhaps the earl wished to keep all
his...*her* options open.

"Your father cares for you. Perhaps that is why he
imposes his will so strongly upon your marital
prospects."

Again, a long sigh. She did a great deal of that as
of late. "I know. But..."

Understanding dawned. "You want a love match."

This revelation gave him pause. Perhaps he ought
to rethink his own designs upon her. He could never
give her what she wanted. He found her desirable. He
found her conversation pleasant, even entertaining, but
he'd lived something of a debauched life until recently.
He was not certain he was even capable of romantic
love—if it in fact existed.

"You also want passion," he added, perhaps to
strengthen his own cause. His eyes dropped to her lips.
His provocative words changed the tenor of their
conversation. Both were very aware of the kisses they
had already shared. The passion he'd brought to a halt.

Her chin tipped up. She held his eyes boldly. "I
do," she affirmed. "Are the two mutually exclusive, or
are they one and the same?" Oh, Lord, this girl had a lot

to learn.

"Yes," Garrett responded, "and no, not at all, in my experience anyway."

"Trade me places. I wish to row." She could be a demanding little wench.

"Please," he corrected her with a stern look. He raised one eyebrow and added, "Please, *my lord*, would you do me the favor of trading seats so I may row?"

Natalie scowled. "Yes, that."

Garrett did not budge. He merely continued looking at her expectantly.

"Oh, fine. *Please, my lord*, would you trade seats with me?"

Garrett laughed and moved to one side, careful to lean inward so as not to tip the boat. Natalie edged around the opposite side, and they managed to exchange seats without mishap. She confidently took the oars and began rowing. She had obviously done this before, as she did not dig the oars into the water too deeply, but just slightly to skim the boat along.

He took the opportunity to lean back and relax. She was strong for a girl. He decided the pink made her look about sixteen. Her exertions, however, brought attention to certain attributes that were most definitely *not* sixteen. His eyes fixed on a droplet of sweat that clung to the top curve of her breast. And then the material of her skirt slid upwards, revealing pink slippers and smooth silk stockings.

They had rowed to the back of the island. They were completely unobserved, utterly alone.

Garrett reached forward and grasped her ankle.

Natalie stopped rowing. Her face revealed uncertainty as to how she might respond to his boldness. He knew she resented him for calling a halt to their other…encounters. Even though it was for her own good as well as his.

His touching her now was an impulsive move. He'd simply had the urge to wrap his fingers around her leg, and the next thing he'd realized, he'd done just that.

"You, sir," she said, "are impertinent."

"My lord," he corrected her again.

"That, too."

Garrett smiled. He could not remember a time when he'd last smiled this much. He leaned forward, sliding his hand to just below her knee. His fingers massaged her calf muscle lightly.

Natalie reached her foot forward. "So this"—she indicated his touch—"is mutually exclusive from love?"

Well.

That was effective.

Garrett released her and sat back on his seat. Did she want an answer?

He searched her expression.

Yes, she did.

"I believe it is." He would not lie. "Unlike that love you told me about that controls a person and leaves them feeling guilty, passion can be exceptional on its own." He shrugged. "I believe passion to be a benefit one ought to experience with a spouse. I believe if one vows to forsake all others, then one ought to have every intention of doing just that." He looked off across the lake, surprisingly not sure where his words came from. "And if there is no passion within the marriage, fidelity would bring with it a great deal of sacrifice for both partners."

This was why he avoided the idea of marriage. Unlike many members of the *ton*, he was not of a mind to carry on with a mistress after he'd taken a wife.

"And friendship?" she persisted. "And trust?"

Garrett lifted his shoulders to show her he'd not considered these questions. "I suppose both of those ought to exist within a marriage."

"Well, my lord, I think if you take passion and throw in some friendship and trust, well, that then is love." She pulled back on the oars again. "You are as much a romantic as I. You wish for love in your marriage as well."

Garrett leaned his elbows on his knees and contemplated her. "Oh, hell."

Natalie continued rowing, smoothly, quietly, both of them lost in thought. A few unthreatening clouds appeared in the flawless sky. Birds flitted from tree to tree, and a wisp of wind rustled the leaves.

"And where does romance fit into this ideal relationship consisting of trust and friendship and passion?" Garrett asked, breaking the silence, as though there had been no pause in their conversation.

Natalie tilted her head and closed her eyes.

" '*The smiles that win, the tints that glow,*
but tell of days in goodness spent.
A mind at peace with all below.
A heart whose love is innocent.' "

Garrett chuckled. "Ah, yes, Lord Byron. That fellow has ruined ladies throughout the kingdom with his drivel."

Her eyes narrowed at his comment.

Yes, yes, a heart whose love is innocent described

Lady Natalie perfectly. He paused, before continuing:

> *'She walks in beauty, like the night*
> *of cloudless climes and starry skies;*
> *and all that's best of dark and bright,*
> *meet in her aspect and her eyes...'*

But the lady Byron refers to has raven tresses, I believe."

"Is that the romance you refer to, *my lord*?" Natalie drawled. "What do you think romance *is,* after all?"

Garrett raised one hand and rubbed his chin in an honest attempt to appear thoughtful. "Flowers? A waltz? Moonlit walks in the garden? Or perhaps around a lake?" He lifted one eyebrow as he made his last suggestion.

"You are hopeless, and a cynic to boot," Natalie said in exasperation.

Garrett opened his arms wide. "At last, you understand me. Although I prefer you think of me as a realist."

> *'So we'll go no more a roving,*
> *so late into the night,*
> *though the heart be still as loving*
> *and the moon be still as bright...'* "

Natalie spoke the words softly.

Garrett knew this one as well.

> *'Though the night was made for loving.*
> *And the day returns too soon.*
> *Yet we'll go no more a roving*
> *by the light of the moon.'* "

Both contemplated the words they'd spoken as Natalie continued to row.

"It isn't all drivel, Garrett Castleton." Natalie broke the silence.

Natalie was tired from rowing but would never make such an admission. Lord Hawthorne had tilted his head back and closed his eyes. No man ought to have such long lashes. Relaxed, sitting in the boat in his shirtsleeves, he looked both virile and vulnerable at the same time. What a pair they were! It seemed that neither she nor Lord Hawthorne knew what they wanted from one another. Well, they did not know what they wanted *long term,* anyhow.

When he'd grasped her leg and slid his hand along her calf, she'd had to call upon all of her willpower not to edge closer to him. A shiver ran through her at the thought of his hand travelling higher up her leg.

Jostling the boat, Garrett shifted and lay back leisurely, resting his head upon his folded jacket. He looked as though he might even fall asleep. How did men do this? Fall asleep in such uncomfortable positions? Her brothers had this same ability. It vexed Natalie that she required the perfect position, the perfect mattress and pillow to even contemplate falling asleep. Tempted to splash Garrett, she examined him instead. Relaxed, his jaw dropped the tiniest bit, parting his lips. His chest rose and fell evenly. Ironically enchanted, she noticed a small dimple just below the right corner of his mouth that she hadn't observed before. She wanted to reach out and touch it. She wanted to kiss him there.

Of course, she would not do so. He had humiliated her enough already.

He'd advised her upon what merits a good marriage could hold. Not to himself. To some other unsuspecting gentleman, one who might allow her as much freedom as she desired.

But she would never desire a man who would allow her such control. What fools women were! What a fool *she* was! She wanted independence, autonomy, and yet she also wanted…something else…If she were honest with herself, she might admit she would like to know more of Garrett Castleton.

She liked his sense of humor. She liked the looks of him for certain. She liked that he was something of a rake, but she also admitted to herself that he *was* a gentleman. He had displayed hidden depths of honor on more than one occasion.

And now he had quoted poetry to her.

Even though he admitted to being cynical—a realist—his voice had caressed her with the poet's words.

Natalie's train of thought shattered as she turned the boat toward the dock and—oh, no—this could not be! Baby Bear was running wildly with Mrs. Tinsdale chasing far behind. The leading string dragged behind the pup, who easily caught sight of Natalie, his mama, out on the lake. With a new purpose and destination, Baby Bear ran to the end of the dock and took a flying leap into the water.

He sank like a stone.

Acting on pure instinct, Natalie threw herself into the water, kicking desperately to reach her tiny puppy. She didn't feel the wet or the cold. Her Baby Bear had disappeared under the water and Natalie needed to find him, *now!*

Frantically reaching through the murky water, Natalie grasped the leading string and pulled the puppy to the surface for some air. In doing so, however, she lost the buoyancy her arms would have provided. She attempted to kick to keep herself from going under, but her dress had wound itself tightly around her legs.

She felt her first moment of fear when she swallowed a mouthful of water instead of air. Oh, no! If she went down, then so would Baby Bear. Her feet were bare, but as hard as she tried to kick herself free of her skirts, they gave no mercy.

And then strong hands grabbed her.

In one sweeping gush, she burst above the surface of the water. She gasped and coughed as her deprived lungs sought to replenish themselves. Baby Bear was kicking and squirming, reaching his little black nose out of the water. Only when an arm wrapped itself around her ribcage did she become aware of the security of a very solid chest behind her head.

"Don't struggle with me. Relax and lean back. I've got you."

Garrett's voice. His deep, gravelly command infused incredible relief.

Trusting completely, Natalie tilted her head back and rested it on his shoulder. He would pull them to safety. Baby Bear crawled up her front and tucked his nose under her chin.

"That's my girl," he said. "Keep your head back just like that, sweetheart." His voice reassured her as he used his other arm and his legs to pull them toward the shore. His breath caressed her nape when he spoke.

The rhythm of Garrett's movements changed when his feet touched bottom. Not releasing her, he slogged both of them to the water's edge. When they reached the shore, Natalie collapsed on the ground in relief, Garrett's arm still around her. He breathed heavily, whether from his exertions or the panic of the last few moments, Natalie did not know. Like a rag doll, she sprawled helplessly face down on the shore. They both lay beached in the mud and slime accumulated there until Garrett rolled her over and studied her in concern.

"You are unhurt?" His voice sounded strained.

She could not answer right away. His gaze was mesmerizing. She liked feeling this close to him. Being held by Garrett Castleton felt safe. It felt right. She wanted to tuck her face into his neck and leave it there forever. The spell couldn't last, however, as she was gradually aware that her precipitous leap had been witnessed by all her mother's guests. Concerned bystanders were about to descend upon them mercilessly. Baby Bear added to the mayhem when he began barking and yelping frantically.

He was very protective.

But Natalie could not look away from Garrett. His gaze burned with emotions she did not understand—tenderness, and then fear, and...anger.

"I shall live." She quipped. His expression remained serious—too serious. In an attempt to tease him into a lighter mood, she smiled hesitantly and added, "Good day for a swim, don't you think?"

Garrett merely shook his head, and a dark scowl appeared.

Pushing himself away from her, he now rested on his heels. His expression lacked any amusement whatsoever. Shuddering, he took a deep breath and then scrubbed his hands over his face.

"What," he growled through gritted teeth, "in bloody hell was that all about?" All tenderness had been replaced with fury. "You did not see Riverton had reached out to pull...*Baby Bear*...out of the water? You risk life and limb for a...for a...What the hell is that animal anyway?"

Natalie suddenly felt the cold.

"Hush," she said. She reached for Baby Bear and pulled him close. The little pup stopped barking and was now shivering from head to tail. Natalie placed some reassuring kisses on the dog's head just as her mother arrived and, in a frantic motion, threw a blanket about her shoulders. Did her mother not see that half of her person remained in the water?

"Natalie! You scared me to death! Why ever would you jump into the water like that?" She looked over her shoulder and gestured for one of Natalie's brothers to come and assist them. Thank God it was Stone. At least he possessed a sense of humor.

"I needed to save my p-p-pup-py." She shivered.

"Stone," Lady Ravensdale addressed her son. "Get Natalie inside at once." She glanced at Natalie where she still lay halfway in the water, very close to Lord Hawthorne and her lips tightened. "Along with everything else we've dealt with, we don't need your sister falling ill."

But that was not why her mother flailed in such a panic. Glancing down at her dress, Natalie saw that the pink material had turned transparent from the water. No wonder her mother had thrown the blanket over her!

As Stone swooped her up and away from Lord Hawthorne, Natalie looked back for one last glimpse of her hero. Although Darlington had tossed a second blanket on the dry ground beside him, he'd made no move toward it. The poor dear looked poleaxed. But that was not all she noticed. His white linen shirt, now plastered to his chest, revealed the stark definition of his muscular build. The sight of a man ought not be able to make a young lady's mouth water, but what was a girl to do? It seemed his legs were not the only part of his body so well honed…

Chapter Fourteen

It took several minutes for Garrett's racing heart to slow down to a normal pace. Despite being just a few strokes from shallow water, he'd felt utter despair when Natalie's blonde head disappeared beneath the murky depths. It was insanely stupid of her to jump into the water wearing so many petticoats and skirts. And to save a puppy! Yes, he'd concluded the creature was a beloved pet to her.

In an effort to clear his head, Garrett shook it side to side and drops of water splattered on the ground around him. Her mother had been none too happy with them, and now Darlington hovered about, scowling. Matters were growing complicated—far too complicated.

Garrett accepted Viscount Darlington's outstretched hand and allowed the man to pull him free of the mud he'd been wallowing in. Damned if his legs didn't feel just a little shaky.

"My sister has some explaining to do," Darlington groused. Natalie's oldest brother spoke evenly, stoically, in fact, but just then, a shudder ran through him. He'd obviously realized the danger his sister had been in. Darlington bent forward to retrieve the blanket and tossed it at Garrett. "My family owes you our thanks. The lake is clouded with mud this time of year, and once a person becomes submerged…"

"She believed her pet to be drowning," Garrett interjected matter-of-factly as he wrapped the blanket around his shoulders. Now that his adrenaline had passed, the chill of the water was setting in. "Damn, I liked these boots," he added, looking downward.

"I was unaware, as was the rest of my family, that my sister owned a pet." Darlington began walking toward the front of the manor with Garrett. "Of all the fool things to do…"

Garrett for some reason felt it necessary to defend her actions. "She must hold a depth of feeling for the little rascal." The image of horror on her face just before she jumped convinced him of this. His boots made a squishing sound with each step he took. Thank God she had not been alone. Perhaps ladies ought not to float about on lakes in multiple layers of fabric and lace. *Damn society and damn fashion.*

Upon reaching the steps, Garrett sat and attempted to remove his boots. It would not serve well to traipse boot-loads of lake water onto the shiny parquet floors for the servants to clean. Viscount Darlington, understanding the difficulties involved in removing a snug-fitting pair of hessians, went down on his haunches and tugged on one of the offending articles. Garrett once again marveled at this family. They lived in complete opposition to the notions his father had valued. Not often did the heir to an earldom perform valet services.

"My thanks, Darlington."

The viscount nodded cordially, and the two men proceeded into the house. The viscount stalked in the direction of the study, while Garrett climbed the stairs to change into dry attire. Not in any way accustomed to having the service of a valet, Garrett was pleasantly surprised to find Marcus already preparing a hot bath and warming towels for him in his quarters. The thoughtfulness brought a calm to Garrett he had not often felt. At least some small things in his life were in order.

Chapter Fifteen

Natalie kept quiet while Tinny assisted her with a long hot bath and then combed out her hair by the fire. Tinny didn't press her nor scold her. Although Natalie insisted she was fine, that there was no harm done from Baby Bear's escape, the older woman remained in an unusually contrite mood.

She'd uttered not a single protest when Natalie asked for one of the dresses from her trousseau. And those gowns had not been designed to be worn by an unmarried girl.

Natalie needed a little extra confidence tonight.

This particular one, made up of a deep brown satin, featured shiny gold embroidery at the hem and around the bodice. The dress, designed to be worn without a petticoat, was refined and stylish. It was something only a married woman might wear or perhaps a widow even.

Turning to admire herself in the looking glass, Natalie's spirit's dipped when her mother entered. Most likely Lady Ravensdale came to scold her.

Except that...her mother wore a look of unexpected approval when their eyes met in the mirror. Lady Ravensdale raised her eyebrows. "I must say I like this outfit more than the confection you wore earlier."

"Tinsdale selected the pink." Natalie inserted just enough disapproval in her tone for her mother to understand. "It is what happens when a lady is dressed by the same person who also once changed her nappies."

Lady Ravensdale's chin rose slightly before dropping in an understanding nod. She then glanced around the room as though searching for something. "And the pup? Are you to blame his appearance on poor Mrs. Tinsdale as well?"

She would not rat Tinny out in that respect. Natalie faced her mother directly. She stood straight, tall, and proud. "Baby Bear is mine. I found him, and I am taking care of him."

Lady Ravensdale looked about the room again. "And where," she asked pointedly, "is Baby Bear now?"

Oh, botheration! Of course, her mother would pounce upon this. "Tinsdale offered to take him outside." Recalling the woman's profuse apologies from earlier, Natalie could not help but defend herself. "Tinsdale's grown rather fond of Baby Bear."

Lady Ravensdale took a seat on a velvet-covered chair near the window. Leaning forward, she rubbed her forehead as though to dispel a megrim. "My darling, I know you are unhappy with the way this summer has materialized. I know you are frustrated at your present circumstances, but really, must you jump into the lake in the middle of my garden party?"

More guilt! She had not meant to embarrass her mother.

She never meant to embarrass any of her family, but that was all she seemed capable of doing for the past few months.

"I didn't plan on jumping in the lake, Mama." She

hoped she could coax her mother into better spirits. "Although the water did manage to rid me of those dratted ringlets Tinsdale gave me earlier."

Lady Ravensdale moaned. "My darling girl, if Tinsdale is not your maid, then what are we to do with her? She has given her entire life to help me raise you children. She has no family of her own and is now past her most productive years. I fear she would decline if there were no purpose in her life. What would you have me do with her?"

"She could be *your* maid," Natalie said, deadpan.

"Oh, do be serious."

"I am being serious, Mother! If you do not wish to have her as your maid, why ever would I?"

This silenced her mother. Natalie took the opportunity to further her cause. "Perhaps Father could settle a pension upon her—set her up in a charming cottage somewhere?" The words landed between she and her mother with a thump. Natalie regretted them as soon as they left her lips.

"You know we cannot," her mother stood, signaling an end to their conversation. "But I will discuss the situation with your father, and he might assist us in finding a better solution to her employment."

As annoying as her parents could be at times, she never, ever, doubted their love. "Thank you, Mama." She rushed into her mother's arms with the intent to reassure her. "And please, do not fret for me. Soon this summer will be over, and then we can go to London for the Little Season. We can shop and make visits and not feel as though we must wallow in the country hiding my shame."

Her mother put one hand on Natalie's cheek. "I have never been ashamed of you my dear. A little embarrassed, perhaps, on a few occasions"—her smile was watery—"but never ashamed."

Natalie blinked away a few tears. "Thank you, Mama." She hoped her papa felt the same.

****

Calm and at peace, Natalie felt unusually graceful as she stepped into the drawing room just before dinner. It was not the dress. It was not the loose chignon Tinny had assisted her with. Nor was it the new pair of gold slippers she wore. No, something inside her had shifted. She was not even embarrassed over the incident at the garden party.

In a distracted manner, she fidgeted with the glass of wine handed to her by one of the footmen and wondered if this was what it felt like to grow up.

Little matters, once so important to her, suddenly seemed trivial.

Very grown up emotions made themselves known tonight, most evoked by Lord Hawthorne.

Natalie had seen a bleakness in his ebony eyes when he pulled her out of the water. He'd been frightened for her, as though he actually *cared* about her.

Which was preposterous, considering his reputation. The man had admitted to consorting with experienced widows, dancers, and opera singers. Natalie was an inexperienced debutante. The extent of her sensual experience could not even fill a thimble, for heaven's sake.

But she could not dismiss what she'd seen in his eyes. Was it merely the effect one felt in the aftermath of a harrowing situation? Would he have viewed Miss Penelope Crone or Miss Abigail Wright with the same gentle sensitivity? The thought alone made something dark and cold curl within her chest.

Ha! Caring indeed! It seemed to her that she might be the one with the unfortunate affliction.

Spotting Miss Crone and Miss Wright sitting on the large wing chairs near the grand fireplace, Natalie approached them with a polite smile and greeting. The ladies stood anxiously, and Miss Wright reached out both of her hands to Natalie.

"Oh, my lady, I do hope you are feeling well after your frightening experience this afternoon? And the little pup, has he recovered too?" Natalie allowed the lady to grasp both of her hands. The fact that Miss Wright included Baby Bear in her concern raised Natalie's regard of her immediately.

"Thank you. And yes, Baby Bear and I are both unscathed by this afternoon's events." In fact, this very minute Mrs. Tinsdale was likely spoiling the little imp.

Miss Wright smiled. It brought a prettiness to her that Natalie hadn't noticed earlier. "Baby Bear is his name? How adorable! I have always wanted a pet, but my mother is allergic and could never tolerate an animal in the house."

Miss Crone rolled her eyes. "Your mother"—she paused for effect—"barely tolerates other humans about—" A warning look from Miss Wright silenced her comment, so Natalie changed the subject.

"Do, let's sit. I do believe summer has arrived." Natalie fluttered her ivory fan before smiling and turning her attention to Penelope. "Did my brother charm you? Please tell me he didn't bore you with statistics and economics. He tends to get carried away conversing on agricultural outputs and trading prices."

Penelope answered in all seriousness. "He was quite charming, but yes, in fact, that is exactly what we discussed. Why would such a topic be considered boring?"

Miss Wright smiled at her cousin. "I'm sure Penelope instigated the topic herself." Ruefully, she added, "Penelope avoids anything resembling flirtation or romance when a gentleman dares attempt such with her. She is determined to remain unmarried."

"And what of you, Miss Wright?" Natalie ventured. "Did you find it necessary to avoid the duke's advances?"

With that, Miss Abigail Wright gave her a sideways accusatory stare. "You were very wicked to pair me with Monfort. A duke, no less! What was I to do when plunked down in a boat with a *duke* of all things, for nearly forty minutes? What does a grown woman, one who is for all intents and purposes on the shelf, speak of with a duke? Very naughty indeed, Lady Natalie," she admonished again. But Natalie's curiosity was aroused.

"What *does* a woman who is practically on the shelf discuss with a duke for forty minutes, Miss Wright?"

The older lady blushed but did not seem to enjoy Natalie's teasing. Some other, unidentifiable emotion crossed the lady's face.

A change of subject was unnecessary, however, when a commotion at the large double doors leading into the drawing room snared their attention. Dressed in travelling clothes and covered in dust, four young men stepped inside of the drawing room. They obviously did not belong in the present surroundings. Their hair, matted from perspiration, stuck out in all directions as they removed their hats and stepped inside amongst the esteemed guests. They must know they were not welcome here.

Natalie did not believe for one minute that her parents would have invited Mr. Damian Farley and his associates to Raven's Park—ever. Farley swaggered in and, catching sight of Natalie and the two other women, leered in their direction. Natalie did not drop her eyes but narrowed them defiantly at the cad. He chuckled to himself and returned her look with a mocking smile. He had lost one of his front teeth since she last saw him. She wondered if it fell out due to decay or violence. It very easily could have been either.

Before Natalie became betrothed, just a few weeks after her come out, Farley had attempted to trap her into marriage to himself. Joseph had been watching out for her, however, and foiled the man's plan. It was only *after* this occurred that Natalie heard of his reputation.

She knew the identity of two of his companions but did not know either of them personally. The Viscount of Trident, although quiet, was stained with a reputation similar to Farley's, but the younger man, the Marquis of Lockley, looked too good-natured to be a threat to anyone. The fact they were in Farley's company, however, gave her reason to distrust the whole lot of them.

Except that Lord Danbury accompanied them. Danbury was a longtime friend of Stone's and an even closer friend to her former betrothed. Just as that thought went through her head, Natalie watched with relief as Stone intercepted the ruffians and steered them back into the foyer.

Miss Crone commented suspiciously. "Wherever did those blackguards come from?" She looked over at Natalie with questioning eyes. "Surely they have not been invited?" Her disapproval was obvious in her tone of voice. Miss Crone had placed her hand atop Miss Wright's fists, which were now clenched in her lap. Miss Wright had gone pale.

"Lord Danbury is a friend of Stone's, but the other three would never be welcomed here. I'm certain Stone is removing them this very moment." She reassured Miss Crone. "My family is aware of Farley and his disreputable ways."

"Trident has more money than sense, apparently," Miss Crone declared, "and now it looks as though Farley's got his hands in Lockley's pockets as well. Lockley came of age this past season. I cannot see his father approving of such a connection for his heir." After a thoughtful pause, she continued, "I agree with you about Danbury, though. I can't imagine what he's doing in Farley's company."

Natalie watched Miss Wright closely. "There is nothing to worry about, Abigail. May I call you Abigail?" At Miss Wright's barely perceptible nod, she continued, "They will not be allowed to stay. My brothers do not consort with such vermin." Thinking that Abigail Wright must be a very sheltered woman, Natalie continued, "They're likely sent back where they've come from already."

But her mother *had* allowed *Garrett Castleton* to come to Raven's Park as a guest. This thought gave Natalie pause. She, in no way, connected Garrett with the likes of Farley and Trident. She considered him a rake, and yet there was something solid about him. He had almost always arrived at *ton* events alone. And she'd never actually witnessed him over-imbibing in the presence of ladies. Since his arrival at Raven's Park, he'd exhibited an uncompromising determination to behave honorably toward her. And even though he looked at her with blatant sensuality, never had she felt she had anything to fear.

He seemed to be trustworthy. No, he *was* trustworthy. The more she came to know of him, the more she felt this to be true. She would never again allow Mr. Farley to get her alone. No, *that one* would, given the slightest opportunity, take full advantage.

Unlike Garrett Castleton. Where was that dratted man anyhow?

****

Garrett left his room feeling more optimistic than he'd felt in a long time. Unfortunately, it didn't last long. At the top of the stairs, he paused silently when he caught sight of Stone with a group of vaguely familiar men. They all looked to be travel weary.

Stone did not appear happy as he addressed Danbury through gritted teeth. Ah yes, Garrett recognized the viscount. Garrett and Stone had known him for years.

Not wishing to draw attention to himself, Garrett watched as Stone pulled Danbury off to the side and addressed him in a tight voice. "What in the hell do you think you're doing bringing these bounders here? The lot of them are nothing but trouble." Stone did not anger easily. Garrett braced himself to assist if necessary.

167

But Danbury looked sheepish. "I didn't plan to bring them here, Stone. Cortland left town, you know, and with the season at an end, I thought I'd remain in London rather than follow my mother and sister back to Land's End." Even Garrett knew that Danbury's mother and sister were the worst sort of matchmakers. It was a wonder the man remained a bachelor.

Pulling a flask from his pocket, Danbury took a long swig of God knows what before continuing. "And then McDuff, Lockley's father, asked if I would keep an eye on him, try to keep him out of any serious trouble. I owed him a favor...I had no idea who I would be up against!" Gesturing with his flask, he glanced toward the room the others had disappeared into. And then, as though remembering something, he drew his brows together. "What's this I hear of Hawthorne being a guest of your parents, Stone? Does your father not know of the insanity in that family? Nothing against Castleton, but not even Wellington could live down Hawthorne's actions." He punctuated his insults with a belch.

Garrett chose that moment to make his presence known. "Danbury." He sauntered down the stairs cheerfully. "Hadn't thought I'd have the pleasure of your company again this summer."

"Ah, well"—Danbury didn't miss a beat—"town becomes uncomfortable during the warmer months."

Garrett nodded, then folded his arms across his chest and leaned against the balustrade.

Stone, looking grateful that Garrett wasn't resorting to violence, turned his attention back to Danbury. The normally well-put-together gentleman had dark circles around his eyes and a sallowness to his skin. "You aren't looking good, my friend. How can I help you?"

Danbury shifted his eyes toward where his companions had gone. "Could you give us a few nights in your bachelors' quarters? I need time alone with Lockley to convince him to forsake Farley's company. If I can get him back to his father, I'll consider my debt to the duke paid in full."

Stone shook his head, reluctance on his face. "Very well. Take the lot of them down there, and do not, I repeat, do not allow them to come anywhere near the house." At Danbury's apparent relief, he added, "I'll send a footman down with provisions, sandwiches, and spirits. But promise me you'll keep them holed up. God knows what kind of trouble those two will make, given a chance."

Danbury grasped Stone's hand. "I'm in your debt for this, my friend." Then, with a sly wink, he added, "Say hullo to your beautiful sister for me, will you? If I didn't have to deal with these idiots, I'd be happy to soothe her wounded heart."

"Don't start, Danbury. I could change my mind yet." Stone did not look amused.

Garrett was not amused either. In fact, he had the sudden urge to drive his fist through Danbury's face.

Which made it all the worse that Farley, Trident, and Lockley chose that moment to return.

They did not, of course, allow Garrett's presence to go unnoticed.

Farley had the audacity to comment first. "What kind of stench is this, Spencer? It seems your servants have forgotten to remove yesterday's rubbish!"

Lockley and Trident guffawed at the statement.

Danbury winced at his cohorts' words. He, at least, knew better.

Garrett, no longer feeling amiable, brushed at some invisible lint on his sleeve before looking up again. Although his glare bore into Farley, Garrett's words addressed Stone. He refused to be baited. "I will not abuse your mother's hospitality, Stone, by responding to your guest's words tonight." He swept his gaze from Farley and Danbury over to Lockley and Trident before settling it back upon Stone. "But if they do not step aside so I might pass, I'm more than willing to meet them in the park at dawn."

Danbury pivoted and pounded his head into the wall three times. Farley, more bluster than courage, stepped back, and his sidekicks followed suit. Garrett nodded in Stone's direction and then brushed past them.

Entering the drawing room, he took a moment to bring his anger under control. The buffoons he'd met in the foyer were of no consequence, and yet he was furious. He was furious with Stone for inviting him here. He was furious with Danbury for his comment about Lady Natalie. But most of all he was furious with himself.

He was furious with himself for caring. When in London, earlier this summer, he'd erected a wall of sorts. Over the past few days, however, it had crumbled.

Without thinking, he ran a hand through his hair and then grimaced as it came away with the pomade Marcus had applied earlier. God dammit! He searched through his pockets, located a handkerchief, and then wiped away the annoying oil. He'd been enraged by Danbury's words implying that Lady Natalie would be receptive to his advances. He clenched his hands to stop them from shaking.

And then a dainty, white-gloved hand settled atop his fists.

He didn't need to look up to see whose it was. He knew her by her scent, by the sounds of her breath, the way her presence changed the air around him.

"They are of no account, whatsoever." She sounded annoyed. "They have not been invited, and I'm sure my brother is this very moment seeing them back to their mounts. He would not abide their presence here this evening." She went from annoyed to outright angry. It was as though she wanted to protect *him*, Garrett Castleton! This thought alone lightened his mood. Earnest blue eyes held concern as she peered up at him.

"You look beautiful tonight." He didn't know where the words came from. They escaped of their own accord. But he could not help himself. She wore her hair in a loose chignon, wavy tendrils caressing her nape. And her dress, rather than compete for attention, enhanced her beauty. Although the bodice was modestly cut, the embroidered design accentuated the delightful curves hidden beneath.

She blushed at his compliment. "My thanks to you. You are looking fine this evening as well, my lord."

He liked it when she "my lorded" him. Not because it reminded him of the title he held, but because she said it when she felt flustered.

Tilting her head, she reached up a hand to his hair. "Except you've mussed your hair here." She removed her glove and plucked and smoothed his hair for just a few seconds. The motion drew them closer together. He wanted to lean down and place his lips on the spot where her neck curved into her shoulder but of course could not. He leaned into her, however, and inhaled her scent.

"There, that's better."

Garrett took hold of her hand. Using his handkerchief, he wiped away the traces of hair treatment, sliding the material between her fingers and then around her palm. He knew she was not unaffected by his touch. But that he could kiss each finger, draw each one into his mouth...

With the fabric still in her palm, she clasped it in her fist and lowered it to her side.

Awareness of their surroundings compelled her to look about nervously. Garrett wondered, too, if their unusually intimate exchange had been witnessed. As luck would have it, a large potted plant blocked them from much of the room. Miss Crone and Miss Wright, however, had observed all. Garrett nodded at them. Miss Wright looked away, obviously embarrassed at being caught, but Miss Crone merely shook her head and then turned back to her friend.

Natalie stepped away. She tilted her head to one side and regarded him again. "I don't believe I thanked you yet for helping me to shore this afternoon. I am normally a good swimmer but never considered the hindrance my dress would cause me." She spoke in a calm manner, not at all willing to admit the peril she'd been in.

Garrett had been furious earlier, but now, seeing her all prim and proper and thanking him so graciously, he could not summon his anger back easily. "Glad to be of assistance, *my lady*. But I have a question for you."

"I will answer it for you if I am able."

"Does your pup, by chance, cry and whimper throughout the nighttime hours?"

"Oh, yes, he cries wretchedly!" As Natalie explained how she'd found the pup and then decided to keep him in her chamber, Garrett thought to strangle her. What he'd thought was her distress had prevented him from getting a good night's sleep as well. Oh, hell…maybe he'd just as well deserved it.

"I would be happy to introduce you to Baby Bear sometime, if you wish—that is…" Her voice trailed off, suddenly unsure. "Perhaps after viewing your mother's paintings?"

He'd nearly forgotten his promise to Lady Eleanor. Had that just been this morning? "I would be delighted." Realizing the other guests were making their way to remove to the dining room, Garrett winged an arm at the lady beside him. "Shall we?"

Something shot through him when she took hold of his arm. Protectiveness? Pride? Tenderness? God help him but he felt all of those. Privileged to escort her, he spent the next few hours playing the part of gentleman to her lady. His father and the *ton*, be damned.

Chapter Sixteen

Her mother's various courses never tasted so divine as they did that night. Except perhaps not because of the food, but the benefit of receiving such undivided attention from Garrett Castleton. He treated her almost as though he were courting her. He was polite to her brother, Peter, who sat on his other side, but included her in their conversation as well. Occasionally, he placed his hand upon her arm in a casual but...possessive manner. He did not, however, attempt to touch her inappropriately, as he had done the night before.

This was almost more tantalizing.

Garrett's demeanor had concerned Natalie when she watched him enter the drawing room earlier. His jaw had been clenched and his eyes narrowed. Immediately, she sensed something untoward must have occurred with Stone's guests causing Garrett to be on the verge of losing his temper. She'd been drawn to his side. She wanted to soothe him. She could not keep herself from touching him. And now, she clutched the handkerchief he'd given to her in her left hand, under the table.

Looking at him now, she could hardly believe anything upsetting had transpired at all. Engaged in animated conversation, he exuded both charisma and charm. The world was a wonderful place indeed, when

Garrett Castleton smiled.

"Shall we? Ladies?" Natalie's mother rose, signaling the ladies leave the gentlemen to their port.

Oh, bother. Natalie would have sat there all night if given the opportunity. Except, perhaps she ought to take a moment to pull herself together. These feelings were too heady, too intoxicating. It wouldn't do for her to fall all over him giddily, like the schoolgirl he'd pegged her for on more than one occasion already.

But he was not treating her thusly tonight. When she rose to leave, he caught her arm for just a second. And he winked at her! Could he read her mind, for heaven's sake?

She did not wink back. Instead she dipped into a quick curtsey, excusing herself, and followed the other ladies out of the room.

Natalie wrestled with a strange hope building in her heart. Was he serious about her? Is that what this meant? Or was he merely being kind for the sake of her father and mother?

She wished she knew.

As the ladies swept into the drawing room, mother instructed the footmen to open the french doors leading to the terrace. The summer sun had warmed the normally comfortable assembling area. The breeze would be welcomed.

Natalie felt stifled, nonetheless.

Far too many concerns filled her mind for her to sit and make polite conversation, Garrett Castleton being the most pressing, and Baby Bear coming in second. She'd left her new baby in Mrs. Tinsdale's care. Tinny had promised under no circumstances would Baby Bear escape from her.

Making a quick decision, Natalie pivoted and then slipped back into the corridor. Baby Bear could make his bow to polite society—on dry land this time. Yes, this was the diversion she needed.

She dashed upstairs and burst into her chamber. There on the loveseat, darning one of Natalie's petticoats and humming, sat Mrs. Tinsdale, Baby Bear tucked in beside her. As a child, on rainy days, or when the boys' teasing was too much for her to handle, Natalie could always find comfort snuggled up next to the dear nanny.

Had that really been so very long ago?

A lump lodged in her throat, and Natalie knew in her heart they could never send the older woman away. It would be like sending away her very own grandmother. Tinny sat the fabric aside and pulled the dog onto her lap. Baby Bear, lolling onto his back, submitted to the old nanny's soothing strokes enthusiastically.

"I had thought to bring Baby Bear down and formally introduce him to the ladies." Natalie didn't want to upset Baby Bear or Tinny but…"It would be good to teach him to behave among genteel company, don't you think?"

"Oh, absolutely." Tinny stood. "The leading string is on the bed. I took him out a little while ago, so he should be fine." Lifting the dog into the air, she looked him sternly in the eyes. "Now don't you be misbehaving, you little rascal." And then Tinny, yes, firm Mrs. Tinsdale, kissed the pup on the top of his head before placing him on the carpet. Natalie knelt beside Baby Bear and tied the string onto the collar Marcus had obtained for him.

"I won't be long, Tinny," she reassured the older woman. "Just a little while—less if he misbehaves!"

Tinny turned back to her mending. "No hurry, my dear. At least this way I'll be able to finish some of this mending. The scamp keeps me from sewing even a single stitch." Her normal brisk efficiency returned.

In the corridor, Natalie placed Baby Bear on the carpeted walkway and allowed him to lead the way to the stairs. But that was the easy part. When they reached the steep staircase, the little pup halted and peered down anxiously. Although a mere six or so inches tall, he was not cowed. Instead, it seemed, he had a plan.

Much like a billiards player contemplating his next shot, the pup paced along the width of the step a few times before making his move. Once ready, he turned, paused, and then daringly dropped his front paws down to the first platform. The second half of his body followed thereafter. He took a second step in a similar fashion.

At this rate, it would take all night to descend the stairs, so, laughing, Natalie lifted him into her arms and carried him to the main floor. "We'll work on steps later, Baby," she told her pet with affection. Once downstairs, she sat him on the floor, and together they entered the drawing room where the ladies were caught up in a spirited game of charades.

Baby Bear let out two quick yaps before Natalie silenced him. Too late. All heads turned toward the cause of disruption.

Most of the ladies spontaneously transformed into pools of mush. Puppies affected people that way. And Baby Bear was all puppy.

His soulful eyes and adorable ears doubled his attraction.

After allowing a few of the ladies to pet Baby Bear, Natalie scooped him up once again and took him to where Miss Crone and Miss Wright sat. There, the pup became the center of attraction once again.

Of course, a few ladies did not care for animals. They pursed their lips and not so discreetly edged away. Nonetheless, they dared not utter their contempt—what with Lady Ravensdale cooing at the pup as though he were her first grandchild.

"He's precious." Miss Wright's assessment agreed with Natalie's own.

"Would you care to hold him?" Although not sorry she'd escaped Monfort's company that afternoon, remorse dogged her for trapping Miss Wright with him. She handed Baby Bear into the other woman's eager arms.

Cradling Baby Bear against her chest, Miss Wright allowed him to lick beneath her chin.

"Oh, Penelope!" Miss Wright's eyes sparkled. "It's like holding a baby!"

Miss Crone's response was classic Penelope. "Ugliest baby I ever saw."

As the ladies joked about the commonalities between puppies and babies, Natalie looked on, satisfied with Baby Bear's success.

And then the gentlemen arrived.

A few were contemptuous of Baby Bear's tiny proportions. They professed to own great-sized dogs, nearly as large as small horses and other nonsense. Natalie ignored them. Baby Bear had pleasantly livened up the evening and done so without making a single diddle. Meeting her mother's gaze from across the room, Natalie felt warm inside, for Lady Ravensdale's expression held an abundance of approval.

An entirely different warmth rushed through her when she caught Garrett Castleton watching her. He lifted one eyebrow and then drifted across the room. In his normal casual manner, he leaned against a nearby sofa. Cradling a glass of brandy, he swirled the warmed liquid absentmindedly, never taking his eyes off her.

"Lord Hawthorne." Natalie curtseyed in his direction. "Come and make your formal acquaintance of Baby Bear." Lifting the pup and holding out one paw, she said, "Baby Bear, I'd like to present the Earl of Hawthorne. My lord, may I present Baby Bear, Lord Puppy of Cuteness?"

Garrett made a small bow in lieu of introduction. Lady Natalie's playful mood charmed him. "Baby bear looks to have survived his swim with no ill effects." Reaching forward, he let the small dog smell his hand before placing it on the dog's furry head and kneading the loose skin around its neck. The dog relaxed into Garrett's touch.

"Oh, he likes you." And then in a near whisper, "My lord." Garrett moved his gaze from the dog to this woman. The quality of her voice spun a web of intimacy around the two of them. It evoked emotions he refused to consider.

Sitting beside her this evening had been a revelation. She'd been unguarded and relaxed throughout the meal. And ever so slightly flirtatious. He wanted to know more about her. He *needed* to know more about her.

In his business ventures, when uncertain of a

proposition, he'd first research all aspects of the transaction.

Perhaps courting Lady Natalie required just such an approach.

"My lady," he said. "Shall we take this pup outside for a short constitutional?" Glancing toward her mother, he added, "We can stay close to the house—for both of our protection."

Natalie glowed. It was obvious he'd pleased her by recalling their earlier conversations. He wondered if the other men in her life did not take her seriously? He wondered if any of them had ever actually *listened* to her.

"Baby Bear would like that very much—as would I." Grasping a leading string, she sat the dog on the carpet and then glanced toward her mother. With her mother's apparent approval, she then took Garrett's offered arm, and he led her out an open terrace door.

He appreciated the boundaries set by her family. She deserved to be safeguarded by her father and mother, her brothers. And she ought to be protected once married.

A warm breeze stirred the air. Garrett inhaled deeply. The fresh unspoiled air was one of the greatest arguments for living in the country. He could also smell a hint of Natalie's subtle perfume. It was difficult to identify the scents it encompassed; it just seemed uniquely her.

She held the leading string with one hand and his arm with the other. Garrett took the string from her. This allowed her to grasp his arm with both hands and lean into him. When Baby Bear began sniffing about suspiciously, Natalie spoke.

"He is shy. He likes to do his business in private." She gestured to a copse of trees off to the side of the manor. This would lead them farther away from the other guests. These evening walks were becoming a dangerous habit.

Garrett allowed the pup to steer them both.

"He is house-trained already?"

"We're working on it." Natalie spoke proudly. "Do you have a dog?"

He had. As a boy, he'd become attached to an unfortunate dog who'd had the audacity to roam onto his father's estate uninvited.

Upon discovering the animal, his father had drowned it.

"A long time ago," Garrett answered. "My father did not approve of his bloodline and killed it." He didn't mean to be so blunt. Saying the words revived unwanted memories.

Natalie walked, unspeaking, and stopped once they reached the trees. Baby Bear was interested in marking several of them one by one. He raised one tiny leg and let out a squirt.

"What did you name him?"

"My dog?" he asked, revisiting that train of thought.

"Yes, your pet."

Garrett looked off into the distance, across the lawn and at the lake. He wasn't seeing any of it though. Instead a memory intruded, of a large brown and black mutt. That dog had followed him everywhere! He'd been on the receiving end of unfettered adoration from…"Ben."

"You named your dog Ben?" she asked with a

laugh in her voice.

"Well, at least it was a name!" Garrett looped the leading string around a sturdy branch and then, giving in to impulse, wrapped his arms around her affectionately. "Your poor pet is bound to go through life labelled as the wrong species! And what of when he becomes a wise old dog? He shall forever suffer the indignity of being called Baby!" Garrett took a few steps forward, forcing her to walk backward until she stood pressed against the trunk of a large oak. Releasing her, he raised both his hands and placed them on the bark above her shoulders.

Laughing, she locked her gaze with his. "Well, I thought he was a bear when I first saw him," she pouted prettily, "and he will always be my *baby*."

Said baby was managing to tangle himself in a myriad of smaller branches.

Garrett leaned forward and placed an open-mouthed kiss on her shoulder. And as if the most natural thing in the world, Natalie tilted her head to the side. Much better, now he could explore the skin behind her ear. The familiarity of touching her so ought to bother him. Being with her was too easy—it felt artless and instinctive. As he swirled his tongue along her neck, she moaned softly.

Somehow, he'd veered away from his plan to obtain information from her. He wished to ask her a few questions, questions that had nothing to do with the sweet softness of her skin beneath his lips. Such a delightful distraction.

He nuzzled her and stepped closer, their bodies meeting, shoulders to thighs. Without moving his hands from the tree, he had her exactly where he wanted. He heard the hitch in her breath and felt the quickening of her heartbeat in the pulse beneath his mouth.

Fragile arms wrapped around his waist. Hesitant at first, they tightened as she grew bolder. Garrett dragged kisses along her jaw, pausing when he reached the tender skin at the corner of her mouth. These inclinations were likely to lead them both straight to the alter.

"Garrett," she breathed. "Garrett, just kiss me already!"

He'd rethink this problem later.

Dropping his arms, he pulled her against him and gave his lips free rein. He didn't need to tease open the seam of her mouth. Her lips were already parted.

And her hands explored him.

He could not suppress a groan when she reached inside his waistcoat and beneath his shoulder blades. A part of him wondered that he had not felt this way with any other woman. This was lust, yes, hot, blazing lust, but there was something else—protectiveness, tenderness, a fierce desire to make love to her and then hold her till she fell asleep.

Garrett broke the kiss and pressed her head into his chest. He could not let this proceed in its natural direction without knowing more.

If he were to offer for her, would she have him? She'd not sounded eager to become betrothed again when they'd spoken of it earlier. Likely he was fooling himself, but he needed to know: could she be happy as his countess?

Breathing deeply, he spoke. "Tell me about your betrothal to the Duke of Cortland."

It took a few seconds for her to comprehend what

he said. She pulled back and looked at him quizzically. Then nodding thoughtfully, seeming to make a decision, she pushed herself out of his arms and stepped over to retrieve Baby Bear's leading string. "I liked Cortland. He was, he *is* an honorable gentleman." Untangling the string, she freed the dog and allowed him to pull them farther into the trees. "He is a good friend to my father, was, anyway. He is pleasant." She took a few steps. "He is good-looking. He courted me formally. Always, *always* we had a chaperone present. The only time we were alone was during the three minutes required to ask for my hand."

"Three minutes?" Garrett asked with raised eyebrows.

"One minute for him to ask. One minute for me to accept. And one minute for him to seal our agreement with a kiss."

They took several steps without talking. And then Garrett delved deeper.

"What about the betrothal caused you distress?"

"I felt no distress at all, in the beginning," Natalie responded. "The wedding was set for a year off, and I assumed I would come to have more romantic feelings for him as the engagement progressed. I hoped so anyway, because—well, the begetting of children and all that." She looked over at him from under her lashes.

"But you did not."

"No." Natalie halted for Baby Bear who'd stopped to examine something curious to only him. "I came to know him better. He was always kind. He was always a perfect gentleman." And then she smiled mischievously. "Unlike other gentlemen I know."

Garrett persisted. "You did not wish for him to be

such a gentleman?"

"That is a good question." She tilted her head back and gazed up at the trees. "With the wedding just a month away, a group of us went on a picnic to my dower property, London Manor. Our party consisted of my brother Joseph and his now wife, Glenda. Also her Aunt Lilly, Lord Danbury, His Grace, and myself."

Lilly, the name sounded familiar. "The aunt? She is the lady Cortland married, is she not?"

"She is. But please, please do not be sorry for me." Natalie grasped a twig and broke it off. "Lilly is my friend. She is in love with Cortland, and he is in love with her. I became certain of it that day. In fact, I sent them off alone in hopes they might work things out. At that point, I was already desperate for Cortland to break things off."

Cortland would never break the engagement. The little Garrett knew of the duke was enough for him to know of his impeccable honor.

Garrett did not speak. He assumed she had more to tell.

"Glenda and Joseph went into the manor, and Lilly and Cortland disappeared into the woods. That left Hugh and me alone."

Oh, hell. Not Danbury!

Garrett knew the viscount as a harmless rake, but he did not like to imagine him with Natalie. Danbury was Cortland's best friend but not considered nearly as honorable as the duke. In fact, he'd frequented a few of the establishments where Garrett had found pleasure.

"What happened?" Garrett prodded her.

Perhaps he did not wish to hear this. The thought of Natalie with Danbury, especially after this evening's earlier confrontation, was enough to make him wish he'd gone ahead and laid Danbury out with his fists after all.

"Unlike my fiancé, Danbury lacked any reluctance to…step out of line with me. Not that he would have done so had he thought Cortland held me in any true affection." She gave Garrett a stern look. "Danbury can be a rake, but he does follow a moral code of sorts."

"Of course," Garrett replied, clenching his fists for the second time that night. Was this jealousy? Garrett dismissed it and returned his attention to Natalie's words.

"It was a lazy afternoon. We'd consumed a good amount of wine and were lying on the blanket in the sunshine." Garrett did not like the scenario she created in his mind. He did *not* like the mental image of another man taking liberties with Natalie.

"And then he kissed me, oh, so very different from when Cortland kissed me. Michael had always seemed to hold himself apart. He is so very controlled. But Danbury, his kiss was savage…carnal even."

Garrett wanted to growl. Instead he asked, "Was it the same as it is"—he stopped walking and kicked at some loose stones in the ground—"between you and me?"

He looked over just in time to see a warm blush crawl into her cheeks. "Oh, no! I mean, it was nice…but not…"—she seemed to be searching for her words—"not at all the same." Her words ended in a near whisper.

"Do you have feelings for Danbury?"

She'd surprised him. He had thought his kiss had been her first.

"Gratitude." She laughed. "For showing me so clearly what my betrothal lacked. For showing me the difference between tolerance and passion." And then she met his eyes solemnly and shook her head. "Nothing more."

Danbury could live, then.

God, he was besotted.

He needed to get back to his original line of questioning. "And so, after the picnic, you were even more reluctant to go through with the marriage?"

"Yes." Natalie tugged at Baby Bear's string pulling him back onto the path. "The thought terrified me."

"What were you afraid of?" There must have been other things that had put her off the marriage so carefully arranged by her parents. "Were you not looking forward to gaining such a lofty title?"

"I looked forward to being a wife. I looked forward to being a mother. I did not look forward to being a duchess." She took a few steps and then turned to look at him. "Do you know that I did not even know which of his properties we would have made into our home? I was expected to begin my marriage in a place where I would be a complete stranger to everyone around me. As a duchess, I would never know if people were friendly to me or to my position." She warmed to her topic. "I was to become involved in large charities and fund-raising. That is what duchesses do, you know."

"And this was not something you wanted?"

"I like visiting tenants with my mother." Natalie scooped Baby Bear into her arms. "I like that she can make a difference in their lives and that they have come to love her for this. It is not that any title matters to me, it is just that *I* wish to matter, *me*, as a person, not just

187

as an asset in a business arrangement." She pulled a face. "I feel selfish when I say it out loud."

Garrett shook his head slowly. "You should not."

The crack of a branch nearby alerted him that their solitude was about to be interrupted. As the sounds drew nearer, the commotion revealed itself to be unpleasant, indeed.

Men's voices rose in slurred, foul, drunken language. Realizing how far from the manor they'd drifted, Garrett took Natalie's arm with the intention of moving her and the dog away from the approaching sounds. He had an uncomfortable suspicion as to whom the voices belonged.

The dog began barking, however, and Farley and Trident stumbled into their path, effectively blocking the way.

Farley, flushed from drink, took in the sight of the two of them together, alone, and spat on the ground. "How the mighty have fallen, Lady Natalie. Now you are not to be a duchess, you're willing to take up with just about anybody?" His eyes gleamed with malice, and he laughed vindictively. "Does your papa know about this tête-à-tête?"

"Step off, Farley. You're foxed and have obviously forgotten you are in the presence of a lady." Garrett would like to have planted the bastard a facer but would not expose Natalie to violence. He was half concerned she would take it upon herself to join in the melee if one were to erupt.

Unpredictable chit.

With a wobble and a belch, Farley reached for the trunk of a tree to keep from tumbling to the ground. "Right you are, Hawthorne. But if that is the case, what is she doing out here with the likes of you?" Trident laughed and whacked Farley on the back.

The hearty slap was more than Farley could withstand, however, and ironically sent him flailing to the ground. Trident's drunken momentum tumbled him into some bushes.

They were too sloshed to present any real danger.

Problem solved.

Shaking his head in amusement, Garrett looked over at Natalie and shrugged. She appeared to be holding back laughter. Best not to linger, though.

With one hand on the small of her back, Garrett steered Natalie and the pup clear of the two fallen cads and back to the house. The men were drunk, but they were also members of the bloody *ton*. This fact was laughable, and yet it illuminated the twisted culture inherent within society. The power wielded by such an institution annoyed him.

Garrett didn't know what these two had witnessed, but if they'd managed to see Garrett kissing Natalie, they would likely not keep the information to themselves. Not that he thought they would even remember the encounter, but if they did, they could instigate all manner of trouble.

The wrong kind of trouble.

Garrett needed to end this...whatever...with Lady Natalie. He could never offer for her. Because he cared for her. If she were to marry him, they would both regret it.

She wanted to be a mother.

She wanted children.

The gravity of this sank his heart like a stone.

He must set her free.

Chapter Seventeen

Something had upset him.

Farley and his cohort had been rude and insulting, but Natalie didn't think that would have put Lord Hawthorne into such a somber mood.

He didn't speak a word as he escorted her back onto the terrace. He didn't attempt to kiss her again nor touch her any more than necessary. Feeling bereft with the sudden removal of his attentions, Natalie hugged her pet under her chin and slipped back into the drawing room. He did not, himself, rejoin the entertainment. He'd given no explanation, only bade her good night.

With the charades game once again in full swing, this time with several gentlemen participating, Natalie's return went unnoticed. As did Lord Hawthorne's absence. To avoid conversation, Natalie sat in one of the window seats with Baby Bear. There, she feigned an interest in the antics of Lord Riverton as he attempted to mime what could only be described as a giant rat.

Was it something she'd said? She massaged the folds of skin on Baby Bear's tiny frame and reflected upon all that she'd told him. He had meticulously interrogated her about her broken engagement. She, in turn, had done nothing to hide her true feelings from him. Interesting that she could be so forthcoming when she'd known him for less than a week.

But why did he care what her feelings were regarding marriage and betrothal? Was he asking in a general sense? Or did he have another motive?

What about the betrothal caused you distress? He asked this question of her when no one, not her father, her mother, her brothers, nor even her ex-fiancé, had thought to ask. Did it matter?

Of course! It ought to have mattered greatly.

There'd been concern for her reputation, concern for the broken contracts, and concern that she find a new suitable betrothed, but no one, *no one,* had bothered to ask why she was so distressed!

So why should Garrett Castleton care?

Were you not looking forward to such a lofty title? Again, a question no one else had bothered to ask. It was as though Garrett saw her as an intelligent but emotional human being. As her own individual person, with feelings and fears and dreams.

And he had held her close. He'd kissed her with passion and, yes, with tenderness!

What did he mean by it?

She did not wish to consider the concept that teased her. It was such an outrageous thought she dared not let it voice itself even in her own mind.

Does he *wish to become betrothed to me?*

There, now she'd done it. She'd allowed the thought to enter, and of course, now it would torment her until she knew the answer.

Her parents would never allow it. Her brothers would chase him off the estate the moment they perceived his intent.

Because...because it was one thing to welcome a

man into your home, quite another to allow him to marry your daughter. Before this week, Garrett had been essentially blacklisted by most of the *ton*. His future wife, although a countess, might very well be banished from society. Garrett's father had been exposed as a madman! Garrett and his children would be tarnished thusly as well.

Natalie touched her abdomen. It would be cruel and irresponsible to have children when they might be born with such a tragic flaw. How must Lord Hawthorne feel then? How must Garrett feel? With that thought, a sharp ache squeezed her heart.

No wonder he seemed so confused. No wonder he did not seek love. He probably considered his own future to be as bleak as his father's had been.

Pulling Baby Bear closer to her shoulder, Natalie located her mother and excused herself for the night. It had been a long day. Of course, Garrett would not be looking for a wife.

As her feet carried her to her bedchamber, the horrible truth hit her. She was a lady. It had been unfair of her to act so recklessly with him. He could not dally with her as he might with a widow or a dancer...or—well, no matter. Gentlemen were to act toward a lady with honorable intentions, and she had made that impossible for him. What had she, in fact, been willing to give?

He'd been right to push her away. When she'd tempted him, he'd played along but not taken advantage of her. When things had gotten out of hand, he'd been the one to call a halt every time. She'd not acted like a lady at all. She ignored the urge to knock on his door to apologize as she'd done two nights ago. Had it only been two nights?

Instead, she entered her own chamber and found Tinsdale reclining on the loveseat with the mending on the floor. Her head tilted back, a low snore escaped from her opened mouth. Her spectacles rested precariously at the very tip of her nose. Seeing Tinsdale this way made Natalie more aware than usual of how the woman had aged. She looked frail, smaller, and vulnerable.

Dropping to the loveseat, Natalie placed her hand upon Tinny's shoulder.

"Tinny? I'd let you sleep here all night, but you'd wake with a dreadful crick in your neck."

Mrs. Tinsdale blinked and sat up. "Just resting my eyes, m'dear." Flustered, she searched for her needle and fabric.

While Natalie bent down and retrieved the garment, Baby Bear hopped into Tinny's lap. Chuckling, Tinny lifted him for a kiss. Speaking to Baby Bear, rather than Natalie, the nanny cooed, "And how did Baby Bear do? Was Baby Bear a good boy?" The puppy answered by licking her on the chin and behind her ears.

Natalie tilted her head and watched as her old nurse poured affection on the pup Natalie had been certain would be *her* very own. Tinny resided in a private suite on the ground floor toward the back of the house. It even boasted an entrance so the elderly lady could come and go from the house without using either the servants' entrance or the main front door. It would be perfect for letting a puppy take care of business during all hours of the day and night.

"Tinny?"

"Yes, dear." Mrs. Tinsdale took one of Natalie's combs and began brushing it through Baby Bear's short dark hair.

"Would you mind if you and I shared Baby Bear?" Tinny peered at her suspiciously. "You mustn't think you have to, mind you. It's just that caring for Baby Bear is much more work than I thought it would be." She had been willing though, *oh so willing*. Natalie's heart broke as she continued, "I think Baby Bear needs two mamas. Don't you? And perhaps he might do better sleeping downstairs with you, so that he can go outside easier…"

Tinny held Baby Bear closely. "Well, that's a good point, my lady. It's mighty grown up of you to realize that Baby Bear may need more attention than you or I could give him alone." She kissed the pup on the head again. "And I wouldn't mind keeping him with me." Was that a tear in the woman's eye?

Natalie blinked away the extra moisture that had accumulated in her own. "I think Baby Bear would like that." She reached forward and rubbed the dog's neck tenderly. "I think he'd like that a lot."

With that, Mrs. Tinsdale stood up slowly. "In that case I better take this little man downstairs and show him his new room! Turn around, and I'll unlace you before I go."

Natalie allowed Tinny to unlace her and before she knew it was left alone holding her dress in front of her. She didn't know when she'd last felt so empty. It seemed she'd not only lost a dog this evening, but perhaps a lady's maid as well. She dared not think about what else she might have to let go of.

Unable to hold back the tears any longer, she fell

facedown upon her bed. Maybe she didn't want to grow up after all.

****

"Did you enjoy your moonlit stroll with that young earl of yours?" Aunt Eleanor's eyes twinkled as she asked the question. Natalie had hoped to slip into the room without being seen.

Oh dear. She and Hawthorne's long absence had been noted after all. Had anybody else made the observation? Aunt Eleanor was more sharp-eyed than most. Shooting the older woman a sober look, Natalie did her best to refrain from blushing. "He excused himself after a few minutes. I spent most of the time walking Baby Bear—alone."

Lady Eleanor's eyebrows rose suspiciously. She must have sensed Natalie's reticence, however, because she changed the subject. "I have so been looking forward to seeing Cordelia's work. I hope Lord Hawthorne has not forgotten."

Garrett would not disappoint the lady. He had more honor in his pinky than most so-called gentleman did in their entire bodies. Natalie forced herself to smile. She did not feel amiable today, but she *had* been excited to see the contents of the old crates.

She anticipated spending more time with Garrett Castleton as well. Even though she oughtn't to—either anticipate it or spend more time with him. As she took a sip of her coffee, her gaze caught sight of his figure entering the morning room. Did her heart skip a beat? Was that even possible?

His hair disheveled and his eyes tired, he did not look well this morning. Acknowledging a few of the guests with a slight bow, he then found a plate and approached the sideboard. When he'd loaded it up, Lady Eleanor beckoned him to sit beside her. She then pointedly set the coffee pot within his easy reach.

"Good morning, my lady." He tipped his head toward Lady Eleanor as he dropped into the chair. "Lady Natalie."

The other members in the room were involved in various random conversations, and his arrival went unnoticed by most. He set his napkin upon his lap, poured some coffee, and dug into his food.

Just when it seemed he was going to sit silently throughout the meal, he set down his fork and addressed Lady Eleanor. "If you ladies are still of a mind to see my mother's artwork, I'll be opening and inspecting the crate's contents when I am done here. I want to get them resealed and loaded on my coach by this afternoon, however, so I can depart tomorrow morning."

At that, Natalie's heart *did* skip a beat. She knew it must have, for why else would it suddenly hurt to breathe in and out?

Lady Eleanor responded for both of them. "That will be fine. I imagine you are looking forward to beginning the renovations at Maple Hall."

Nodding silently, Garrett went back to work on his food. He'd not spoken one word to Natalie, really. And he hadn't even looked at her when he'd oh-so-casually mentioned his plans for an early departure.

"You are leaving?" The question slipped out before she could stop it. Foolish girl, for imagining that he might have a *tendre* for her. "You are leaving tomorrow?"

Garrett paused his fork for a moment, long enough

to glance up. "I have a great deal of work awaiting me." When he looked back down at his food, he frowned. "It's best I don't waste any more time." With that, he stabbed his fork into a piece of sausage. He was not in the best humor this morning.

Natalie looked back down at her plate.

She was no longer hungry. Even her coffee lost its appeal.

Chapter Eighteen

Mixed feelings plagued Garrett at the thought of
spending the morning with Natalie. Being near her, but
unable to touch her, would be…frustrating. Staring into
his coffee, he pictured Natalie as she'd been last night,
sweet and trusting, leaning against the tree. Her skin
beckoned him, invited him. One taste would never be
enough.

So soft. So fragrant. So enticing.

When he'd first laid eyes on her, over two years
ago, he'd made the judgment that she must be one of
the most pampered and selfish debutantes of the season.

Ah, but he'd been wrong. She worried she had
been selfish to insist upon a marriage that would meet
her needs. As beautiful on the inside as the outside, she
was smart and compassionate and sweet.

And yet, to even consider a future with her was
impossible. Having come to this conclusion, he did not
wish to listen to her laugh, or smell her hair, or touch
her hand. He needed no further reminders of her
feminine delights.

They had finished breakfast and were now headed
upstairs.

And of course, her dress caressed and molded itself
to her body while she walked in front of him.

Garrett had another reason for dreading this
morning's task. Dredging his mother's artwork up, after

all these years, gave him a somewhat sickening feeling. The reason for this eluded him.

He hadn't looked at the paintings when he'd retrieved them from his mother's agent. They'd been gifted to him, put into trust by her. Just after he'd come of age, a solicitor had contacted him. He'd been ordered to give the paintings to her child when he reached his majority.

As though she had known she was going to die.

For a storage fee, Garrett had left them in care of the solicitor until a few years ago, when the man himself passed away. Reluctant to store them at Maple Hall, Garrett had quickly accepted when Stone offered to keep them here, at Raven's Park.

Since the day he'd been notified of this strange inheritance, he'd felt a dread at opening them—as though he would be opening a door to the past—a past that included his father. Was he perhaps afraid to find that his mother might have been as insane as her husband? She'd married the man, after all. She'd borne his father a son. It had been the very last thing she'd done on this earth.

Garrett dismissed his misgivings as Natalie led the way. She knew where they were stored and strode purposefully through the corridor. Garrett vaguely remembered assisting in their placement, but that had been some time ago, and he could not remember the exact location of the room. When they reached the door, he waited in the corridor while Natalie turned the knob and pushed it open. The ladies entered first. Holding a large crowbar in his right hand, Garrett followed hesitantly. Lady Ravensdale had offered to send a servant along to assist, but Garrett would open them himself.

He found it oddly comforted that he was not to do so alone.

He stepped into the room and paused as Natalie opened the thick drapes blocking the morning sunlight. Lady Eleanor removed a dust cover from a high-backed brocaded seat and perched herself on its edge. Looking at him, she nodded encouragingly.

Taking a deep breath, Garrett examined the nearest wooden crate. It was one of the larger ones but opened easily when he pried at the seams. With one corner dislodged, Garrett pulled the wood away and leaned it against the wall. He then unwound the burlap cloth that had been wrapped around the cargo so very long ago. Was his mother the last person to have touched these contents? He inhaled deeply, thinking there might be a hint of her perfume, something of her person. But all he could smell was dust and paint. What had she been thinking when she'd stored these items? Did she know she would not live to know the child she carried?

The first painting appeared to be a rendering of Hyde Park in the springtime. Abstract colors, chosen by the artist, softened the realism. Garrett's eyes drank in the image. It was as though the woman who had been his mother could finally share this memory. Natalie walked over to the painting and knelt on the floor to get a closer look. She reached out a tentative hand and touched the frame.

"Oh, Garrett, it's stunning." Her voice fell to almost a whisper.

Forging ahead, Garrett moved the painting and leaned it against the wall. Natalie rose again and removed the burlap from the painting behind it.

"Oh, that is the one!" Lady Eleanor cried out. "That is the one I told you about, Natalie. Notice the life in it. I've always remembered how this painting made me feel. It is as though she were painting the colors of the sun itself, during autumn. You think you ought to be able to smell decaying leaves. *It is so…alive.*"

The large lump that formed in Garrett's throat threatened to choke him as he uncovered the paintings. All in all, there were over twenty, each of them a great work to be appreciated. These were created by his mother. *His mother!* His initial reaction of a connection with his long-deceased mother was gradually replaced with a sense of awe.

She was not only an artist; she'd been a genius.

Natalie opened the last container, a trunk, and after removing a few gowns, pulled out some stacks of paper. "Oh, look, here are some drawings of people—portraits. Such talent, Garrett!"

Lady Eleanor had been staring at one of the paintings, but upon hearing Lady Natalie's words she walked over to look through the drawings. Grasping one of them with shaking hands, she let out a soft exclamation, "Oh, Arthur!"

Natalie examined the portrait. "Do you know him, Lady Eleanor?"

The older woman blinked back tears. "My brother," she said. "He is Arthur, my brother."

Sifting through the papers, Natalie placed several of them atop a table near her. "There are others of him, Lady Eleanor. All of these! They are all portraits of your brother!"

Garrett peered over Natalie's shoulder to get a

better look at the drawings. They were all of a young man in several different settings, drawn from different angles.

"He was very handsome, Aunt," Natalie said as she examined a few of them. And then she jerked back and hastily stuffed the rest of the pages into the bottom of the trunk. Lady Eleanor did not notice. She simply gazed at the first couple of pages, perhaps lost in her memories.

"My dear Arthur," she said softly, touching the drawing as though she could caress the face of the man within it.

Garrett retrieved the stack Natalie had discarded. The portraits were of the gentleman in the nude. He smiled for the first time that day. No wonder she'd put them down so quickly.

"What happened to your brother, Lady Eleanor? Why would Lady Hawthorne make so many renderings of his likeness?" Natalie asked the questions before Garrett even considered them.

Lady Eleanor found the chair she'd uncovered earlier and sat heavily upon it. Looking at Garrett, she hesitated before speaking. "Before Lady Cordelia married Lord Hawthorne, she and my brother had formed an attachment."

Natalie regarded one of the drawings with a perplexed frown marring her smooth forehead. "What happened, do you know?" Natalie prodded Lady Eleanor.

"Arthur was killed." She stared at one of the drawings and brought one trembling hand to her mouth. "I have not seen his likeness for so many years. And it is such a wonderfully accurate likeness."

Garrett stepped forward and crouched in front of the older lady. She was quite shaken by this discovery. He'd not realized that there had been such a connection between his mother and Lady Sheffield's family. It made him feel closer to the elderly lady somehow. "Would you like to keep them?" He indicated the drawings. "They are of more value to you than to me."

She reached out her hand to touch him on the cheek. "You are such a dear young man. Cordelia would have been so very proud of you." And then, before he could feel awkward, she dropped her hand. "I would be grateful to keep a few." She turned back to the drawings and pulled out three. "Just these, if you wouldn't mind."

"It is my pleasure to give them to you." His sentiments were sincere. Lady Eleanor did not have a great deal of family left. He was glad to give her such a touching reminder of her brother.

Blinking, Natalie made a fuss of brushing the dust from the front of her dress. "I believe that is everything. Shall I send for some manservants to repack these?"

Garrett considered the room's contents. "No, I'll see to them myself." In fact, he needed to spend time with the paintings alone. He reached out and grabbed Natalie's wrist to keep her from hurrying away. "Thank you." He wanted her to know he was glad she'd been with him today. He held her gaze and hoped she understood.

With a rueful smile, Natalie nodded slightly. "Thank you for sharing them with me, with us." Lady Eleanor stood by the door. Natalie pointedly glanced at her wrist and, feeling reluctant, Garrett released it.

When she reached Lady Eleanor, Natalie took the

older lady's arm and then turned back to Garrett for a moment. "I will have somebody come, after a while, to see if you need any additional supplies."

And with that, she took her leave.

After the door closed, Garrett sat on the chair vacated by Lady Eleanor. He looked around at the amazing artwork his mother had left to him and wished that instead he could have known *her*. The paintings, though, made her seem more real to him than ever before. His father had ordered portraits made of her so Garrett knew what she'd looked like, but these paintings, they were a part of who she was. She'd poured herself into this work. She'd loved nature and the passionate wildness it possessed. She'd seen the world in a unique light, in unique colors.

Remembering something important, Garrett turned back and held up one of the gowns which Natalie had set aside. He unfolded it so that the hem fell to the ground. The dress consisted of ivory satin and lace, with tiny pearls decorating the neckline and bodice. Was this her wedding gown?

Garrett brought the garment to his face and inhaled deeply, again hoping to catch a lingering scent of the perfume she might have worn.

It smelled of camphor and decay.

The lump in Garrett's throat won. He sat down and allowed something to break inside him.

He wept.

Chapter Nineteen

Garrett needed time alone, and furthermore, Natalie was not ready yet to abandon Aunt Eleanor. What a shock it must have been to see the image of a brother who'd been dead for many years. How many years, she wondered.

With Aunt Eleanor leaning heavily upon her, Natalie escorted her to the chamber she always stayed in while visiting. As one of their more elaborate guestrooms, it boasted a small sitting area. Natalie assisted the suddenly frail woman to the comfortable settee. She then fetched a shawl from the dressing room, wrapped it about Aunt Eleanor's shoulders, and finally reached for the bell pull. When one of the housemaids arrived, Natalie ordered tea and sandwiches. She did not think her godmother would be up to partaking nuncheon downstairs with company.

Content in each other's silence, Lady Eleanor rested her eyes while Natalie drifted over to the window. Gazing out upon the landscaped gardens, she contemplated her own brothers, and how she would grieve if something tragic were to befall any of them. And she'd been blessed with four of them! As much of a blight as they might be, they were each, every one of them, so very dear.

And in what was becoming a normal occurrence these last few days, her thoughts returned to Garrett. He had been very quiet examining the paintings. But, watching him, she'd known he was greatly affected. Each time they'd revealed another painting, she'd sensed a new wave of emotion sweep over him.

He'd never known his mother. She knew his mother had died in childbirth. Garrett Castleton had lived most of his life alone in this world.

When the maid arrived with a tray of food and tea, Natalie poured cups for them both, adding liberal amounts of cream and sugar to Aunt Eleanor's.

Leaving the sandwiches untouched, they drank quietly for several minutes.

It was Lady Eleanor who finally broke the silence.

"He died in a duel," she said. And then, almost as an afterthought, added, "With the late Earl of Hawthorne."

Natalie swallowed her tea and sat up straighter than normal. She could not help imagining one of her brothers being killed on the field of honor. Or her father. Or Garrett. It was every woman's greatest fear. Honor be damned.

"The old earl killed your brother?"

With a resigned nod, Lady Sheffield leaned into the cushioned back of the settee and rehashed the great scandal of 1793.

"I am not a lady by birth," she began. "I came by my title through marriage to my late husband. We were gentry, not nobility. My brother, Arthur, was a barrister.

"Lady Cordelia was the only child of a duke. Naturally, her family had high expectations for her. Throughout her youth, they anticipated her marrying an earl or higher. Perhaps a viscount if the title was an old one and the estate very wealthy.

"Knowing this, one would have expected her to be very high in the instep, nose in the air. But I came to know her as a lively, tenderhearted, and delightful young woman.

"My brother and Broderick, your father, befriended one another at Eton. After your father became the earl, he did not sever the connection as many others might have.

"If not for your parents, Arthur and I never would have come to know Lady Cordelia. We attended many *ton* events, and Lady Cordelia came to be one of my closest friends. At these same social gatherings, Arthur and Cordelia developed an attachment to one another."

Wiping a tear from her face, Lady Eleanor went on. "I blame myself for Arthur's death. Thinking it romantic and exciting, I made it possible for them to spend time together alone. I distracted our chaperones, and they fell in love.

"So very, very stupid. Arrogant of me to think with my help, true love would conquer all. If I'd but known what the consequence would be, I would have done everything in my power to keep them apart."

Natalie reached out and covered the woman's powdered dry hand with her own.

"They attempted to elope." Lady Eleanor shook her head sadly. "Sometimes, I think it was the bravest and most wonderful thing Lady Cordelia ever did, whereas the worst decision she ever made was to tell her maid.

"Lord Hawthorne and the duke apprehended them a mere twenty miles out of the city. Arthur's second-hand carriage and pair of old hacks were no match for the duke's magnificent team. They were overcome a few hours after they attempted their escape."

Natalie surmised the situation, "And the earl challenged your brother?"

"He did." Reaching for a sandwich, Lady Eleanor took a moment to chew the fine meats and fresh baked bread. "My brother loathed the notion of fighting. But he had no choice. As the challenged, he chose the weapon." She looked over at Natalie. "My brother was an academic his entire life. He was slim and fit; he was not brawny."

"He chose pistols," Natalie guessed.

"He did." Setting the crust of her sandwich back down on a small plate, Lady Eleanor brushed some crumbs from her hands. "The irony is he drew before Hawthorne. The first shot was his."

"He deloped?" Natalie asked.

"Yes. Shot straight into the air. But the earl, such a horrible man—evil—aimed right at dear Arthur's heart." Taking another sip of her tea, from a shaking hand, Lady Eleanor came to the end of her tale. "And shortly afterwards Lady Cordelia and Lord Hawthorne married and then retreated to Maple Hall. I never saw her again. Unfortunately, I cannot say the same of Lord Hawthorne. And then what he tried to do to my very own niece, to Lilly…"

Lilly was lucky to be alive.

"I met the man on a few occasions but never came to know him in any way. I must admit, I am thankful. He sounds like the devil himself!"

"He was."

Natalie felt utterly drained. She was shocked and exhausted by the recounting of Mr. Winter's death. "Would you care to rest a while, Aunt Eleanor?" Natalie stood, preparing to take her leave.

Her godmother grasped her hand. "Natalie, Garrett Castleton will be a wonderful earl. He will bring honor back to his inheritance. Do not judge him by the acts of his father."

Natalie looked into the woman's watery eyes. "Of course."

Walking back to her own chamber, Natalie shivered. Garrett's own father was a murderer. He had murdered more than once. He would have killed Lilly if she hadn't escaped first.

Were such traits hereditary? Before she could even contemplate the notion, the memory of Baby Bear licking Garrett's hand intruded into her thoughts.

Garrett was not like his father. He was not!

Upon reaching her doorway, she nearly ran right into Marcus as he exited Garrett's room.

"Forgive me, Natalie! My lady," he corrected himself with a wink.

"Why are you rushing about?" At sixes and sevens, her good humor escaped her in that moment.

But Marcus was oblivious. In fact, bursting at the seams with excitement, he rushed to tell her his news. "I cannot thank you enough for suggesting to your mother that I valet for His Lordship." A grin spread across his face. "I am to valet for him henceforth! He has asked me to travel with him to Maple Hall and take up the position permanently. We leave at first light, tomorrow."

It was odd, experiencing both sadness and joy at the same time. Knowing Marcus was leaving hurt nearly as much as Joseph marrying. Except with Joseph, she had gained a sister, and hopefully would one day have nieces and nephews to look forward to.

But with Marcus—well, he was simply leaving. Leaving her behind.

Oh, but she was so pleased for him. He'd always wanted this! And she could take a certain comfort in knowing he would be watching out for Lord Hawthorne.

Garrett needed taking care of, loath as the man would ever be to admit it.

Natalie clasped both of Marcus's hands in hers. "Oh, Marcus, that is wonderful! I will miss you, but I am so pleased. Lord Hawthorne is lucky to have you."

"My pa is proud near to bursting," he said sheepishly. "And His Lordship is not overly demanding or fussy. I think we will get on together very well." He turned her hands so that they were cradled in his. "Aside from my pa, I will miss you the most. You have always treated me as a friend. I will remember you fondly. I hope you will think fondly of me, as well."

Feeling a little awkward, because their relationship had always consisted more of teasing and pestering, Natalie smiled back at Marcus. "You know that I will, and of course you will return to visit your pa every so often. This is not goodbye; it is farewell." She pulled her hands back to her side. "And please try not to cut the earl's face too much or tie his cravats into anything a dandy would ever wear." The teasing felt more normal.

"I shall make certain he never appears looking anything but a perfect gentleman," he promised and then, walking backward, added, "I already have the earl's belongings prepared for travel, but I've my own belongings to pack this afternoon."

"Well, off with you then, Marcus.

And...congratulations. I think you are going to do wonderfully. You are the perfect valet for Lord Hawthorne."

And so, Marcus, too, would be leaving her.

Natalie entered her room and then called for a maid to assist her in donning her riding habit. She could not stay in the house this afternoon. She needed to take flight. A good ride was what she needed.

****

Garrett did not allow himself to grieve for long. Shaken by his emotional outburst, he put himself to the task at hand and resealed the paintings as they'd been before. Refusing assistance from the servant who'd been sent by the countess, he did his best to secure each crate so that the contents would be protected, even if exposed to rain on the journey to Maple Hall.

Lastly, he returned the dresses and drawings to the large trunk. Not even a quarter full, it posed no difficulty as Garrett carried it outside to the back of the carriage house where his traveling coach was parked. By late afternoon, he'd packed everything securely. The physical labor had been just what he needed.

Satisfied that preparations were complete, Garrett went around to the other side of the carriage house to check in on Rumble.

The horse was just finishing off the apple Garrett had brought for him when Natalie appeared atop a gorgeous chestnut mare. Sitting sidesaddle in a regal posture, she looked magnificent. Of course, as Ravensdale's daughter, she would be an excellent equestrian. Garrett waved the groom away as she rode over to the mounting block so he could assist her down himself. Flushed from her exertions, she brushed away some wisps of hair that had escaped from beneath her riding hat. Her eyes burned bright, even as they looked at him warily.

He gave her his hand so she could dismount from the impractical sidesaddle—another stupid and cruel societal standard. Not only was it hazardous for the women riding but it also endangered the horse.

Natalie addressed the groom who had stepped back. "She behaved beautifully today, Tobias." The horse was covered in sweat. She'd not ridden for leisure.

"I'll rub her down, my lady." The groom took the horse's reins to walk her back to the paddocks. He patted the mare fondly.

Accusing eyes met Garrett's. "You are returning to Maple Hall tomorrow?"

Garrett nodded. Best to leave Natalie to her parents, and to their…dukes. She deserved a proper husband and a proper family—two things he was unable and unwilling to give.

He ignored the urge to remove her hat and pull out the pins restraining the rest of her hair. Nor would he carry her up to the loft and lay her down in the hay.

"You have hired Marcus. I think it's wonderful for both of you." She didn't fool him with the false cheer in her voice. And the sadness behind her gaze belied the poor attempt at a smile.

Ah, yes, he would put an end to this attachment they had formed. He would return to his room, go over some reports, dress for dinner, and then retire for the night before making the journey to Maple Hall tomorrow. He did not plan on stopping. It would make for a long day, but barring any complications, they ought to arrive before darkness set in.

He would tell her goodbye and then set himself to the challenges that lay ahead. He would not allow himself to be alone with her. He would not allow himself to touch her.

"Walk with me?" he said, reaching out a hand. Reports be damned.

She did not move. Raising her lashes, she searched his eyes.

And then she reached out and took his hand. "Yes," she said.

Chapter Twenty

They slipped out the back of the stables and headed toward one of the less-utilized paths. The trees were dense and the trail overgrown making it difficult to walk side by side. Nonetheless, leading the way, Garrett reached behind and grasped her hand firmly. When they came to a small clearing, she walked abreast of him.

The meadow, covered in wild flowers, promised peaceful privacy. Hand in hand, they stepped off the path and picked their way into the blossoms until they found an inviting patch of grass. Garrett wore only his shirtsleeves, having removed his jacket and cravat much earlier while working, so he had nothing to lay on the ground for her to sit upon. Natalie stood before him in her full riding habit.

"You must be uncomfortably hot."

It was ill mannered of him to make such a comment. It was also ill mannered of him to appear in his own state of undress—shirt unbuttoned, lacking both his jacket and cravat. But she would not be offended.

Without answering, Natalie pulled off her hat and tossed it to the ground.

And then, from beneath her lashes, she sent him a knowing look. Such an enticing combination of sweetness and fire! Taking hold of her shoulders, Garrett turned her so her back was to him. He inhaled deeply, experiencing an unusual need to steady himself. He could not imagine another woman in the world making him feel the way he did now.

She stood unmoving as he pulled out each jeweled pin securing her coiffure. As though opening a gift, he watched in awe as blond tresses tumbled down her shoulders and back. Still, neither spoke. In this moment, they would communicate with touch, only with touch.

When he'd removed all the pins, he tucked them into his pocket but did not release her. Instead he reached his arms around to unbutton the jacket she wore over her habit, pulling her against his chest. Her feminine curves melted into him. "Ah, Natalie."

She tipped her head back, her breaths more labored than they had been before. Her eyes closed, and a tear escaped. Garrett caught it with the side of his thumb. "What is this?" Whispering, he did not wish to break the spell which had taken hold of them both.

Natalie shook her head.

The skin along her face shimmered, fragile as a butterfly's wings. He caressed her cheeks, her chin, and then his thumb trailed along the seam of her lips. When they parted, the velvety warmth of her tongue sent a surge of heat through him.

Garrett allowed her to taste and caress the tip of his thumb until she tugged on him with a sweet sucking motion. If this continued, he would embarrass himself, and quite likely her as well, within minutes.

And yet, he was not dissuaded. He peeled her jacket off and tossed it to the ground where her hat already lay.

Familiar with the workings of such feminine contraptions, he deftly undid the fasteners of her dress.

She stood, unmoving with her head bent forward. When he pushed the sleeves down her arms, the dress caught at her elbows. He paused only long enough to place kisses on her bared shoulders.

All his intentions to avoid succumbing to this need, this hunger for her, had fled. He could not stop himself.

Freed from the heavy garments she'd worn, the plump mounds of her breasts drew his gaze, just visible beneath her chemise and pushed up by her stays. Hungry to see every inch of her, he pulled her hands downward causing the habit, as well, to join the other clothing on the ground.

"Does that feel better?"

Natalie nodded silently. Where was the bold girl of a few evenings ago? She truly was an innocent.

And then she said, "Will you untie my stays, please?"

Ah, there she is.

Unwilling to release her, he turned her to face him, still within his embrace. Reaching around, he undid the tight laces with surprisingly shaking hands. She took a deep breath as the garment loosened.

It, too, was destined for the ground.

She stood before him, now, in her very thin chemise, stockings, and a pair of half boots.

With both her hair and her body unbound, she was all grace and womanly curves. Gloriously female. Garrett would love her, but he would not take. He could not take what he wanted so badly.

But he would give her the passion she desired.

He would show her some physical love.

The grass was dry. There hadn't been rain for over a week. Kneeling before her, he unlaced her boots and pulled them off. He wanted her to be comfortable. He removed his waistcoat and then reached over his head and pulled off his shirt. Spreading it on the ground, he laid it out to protect her from the dirt and grass. He then lay down and beckoned her to join him.

They now lay, side by side, facing each other.

Pressed against one another from head to toe, he finally lay siege to her lips.

He teased, he explored, he tasted. And then she was with him. With her hands clutching at his hair, she pressed herself into him, arching to be closer. He fought the urgent need to rip open his breeches and take her innocence for himself. Everything else be damned.

Natalie fought the tears threatening to spoil this moment.

He was leaving.

This ought not to make her feel as bereft as she did. Although she had known of him, she'd only really known the man, Garrett Castleton, for less than a week.

So why should his leaving upset her so?

When she'd returned from her ride and found him in just his shirtsleeves, offering his hand to assist her off her mount, she'd kept her dignity and forced herself to endure a polite goodbye. For she'd seen it in his eyes—the resignation. His decision to walk away.

But he had not.

And now she lay on the ground in only her chemise! Practically naked! Pressed against his bare chest. He still wore his breeches and boots, but his arousal pressed into her.

She would not contemplate what this meant. Or what they were doing.

She only wanted to feel.

Let tomorrow take care of itself. She'd not known it, but she'd waited for *this* her entire life. Blood roared through her head as she caressed the smoothness of his back. Sliding her hand downward, she explored the sinewy paths of his muscles.

"Natalie." He shuddered, removing his lips and lowering his head.

Oh God, his mouth on her skin felt like heaven. She wanted to be closer. He gave her a gentle nudge, and she found herself on her back, looking up at the sky.

Pulling away, he gazed down at her. Desire flared hot in his eyes. But there was also tenderness there. "Do you trust me?" His voice came out raspy and hoarse.

"Why?"

"I'm not going to make love to you, but I will show you something beautiful if you will allow it."

He'd already saved her from herself more than once. "I trust you, Garrett Castleton."

With that, one of his hand drifted downward to the edge of her chemise. Without looking away from her face, he grasped the hem and slid it upward. The summer breeze touched her knees, her thighs, and her most intimate of places.

Still, Garrett lay beside her, staring straight into her soul.

His hand grazed over the bone at her hip and then around her navel. The swirling caresses gathered a warmth to pool at her core. She squirmed and gasped, but he did not stop his exploration. Sliding past her rib cage, he then cradled the underside of her breast. She squirmed some more and then moaned as his fingertips pulled and teased its rosy tip.

Unable to help herself, she arched into his touch. She could no longer return his gaze. Torn between a tortured longing and acute embarrassment, she closed her eyes and focused on the sensations of his touch.

And then his mouth took the place of his hand, hot, demanding, wet. Embarrassment forgotten, she let her knees fall apart. She needed him to touch her *there*.

He would not disappoint.

A longing swept through her, so intense as to be almost painful. But it was an excruciatingly good sort of pain. She pushed into his hand, reaching for him. Suddenly, she understood so very much. This was why a woman would want intimacy with a man. She wanted him to put himself *inside* of her.

Such a revelation!

Everything he did created a frenzy of wanting, of needing, of craving. When she felt something slip inside, she pushed forward and demanded more. He touched places that had never been touched, moving in a rhythm as natural as the tide. She was so close. Her head tipped back, and she gasped for air. Slowing for a moment, he stretched her wider. Natalie thrust her hips off the ground as she reached for completion. His thumb moved as well, rubbing and massaging, building within her an even more exquisite hunger.

And then the wave crashed, and all of her senses came to life at once. Roaring sounds, flashes of light, the fragrance of grass, and the taste of passion. As though falling, she shuddered and let go of everything. And when she landed softly back into reality, her satisfaction still pulsed as it slowed and then drifted away.

Awareness returned when warm lips tasted hers.

Garrett had long since stilled his hand. He'd been kissing her face and murmuring endearments.

She lay back and relaxed, utterly boneless. She ought to have been embarrassed when she opened her eyes to see him staring down at her. But she was not. She simply gazed back at him, feeling closer than she'd ever felt to any person in the whole world. He now rested his head on his hand, propped on one elbow, still lying on his side.

His other hand remained partially inside her. Tenderly, he removed his fingers but left his hand on her hip, in a slow, loving caress.

He looked rather satisfied with himself.

Which perplexed her as she knew he'd not found his own release.

"What was that?" she asked sleepily, in awe.

"The French call it *la petite mort*." He smiled and leaned down to place his lips upon hers. Speaking into her mouth, he said, "The little death."

Natalie kissed him back, openmouthed. "And now, I am still here. I must be reborn." She felt reborn, no longer a girl but a woman. Twisting and writhing, she stretched like a cat. He removed his hand and pulled her chemise down to cover her. As he moved to sit up, she could not help but ask, "What about you?"

Garrett shook his head. "I will be fine." It was then Natalie sensed a change in him. Sitting back from her now, he rested one arm upon his knees and looked away from her, off across the meadow.

His easy smile had disappeared. As though fighting a battle within himself, he grudgingly spoke his next words. "I will marry you if you feel ill-used. But I know it is not something you or your family want." He forced his gaze to return to hers. "I haven't much to offer, but what I have is yours, if you wish."

She had not felt *ill-used*.

Not until he chose to speak to her with all the romance of a mallet!

His words hit her like a bucket of ice water. The closeness vanished. She suddenly, ridiculously, felt alone and exposed. He'd gone from lover to stranger in the blink of an eye.

She would not give him the satisfaction of seeing how much he'd hurt her.

"Have I fallen so low, then?" she asked, with as much disdain as she could summon while sitting on the crushed grass in her chemise. "That I am to consider a proposal, a boorish and grudging proposal, from one such as you? From the Earl of Hawthorne, no less?"

Scrambling to her feet, she gathered her stays about herself. If only she could simply walk away from him. But she was unclothed, and she could not make herself presentable without assistance. "Help me with this," she commanded. "And don't look at me like that, as I'm not about to say 'please' or any other such nonsense."

She clenched her fists at her sides, her fingernails digging into her palms, as Garrett tugged at the laces of her stays. How had he expected her to respond? Nearly shaking in her anger, she barely noticed when he gathered her dress from the ground and brushed the grass from it. Without a word spoken, he dropped it over her head. She pushed her arms into the sleeves, and he fastened it as well.

"I do apologize," he said. "I had not thought my proposal would be such an offense to your dignity."

Natalie wanted to put her face in her hands and

221

weep. What a stupid, stupid man! Oh, how she hated him!

"Perhaps, my lord"—she would not look at him—"it was not the proposal itself, but the manner in which the gentleman presented it." She snatched up her jacket and hat and would have stormed off if only she could locate her boots.

Oh, where were they? She glanced around to no avail.

"Looking for these?" Garrett had a sad little smile on his face as he dangled her half boots by their laces in front of him.

When she went to grab them from him, he seized her wrist and stepped toward her instead. "You know it is not what you want." He pulled her close and held tight to her as though she were a child in need of comfort. "You are just recently free of an unwanted betrothal."

Natalie did not know what to say. Should she tell him she loved him? Did she? Upon such short acquaintance was it even possible? Or had the furtive glances and seductive stares they'd exchanged throughout the previous two seasons begun all this long ago?

Could she attach herself to a man judged to be a pariah by society? A man who carried tainted blood? A sob escaped her.

She did not want to cry.

"I do not feel ill-used by you," she said. "I think you an honorable man." He could have taken her completely. She'd offered no resistance and probably would not if he chose to do so now.

She felt his lips move, pressed upon the top of her

head as he spoke. "I know you want a love match. I know you wish for a family. It is not possible." He pulled her down to the ground, into his lap.

"My father was not just an evil man, but a mad one. Something was broken inside of him. As a youth, there were times when I thought he ought to be locked away from other people. But he always returned to his own strange type of normalcy, and all seemed settled." He rocked her as he spoke. "He could be violent, and he could be oddly tender. There were periods when he would work in his office, drafting bills and documents for Parliament as though the fate of the world rested upon his shoulders, and then there were other times when he would not come out of his bedchamber for days. As a boy, I was terrified of him."

Natalie understood. "You are fearful that his disease could appear in your own children."

He exhaled long and slow. "Yes. Or even in myself."

Blinking away tears, Natalie twisted around to look at him. She did not know very much about this. But just as her brothers shared similarities in appearance with their father, and she shared the good looks of her mother, she presumed it was possible to share other traits as well.

"You will never have any children then?" she asked.

"I will do what I can to help the tenants and the workers prosper on my father's properties, but the title will go into abeyance upon my death." She did not like to hear him speak of his own demise. His words made her overwhelmingly sad.

To think he would never be a father nearly broke

her heart. She remembered the gentleness in him when he'd handled Baby Bear.

This was a travesty! No, a tragedy—for God help her, she loved him! She'd fallen in love with Garrett Castleton, the Earl of Hawthorne.

Had she told herself she would feel thusly, a sennight ago, she would have been the first to laugh. Well, the joke was on her.

Because she wished for nothing more, in that moment, than to place her hand in his and promise to love him and to help him, for the rest of their lives.

"That is why I could not love you properly this afternoon. It is why I cannot offer myself to you as a proper husband."

He *could not love her properly*...Did he love her at all? He'd never said so.

Was this merely a handy excuse on his part? A pretext for avoiding the parson's trap?

"A proper husband." She repeated his words thoughtfully. The words left a bitter taste in her mouth.

Garrett ran his fingers through her hair and began twisting it into a knot. Reaching down, he pulled something from his pocket, and she felt him slipping the pins back into her hair.

"I could use a new lady's maid." She could jest. Otherwise, she might burst into tears. Today had been distressing. And now she felt his lips trailing along her nape. Oh, how he knew her weaknesses!

Garrett settled her hat upon her head. "I would suggest foregoing the jacket." He sounded far too practical. "I don't want you fainting from the heat."

He turned her head so she would look at him again. "And if there isn't a duke out there waiting for you, I trust there will be some other, equally lofty young man who will love you for yourself, who will give you babies and romance and everything you long for."

He was going to make her angry again.

He could not love her if he was so eager to thrust her upon any other man who might happen along. Very well then. She was not so very needy.

"Well, allow me to thank you then, for introducing me to *la petite mort*. For I now know what one of my demands will be before I commit to another betrothal." She pushed herself away from him and donned her boots. Standing, she brushed at her skirt and then offered him her hand.

He stared blankly at it for a moment before grasping it in his and allowing her to pull him up. Once standing, he held out his arm, but she ignored it and walked away from him instead.

Striding through the dense trees, she couldn't help thinking there was more than one type of *petite mort*. For a small piece of her heart seemed to have died just now. She would not cry. She would not.

Chapter Twenty-One

Garrett followed her until they came into view of the house. Knowing she was safely returned, he allowed her to stalk off without him.

She'd called him a gentleman on more than one occasion. She could not be more wrong.

In frustration and guilt, Garrett shoved a hand into his hair, pushing it back from his forehead. He needed to clean up and attend dinner as though nothing earth-shattering had occurred.

He'd hurt her, but what else could he have done? He'd been honest. He'd offered himself but done so bluntly. He'd revealed the truth, in case she was under any misapprehensions regarding his situation. She was not. She was not dull of mind. Quite the opposite, in fact.

After rechecking the baggage coach, Garrett located his waistcoat and jacket in the stables and proceeded to the main entrance of the house. Although the sun hung low in the sky, the persistent heat had left the estate unusually quiet. His heart felt leaden. He was covered in sweat and dust.

And she'd let him touch her! The bastard that he was.

He could no longer convince himself his emotions were fleeting. He wanted to make love to her, in truth, but he wanted more. Oh, hell, if he were going to be honest with himself he'd have to admit that he wanted to give her a permanent place in his life, to fall asleep each night knowing she would awaken beside him.

He wanted to show her his home and have her opinions in the rebuilding of Maple Hall. For she would not sit idle while he made all the decisions and then executed them. She possessed an energy that needed a productive outlet. Her father was correct in his assertion that she would make an excellent countess. Ravensdale had not, unfortunately, considered the implications of his daughter becoming the Countess *of Hawthorne.*

It was unusual for the earl not to think the entire situation through to its natural conclusion, for if he'd done so, he never would have made the suggestion. He would not wish childlessness upon his daughter. Or worse.

Then again, perhaps Garrett had misunderstood the earl that morning.

Likely the earl would call him out if he knew what Garrett had done.

He'd touched her intimately. Had it been a mistake? It had not been all about his own lust, had it? His breath caught. God, but the way she'd moved, the sounds she'd made. Touching her, tasting her, had been better, by far, than he could have imagined. Awakening her passion, seeing Lady Natalie Spencer relax her sensual inhibitions had been a revelation.

In his mind, he replayed their moments together in the meadow. He remembered her eyes, unfocused and fluttering as she relinquished control and moved with him. He remembered the soft moans and cries that escaped her lips, lips that had been his to taste and invade. He remembered the feel of her skin, the silken moisture as he touched her where no one before him had.

Now, she knew some of it.

She knew there ought to be evidence of passion between herself and the one she would eventually marry.

But thinking of some faceless man, not the Duke of Monfort, but a younger, warmer man, touching her, caressing her as he had, left a cold sick feeling inside him.

He both looked forward to and dreaded spending one last evening in Natalie's company. He must keep himself away from her. He mustn't allow his gaze to follow her the entire time. One more evening, and he would be free to set himself to work. And to set himself to forgetting.

Mr. Winston opened the door before Garrett could do so himself. How the devil had the butler known he was there? Looking about, Garrett searched for a small window that Mr. Winston might have used to watch for visitors. "Marcus is awaiting you in your chambers, my lord," he said. "Dinner is formal this evening."

Garrett nodded. "I wish to speak with the earl. Is he in his study?"

"He is. Can you find your way, my lord?" Another group of guests had just returned for the day, and they looked to be carrying several items that would need the butler's attentions.

"Of course, Winston." Garrett followed the corridor toward the office where he'd met the earl on previous occasions. He'd personally informed the earl he was leaving the next morning. And thank him for his hospitality. He would not be asking permission to court his daughter. He would not.

As he neared the entry to the study, however, Baby Bear came dashing out, leaving the door ajar. Voices carried outward into the hallway. The sound of his own name stopped Garrett from turning and leaving immediately.

"I can only be grateful," Lord Ravensdale's voice boomed, "that Garrett Castleton is leaving us tomorrow, young lady." Was he speaking to Natalie? He must be. "You have shown no regard for propriety where that degenerate is concerned."

Garrett could barely make out Natalie's response. "He is not a degenerate…" Garrett's mouth twisted into a wry smile. She ought not to defend him.

Lord Ravensdale continued, "I have allowed his presence here as a concession to the numerous times he assisted me in business. But I will not have him dallying with my daughter. I will not have him anywhere near my daughter, is that understood, young lady?" Why would he take this up with Natalie? Why did he not call Garrett out on these matters?

"You need not worry on that account, Papa," she said. Wise girl.

Garrett had obviously been wrong in his interpretation of Lord Ravensdale's words the morning of the irrigation tour. Even so, it hurt. What exactly had the earl told him just a few days ago? A good lady at his side…Perhaps the lady he needed at his side could be found in the country. Of course, the earl had not been referring to his own daughter! It was just that Garrett had spent so much time thinking about her, he'd jumped to the wrong conclusion. *Of course*. Garrett felt foolish for voicing his thoughts to Stone. Stone must have felt pity and not wished to embarrass him. He'd been quick to discourage—of course!

But Garrett had begun to believe the Spencers were different from the rest of the *ton*. The rejection left a bitterness in his heart. He was disappointed but also angry with himself for caring.

Damn! He was done with all of it.

Garrett turned on his heel, not wishing to hear anything further, and strode toward his chamber. His time here was over. Tonight promised a full moon. He would leave right away. By God, he would not play games with these people any longer.

****

After being duly chastised by her father, Natalie was more distraught than before. Unable to face anyone, she asked Tinsdale to tell her mother she would not be attending dinner that evening. She would have a tray brought to her room. She told Tinsdale she'd taken too much sun that afternoon and needed to retire early.

She could not face him.

She had known, yes, she had known about his father, about the insanity. But none of it had stopped her heart from falling in love with him.

And he'd not once admitted to feelings of affection for her. Since that very first night of his arrival, she'd made herself available to him. She'd thought herself so wise, when in fact she'd been quite the idiot. She had thought to experience a thrill, find some excitement for herself. But instead she'd only brought more—no, not more—but *true* heartache upon herself. For she now knew Garrett as a man of sensitivity and honor. He was more than a rake—more than the son of a scandalous murderer—he was flesh and blood male. *He was*

Garrett!

She loved him. She wanted him. She needed him. He would deny all of this.

Perhaps he wanted her—well, no perhaps about it. He'd very obviously wanted her on more than one occasion. Even her limited experience didn't keep her from knowing that.

But he did not need her. And he did not love her.

Changed into nightclothes, Natalie lay back upon her bed and closed her eyes.

Surprisingly, in her mind's eye, she pictured one of the portraits of Aunt Eleanor's brother. Arthur? Yes, it was Arthur.

This day felt like a lifetime.

When she and Lady Sheffield left Garrett alone, she'd known he'd nearly been overcome by his emotions. What must it have been like to grow up without a mother? And then, seeing her artwork, Natalie had felt as though they'd all been given a glimpse of her soul. Garrett had likely experienced both joy and pain. Perhaps one day he could experience only joy—and pride—when in the presence of his mother's work. Right now, it was too raw. Especially with the death of his father so recently.

Did Garrett mourn his father at all? Natalie did not think so. He must have mourned his father long ago, at a much younger age, when he'd realized the extent of his father's depravity. What a horrifying childhood!

Garrett's words regarding his father had been blunt. "He could be violent, and he could be oddly tender," he'd said. "As a boy, I was terrified of him."

He'd also told her he could never be a proper husband to her. Or anybody, she supposed. He would

231

let the title go into abeyance. Tears, ah, at last her tears came. He would not allow himself to sire an heir. There would be no little boy running about with wicked black eyes, wiry strength, and a small dimple at the corner of his mouth. She pictured Garrett as he must have looked as a child.

And then bolted upright as something struck her. What was it? What was it?

Something about those drawings; something about those portraits.

Natalie needed to look at them again. Donning her dressing gown, she slipped into the hallway and headed for the stairway that would take her to the third floor.

Was her mind playing tricks on her? She needed to see now!

She dashed up the stairs and ran to the end of the corridor. The sight that met her upon bursting into the room, however, sent disappointment coursing through her. Garrett's items had all been removed and the furnishings once again covered with clean white sheets. Oh, damnation! Of course! Garrett had already removed them. Where were they now?

On his baggage coach. She belatedly remembered seeing the large trunk strapped onto the back of the coach when returning from her ride. How stupid of her not to have thought about that first. Breathless, Natalie retraced her steps, descending all the way downstairs this time, and slipped out one of the back doors to head toward the stables.

As luck would have it, everybody was either dining or serving dinner. The stable hands must be taking their meal as well. Nobody witnessed her foray outside in such a state of dishabille. She ought to have gone back to her room and pulled on one of her day dresses, she admitted to herself, but this could not wait! She picked her way barefoot over the driveway and around to the back of the stable.

Yes! There it was. She stepped up and untied the knot securing the trunk to the carriage. Since it hadn't been locked, the lid opened easily, but she couldn't reach inside. It was too high. Hitching up her gown, she climbed all the way onto the carriage and stepped into the half-empty container. Where were they? She dropped to her hands and knees and shuffled the dresses around in search of the drawings.

There they were. She flipped through them until she found it.

She hadn't been mistaken!

But what did it mean?

And then before she could contemplate her discovery, the lid of the trunk dropped. Sharp pain felled her as it struck the top of her head, pushing her down into the trunk. Stunned, she curled face down into the musty-smelling dresses.

Natalie lay still for a moment but for the hand she moved to rub the back of her head. With cautious fingers, she felt around in her hair where the lid had struck. Finding a wet and sticky spot, she flinched. She must be bleeding. Natalie didn't like blood. Especially her own. The smell inside the musty old trunk wasn't helping matters.

Even lying down, she felt dizzy and nauseous. Air. She needed air.

The lid must have been propped open precariously and then been unbalanced by her weight, causing it to close. But when she pushed against it, it did not move.

She pushed harder. It didn't budge.

"Hello!" she cried out. Surely there was somebody nearby? "Hello," she called out louder.

Panic crept into her. "Hello! Help me! Somebody!"

Her breathing felt shallow. She tried to take in a deep breath but could not. *Oh, dear God, is this trunk airtight?* Terror threatened to engulf her completely as tears overflowed. She pressed her entire body against the lid of the trunk but to no avail. She pushed with all her might. Again.

Again.

By now she was sweating profusely and gasping for breath. "Hello! Help me!" she yelled over and over, her voice growing hoarse.

She imagined Garrett opening the trunk to discover her dead, lifeless body within. She imagined her family and how they would react once learning of her death. They would not blame Garrett, would they?

Of course, they would! Especially after the words her father had spoken to her this afternoon! Her father would kill him! But he mustn't!

Oh, dear God, she mustn't die! She mustn't allow Garrett to be labelled a murderer!

Her panic crescendoed as terror took root. Such a stupid thing to happen! Tearful calls for help turned to forlorn cries.

Sobbing, she collapsed into the bottom of the trunk with her knees tucked beneath her. Exhaustion and the pain of the blow to her head thankfully stole her consciousness.

Chapter Twenty-Two

Garrett changed into traveling clothes, the ones he'd worn only a few days ago when he'd arrived. He allowed himself just a moment to glance around the chamber before closing the door behind him.

The room itself haunted him with her image. Too much had occurred in such a short time.

He placed his hat on his head and stared at his boots. He'd thought his attire would be proper for mingling with the aristocracy in the country. How wrong he had been.

He'd sent Marcus to make his apologies to Lady Ravensdale. He must attend to urgent business, he'd informed Marcus. They would be leaving presently.

Using the back stairs, he'd avoid making any explanations to other guests. This tactic worked until he reached the stables, but damned if it just wasn't his day.

Another party readied for departure as well. The earl's stable hands were busy, not only assisting Garrett's men with his carriage and mount, but assisting Farley, Trident, Lockley, and Danbury.

Stone watched the activity warily. Most likely assuring himself of their departure.

He did not appear pleased with the world in general. "So it is true, then, you are cutting your holiday short?"

"I am." Garrett pushed aside any resentment he

held for the earl and grasped Stone's outstretched hand. He'd always been a good friend. "Duty calls at Maple Hall."

Danbury stepped forward to join them. "Hawthorne, good to see you," he said, as though the meeting the previous night had never occurred. "I see you are taking advantage of the full moon as well." He gestured toward the young marquis. "Lockley and I are returning to London."

Garrett was more concerned with the other two's destination. "What of Farley and Trident?"

"Farley mentioned a house party up north. From what I gather, they've a few days' ride."

"Danbury and Lockley are heading your direction, Hawthorne, "Stone interjected. "The three of you ought to travel together as far as Reading. Safer for the lot of you."

"I'll be riding alongside my baggage coach," Garrett said. "They'd make better time without me." He did not wish for company.

Danbury brightened, however. "We'll hold back with you, Hawthorne. Spencer, here, is correct. Much safer."

Danbury looked exhausted. Dark shadows encircled his eyes, and his mouth was pinched. Keeping company with villains had taken its toll.

"Very well," Garrett acquiesced. Safety in numbers couldn't hurt.

The various travelers mounted their horses while Garrett's driver checked the harness on the baggage coach. Ravensdale had given Marcus a gelding of his own. It was a very generous going-away present.

Already mounted, Trident and Farley made

particular nuisances of themselves. They allowed their horses to dance about recklessly, while they smiled and wished Danbury, Lockley, and even himself safe and happy travels. Feeling uneasy at their feigned graciousness, Garrett felt relief when they finally departed. They were annoying, but most likely harmless.

Other matters beleaguered his thoughts.

What was she doing now? Was she sitting beside Monfort? Perhaps locating a crack in his icy demeanor?

He warred with his imagination.

It would do him good to remove himself from Raven's Park—even though it felt he was leaving something very important behind.

They had good light for travel, a full moon illuminating the sometimes rutted and gnarled road. Such conditions quickened the journey. Just before dawn, Garrett and his entourage turned south on a road near Reading while Danbury and Lockley continued to London. They'd ridden mostly in a comfortable silence, except for a few periods of spontaneous conversation.

Danbury had enlisted Garrett's assistance in dissuading Lockley from associating with Trident and particularly Farley any longer. Garrett didn't offer much but agreed on several points, especially when Lockley made it known that Farley expected him to pay off several of his own gambling debts.

The young Lockley had been too easily ensnared in the older gentlemen's sophisticated lifestyle. Having just come of age, without his father in town as a calming influence, he'd allowed matters to get out of hand quickly.

Garrett hoped the younger man appreciated

Danbury's efforts to remove him from such unfortunate connections.

Once on the less travelled, unmaintained southbound road, their pace slowed significantly. Arriving long after sunup, the weary travelers were sleep deprived and fatigued when they finally drove into the park of the once-grand estate.

Ominous skies hovered, so Garrett instructed his driver to bring the baggage carriage around to the dower house. This way the artwork could be unloaded without delay and stored before the rain came.

In his care, the treasured artwork left by his mother would be protected. Thunder resounded in the distance, and black clouds gathered on the horizon.

The last family member to have dwelt in the dower house had been his grandmother, on his father's side. She'd died before Garrett was born. The dower house, a two-story brick Tudor built a few hundred yards behind the charred manor, was the only habitable structure available.

Although the house suffered from considerable neglect, the current caretakers, Mr. and Mrs. Hampden, had managed to keep the main rooms in reasonable repair. Garrett had ordered the main suite to be put to rights when he'd been here earlier, one short week ago. He hoped to find progress well underway. Marcus would need a room as well. Although many of the servants had abandoned the estate following the fire, some old retainers remained, whether from loyalty or lack of accommodations elsewhere, Garrett did not know.

A few stable lads were on hand and took control of the tired horses while Marcus and the outriders unloaded the crates. Handing Rumble over for a good rubdown, Garrett himself walked over to unstrap the half-empty trunk from the back ledge of the carriage. Best get the lot of it inside. Feeling the wind gathering strength, he figured the storm would arrive within minutes.

Marcus oversaw the outriders as they carefully pulled one of the crates from the coach. He looked exhausted but was determined to please his new employer. Garrett appreciated the young man's loyalty. He smiled to himself, thinking again of how he'd found himself in company with the eager valet. It seemed he could not go a moment without some thought or other of Lady Natalie Spencer coming to mind. He hoped this phenomenon would diminish with time.

As he went to loosen the strap, which he'd tied himself the previous afternoon, a twinge of foreboding crept over him. The knot was not the one he'd tied. And the trunk had since been locked as well.

When he'd loaded it, he'd purposely left it unlocked.

Garrett painstakingly unknotted the gnarled bundle of rope and then went to remove the trunk itself to the ground. Expecting it to be only slightly heavier than the container alone, as it had been when he'd loaded it, he grunted when it strained his muscles. What the devil?

"Marcus!" he shouted. What had been added to the trunk? Thoughts of Farley lurking about with a smug grin taunted Garret. It would be just like the louse to pilfer something from the Spencers and plant it on him. It was the sort of thing that little weasel would do.

Marcus rushed over and went to grab one of the handles of the trunk. "I thought there wasn't much in this one, my lord," he said as they both heaved the trunk off the platform.

"Careful, now," Garrett said, in case the unknown contents were breakable. He could not for the life of him imagine anything of his own that would have added such weight to the trunk. "You did not store your belongings in here, by chance, did you, Marcus?" That would be an acceptable explanation. But he hoped not. He'd ordered none of these items be touched by anybody. Marcus would need to be admonished.

But Marcus shook his head vigorously. "No, my lord."

They set the trunk on the ground, and Garrett regarded it skeptically. He did not possess any key that might unlock it, so the catch would have to be broken. Eyeballing the dark clouds nearly upon them, he reached back down to grasp one of the handles. "Let's get everything inside for now. Then see if you can locate a crowbar or hammer—something to break the lock."

As they hefted the trunk to carry it inside, Garrett was again perplexed by what the devil could be stored within. The damn thing must weigh ten stone more than it had when he'd carried it before.

Chapter Twenty-Three

The heavens broke loose just as the stable hands carried the last of the crates into the foyer of the dower house. Garrett had just brushed the dust and dirt off his hands and turned to head upstairs when Marcus found him.

"I'm having a bath prepared for you, my lord," Marcus said. Entering the foyer, he surveyed the various crates. "And I've a crowbar sitting on that trunk. Can't imagine what could be inside it. Would you like my assistance before I go up?"

In the midst of the rush to get everything inside, Garrett had forgotten about the dratted thing. "No, I'll take care of it. You settle in upstairs. I'll be there momentarily."

Remembering they'd put the trunk in the parlor, just off the foyer, Garrett slipped around a few crates and entered the room. He was exhausted and reluctant to discover whatever problem would surely be found inside.

A crowbar balanced on the lid.

Taking a deep breath, Garrett wedged the bar under the lock and pried off the fastener holding it in place. Setting the bar on the floor, he then reached out and lifted the lid.

It took a moment to process the contents. His mind did not wish to accept the reality of what his eyes saw.

And yet, the startling image of tangled hair and bloodied white linen was very real. Patches of blood marred the material. The tangled hair was blonde. A sticky mass of dried blood had congealed in the woman's hair.

The hair was *blonde*!

"*Oh, dear God, no.*" Falling to his knees, Garrett reached inside and touched her back. No response. Frantic, he pushed the tangled hair aside and found the tender skin of her neck.

It felt warm.

His fingers searched until he located a pulse, weak and fluttery, but a pulse nonetheless. It had been strong and even not a day earlier, when he'd pressed his lips against it.

"Marcus! Mrs. Hampden!" he bellowed hoarsely. "Send for a doctor at once! Immediately!" He bent over and wedged his hands and arms beneath her. "Oh, my darling," he whispered. "What has happened to you?" His lungs constricted. His eyes stung.

He could not bear to think how she came to be inside the trunk. Locked inside! The outer rim of his vision turned red with anger at the thought.

But his hands and voice remained tender.

She'd been trapped. Perspiration dampened her gown as well as the soft hair around her face. She must have been terrified!

Taking exquisite care, Garrett wedged his hands beneath her. Reaching under her knees and back, he then lifted her out of the confined space.

As he stood, Marcus appeared in the doorway. His countenance revealed both horror and concern. "Oh my God! Natalie? What's she doing in there?" he gasped, rushing forward to assist Garrett in laying her on the settee.

"Has a doctor been sent for?" Garrett ignored the question as he propped a small pillow under Natalie's head and knelt. She did not stir.

Marcus looked pale but nodded. "Mr. Harris left for the stable as soon as you cried out. He's taken a carriage so they can bring the doctor." Then Marcus, too, knelt alongside Natalie's inert form. "How in God's name did this happen?"

Garrett shook his head. "The gash on her head must have been violent...so much blood." The head wound appeared to be the only source of the vast quantities. Garrett forced himself to think clearly. If he focused on her pale face and shallow breaths, he would drive himself mad. Something must be done until the doctor could be fetched!

"Have Mrs. Harris bring washcloths and towels to my suite. I'm going to clean the wound and make her more comfortable. With this nuisance of a storm, who knows how long it will take the doctor to arrive?"

Garett was already cradling Natalie once again. He would not have her laid out in the parlor as if...no...he mentally shoved the thought aside. She would be all right. She would be well. She must.

Carrying her upstairs, he noticed her gown was torn and her knees chafed. Good God, how long had she been cramped in there? The last time he'd seen her she'd been fleeing from him out of the woods.

And then he'd overheard her defending him in her father's study.

But why? How?

When he'd first placed her on the settee, her face

had been flushed. Now she'd gone pale, her lips colorless. Tamping down his fear, he entered his suite and positioned her on one side of the tall, canopied bed. The counterpane and sheets were already drawn back. Garrett rolled her onto her side, so he could examine the wound on her head more closely.

Mrs. Hampden entered the room just as he turned to get a washcloth. Upon seeing Natalie in her torn and bloodied nightdress, the housekeeper's brows rose questioningly, and she scowled at Garrett. "You might be the master, my lord, but I'll not take part in anything criminal. We put up with enough of that from your father. I hoped things would be different around here now." Nonetheless, the woman placed a towel over the pillow while Garrett wet a washcloth and set to cleaning the wound. And then, apparently realizing that Garrett would not be demanding treatment for the patient if he'd committed the crime in the first place, the middle-aged woman sighed. "What happened to the poor girl?"

Parting Natalie's hair and smoothing it away from the gash, Garrett swallowed hard. "I wish I knew, Mrs. Hampden. She managed to get herself trapped in one of the trunks we traveled with last night." The cut was still inclined to bleed. "Do you have something we can put on this? Some honey or ointment?"

"On the table, my lord. But let me do it. And I'll get her in a clean gown, too. It isn't proper for you to be here right now." Mrs. Hampden touched the fine material of Natalie's nightgown. Trimmed in a delicate lace, the neckline had tiny flowers embroidered along the edge. Garrett remembered her wearing it the first night he'd stayed at Raven's Park, when she'd invaded his bedchamber.

"Her being a proper lady, I imagine her reputation will be in ruins after this business."

Garrett did not want to leave Natalie alone, but he stepped toward the door. Mrs. Hampden's assessment astutely described the situation. "Please call for me if, *when*, she awakens. I'll be downstairs to receive the doctor.

Garrett stepped into the corridor and closed the door behind him. He meant to head downstairs but instead found himself bent over, his hands on his knees as though he'd taken a blow to the stomach. Terrified, he pressed the heels of his palms into his eyes and took in a few gulping breaths.

Somehow this was his own fault! He didn't know how, or why, but he ought to have protected her. He'd suspected something awry but, with his emotions in such a tailspin, had ignored it.

When Farley'd acted so strangely, Garrett ought to have trusted his instincts. He should have unloaded and inspected the contents of the baggage then. He should have sent a maid inside to check on her.

He should have gone to her to say goodbye.

That was it. If he'd taken the time, ignored his inappropriate feelings, and taken proper leave of her, her absence would have been discovered right away. None of this would have happened. Imagining such an ordeal as she'd gone through, trapped in that damned trunk, Garrett felt sick. She must have been terrified.

Thank God it was not airtight! That had been his fear when he'd first touched her. If she did not make it…If she were to die…

But no, Garrett forced himself to stand again. He

could not allow himself to dwell on things that were not going to happen. He must remain calm.

He must notify her family immediately. The earl and countess were most likely panic stricken. Rushing downstairs, he located parchment and a pen, but then paused. What to say? How did he tell a man he'd unknowingly kidnapped his only daughter and her condition was yet unknown? Damn! He'd best wait until the doctor gave them a prognosis.

Garrett walked to the window and peered out into the storm. Where was the damned physician? He cursed the roads. He cursed the rain. He cursed Farley, if it was, in fact his doing.

But most of all, he cursed himself for remaining at Raven's Park in the first place.

With a light knock on the open door, Marcus hesitated before entering. "Did she awaken yet, my lord?"

Garrett turned to the boy who'd known Natalie for most of her life. "Not yet." His voice choked. Not knowing her condition would take its toll on both of them.

Walking over to a tall cabinet, Garrett retrieved a decanter of brandy and poured a splash into a short glass tumbler. He handed it to Marcus. "Drink up. It's been a long night and a hellish morning." Garrett would not drink. He must keep his wits about him. "She must have been terrified." He stared out the window again.

"I thought, for a moment, she was dead," Marcus admitted. "But she is breathing. She will be all right?" He wanted assurances from Garrett—assurances Garrett didn't have.

"I think so," he answered. "God, I hope so." And

then, he voiced his earlier thoughts. "I need to notify Ravensdale." His gaze fell on the blank parchment. "I shall wait until we have news from the doctor, though, before sending out a courier."

"The countess will be beside herself with worry. What will they think? That she has been kidnapped?" Then, glancing at Garrett with startled eyes, the newly hired valet seemed to comprehend that his new employer might be in a good deal of trouble.

"First my father and now his degenerate of a son, eh?" Cynicism laced his voice. He did not wish to consider what Lord Ravensdale's response would be. Garrett would focus all his energy on Natalie's recovery. "Where is that damned doctor? Did they have to travel all the way to London, for God's sake?"

Marcus dropped into the nearest chair. "Mr. Hampden said the doctor lived in the village south of here. Most likely, they are delayed by the rain." And then, exhaustion obvious in the slump of his shoulders, Marcus addressed Garrett again. "Is there anything I can do, my lord?"

The young man was anxious and weary. Perhaps the midnight journey had been a huge mistake. No perhaps about it. If they'd waited until morning to depart, Natalie's absence would have been discovered. "There are empty rooms on the second floor, Marcus. Take one near my chamber and get some rest. God knows you need it."

Marcus required no further urging. "Yes, my lord," Pausing at the door, he turned and then added, "Please wake me if you need anything."

Garrett dipped his chin in acquiescence.

He could not sit here doing nothing. Mrs. Hampden

be damned; he needed to check on Natalie again.

It being his own chamber, he did not knock before entering, which earned him a scowl from the housekeeper. She had removed Natalie's torn and bloodied gown already, however, and exchanged it for a clean one. Accustomed to Garrett's father, the woman had good reason to be wary of his motives. Gathering a dirtied bin of water and some soiled washcloths, she moved about the room nervously. Garrett noticed she'd cleaned Natalie's wound and wrapped it with a strip of muslin.

"I'll sit with her until the doctor arrives." His tone left no room for argument. When the woman hesitated, he added, "Leave the door open if you must. I'd appreciate some hot tea and sandwiches, and see that the new valet locates a chamber for himself, as well."

The protective housekeeper needed something to do or else she'd hover over him incessantly. It was obvious she objected to his presence.

But he needed to be here with Natalie.

"Very well, my lord." But she clicked her tongue in disapproval.

Garrett would not be moved.

When she finally heeded his dismissal, Garrett closed the door and dropped into the chair beside the bed. Pale and unmoving, Natalie's fragility called out to him. Garrett wanted to remove his boots and lie down beside her. He wanted to wrap her in his arms and murmur reassuring words into her ears until she came awake again.

He took her hand in his and raised it to his lips.

"Come back to me," he said instead. "Come back."

****

Natalie was dreaming.

The sun shone brightly in a brilliant blue sky. Dark-haired little boys scurried about in a meadow, tumbling and rolling on soft, thick grass with a man—with their father. Laughing, they climbed on the man and demanded pony rides. The exuberant bundle consisted of wiry little bodies, unruly hair, and familiar black eyes. When the smallest child looked at her and smiled, a slight dimple appeared near the corner of his mouth.

In between their play, they called her "Mama." She sat stringing together a chain of daisies feeling perfectly content. And then she wanted to be closer to the man and her children.

She tried to join in their games but could not move. She was trapped——in a box——with no sunlight and very little air. And pain—blinding pain. Where did the children go? She couldn't move. She tried to break her way out but could not. She began gasping and crying. Something was crushing her.

"Shhh…it's all right, love. I'm here. You're safe now…" A cool cloth pressed against her forehead. A man's voice spoke in soothing tones by her ear. "Hush, sweetheart, you're safe now." She tried opening her eyes, but when she did so, the light caused stabbing pain. Ah, but the man beside her was Garrett Castleton. *Garrett.* She must be safe.

He placed her hand upon his face. She could feel the rough texture of his beard beneath her fingers. "Garrett," she rasped. She moved her fingers tentatively. She felt his face turn and hot breath upon her palm. Moist lips dropped a tender kiss there. And then he lay her hand back upon the bedclothes.

The wet cloth dabbed at her mouth and a few drops of cool water were squeezed onto her lips. "Are you thirsty, sweetheart?" He wiped the cloth around her face. It felt soothing. But she did not feel well.

"I'm going to be ill." She ought to be mortified but could not muster much other than the energy to warn him. Before she knew it, her body heaved, and she retched into a pot while strong hands supported her. The violent movements caused her head to pound even worse.

When it was over, she lay back and the soothing washcloth again dabbed at her mouth. Somebody else entered the room. A woman and another man. The pain in her head made it difficult to pay attention to their words. She allowed herself to be enveloped by sleep once again.

Chapter Twenty-Four

After showing the doctor out, Garrett returned to his desk and slumped down in relief. She would live. The blow to her head was her only apparent injury. The trunk was inspected and found to have slight gaps along some of the seams. Thank God, she had not been deprived of air. Her head injury was worrisome though; she was to be watched and wakened often. The doctor had said to keep the room darkened and quiet. He would return tomorrow, but meanwhile she was not to be moved. They would know more later, the doctor said.

Garrett opened a jar of ink and then wrote a note to be delivered to Raven's Park. He outlined, as concisely as possible, the events of the past twelve hours. He wrote that Natalie had suffered an injury, but the doctor assured him she would recover fully. The rain had passed, and a servant could be dispatched right away. He pulled the bell pull and handed it to Mr. Hampden with strict instructions.

And then, in his exhaustion, he contemplated his own circumstances. He'd made off with a lady of noble birth—overnight—a lady who now lay injured in his very own bedchamber. He'd not, truly, been alone with her. He'd not thrown her over his mount and made a run for Scotland. It was all simply a mistake—a criminal mistake. Would he be absolved? Would the events be considered scandalous? Not that he gave a shilling for his own standing, but he minded for Natalie. Her reputation already hung in peril—would she be ruined by this? His mind teased him with the thought that they would be forced to marry.

But would Ravensdale countenance it? Would she? Garrett felt beyond tired. Chasing these thoughts around his already muddled mind was useless. He removed himself to the leather couch, near the fireplace, and collapsed. It took but a few moments before he fell asleep, boots and all.

Garrett had not slept long before being awakened by a loud pounding. Hearing a familiar voice in the foyer, he had no doubt who had arrived. God, he needed a bath. He'd forgotten all about the one Marcus had drawn for him earlier. But even a tepid bath would feel good at this point.

Despite not having imbibed any spirits recently, his head throbbed as though he'd spent the previous night soused. Rubbing his hands over his face, he rose reluctantly to face one of Natalie's brothers.

"Darlington." Garrett spoke quickly, not wishing his housekeeper to become any more flustered than she already was.

The viscount turned and, catching sight of Garrett, narrowed his eyes. Soaked through with mud clinging to his splattered boots, Natalie's eldest brother must have travelled straight through. Garrett ignored his guest's appearance though. He found the murderous intent in the gentleman's eyes a more pressing concern.

Garrett braced himself, knowing what was coming the split second before his head snapped back from the well-deserved blow.

Darlington had obviously frequented Gentleman Jackson's sometime in the recent past for the well-placed punch landed soundly. Upon impact, light exploded in Garrett's head.

Stumbling slightly, he rubbed at his jaw and prepared to defend a second attack.

But the viscount seemed satisfied as he examined his knuckles casually. "Hawthorne," he nodded.

Garrett took a moment to gather his wits before speaking. Pain spread through his jaw and into his left eye.

"Did you, by chance, happen upon the courier I sent a few hours ago?" Without waiting for an answer, Garrett led the viscount into his study.

"I did," Darlington answered from behind. "I sent him along to notify my parents of Natalie's...situation—and of her safety." Eyeing the makeshift room, Darlington asked, "Shall we obtain the special license from London? Or do you think one can be had in Reading?"

Garrett shook his head wearily at the question. Before falling asleep, he'd decided on one thing. Only as a last option would he allow the two of them to be forced into a betrothal.

Furthermore, he would insist that all possible alternatives be discussed with both her father and the lady herself. He knew Natalie would hate having such decisions made without her consent.

Perhaps she could travel to the Continent for a year or two until the scandal blew over. She herself had once told him there were other solutions for such situations. The *ton* was a fickle group. What enraptured them one moment could be forgotten in the next. Besides, who could know of her presence here? Surely no more than a few servants and her family.

Darlington shattered that assumption with his next words. "The entire house party knows she went missing last night. Many assisted in an all-night search. On the heels of her broken engagement, she is ruined." As angry as the man had appeared moments earlier, he merely looked resigned now. "You are the last person I would have chosen to marry my sister, Hawthorne, but if there isn't a marriage, and a quick one at that, she'll never be able to show her face in society again." And then, walking over to the window, he let out a heavy sigh. "Where is she now? The doctor seemed convinced of his diagnosis?"

Garrett felt a grudging sympathy for the man. He'd obviously had no sleep himself and had been forced to travel after a frantic search throughout the night. "Sit down, Darlington. She is sleeping. The doctor believes she was concussed. We are to awaken her every hour or so."

Torn between defiance and fatigue, Darlington hesitated before fatigue won out and he dropped into the chair. "What the hell happened? The note said she had been trapped inside a trunk?" His eyes narrowed threateningly again. "She was borne away on your carriage. You must know how this story will play out."

"Until we speak with Natalie, I am as in the dark as you, but"—he met the viscount's gaze squarely—"I have suspicions, not based on anything solid, rather a gut feeling. Farley and Trident were hanging about the stable block when I bid your brother farewell. And Farley, in particular, appeared a tad smug for someone being turned off the property."

Garrett paced to the fireplace and stared down at the diminishing flames. "I don't know how he would have done it, or why, but I'd wager the estate he played some part in it. When we came across him the previous evening, he was not well disposed toward your sister." Pounding his fist on the mantel, he added, "Nor myself. But this prank of his could have killed her!"

"Natalie has been unable to tell you herself?" Darlington's brows lowered in concern. "She is not coherent when she wakes?"

Wretchedly, Garrett shook his head. "She is not."

The viscount watched Garrett searchingly. "You have an affection for her. I thought so when you fished her out of the lake. You will give me your word that you did not take her intentionally? You have not done this to trap her into marriage?"

Garrett laughed at the irony. "You would accept my word? Honor from the son of a madman?" He found the demand intolerable. But it was what he expected. He steeled his gaze upon Natalie's oldest brother. "I will do all in my ability to *avoid* matrimony with your sister, Darlington. You have my word on that." And, in a barely audible voice, he added, "I wouldn't wish that upon my worst enemy."

"So you do care for her."

Garrett paced to the desk. He felt like a caged animal. "Of course I care for her." He shoved his hands into his pockets. The memory of Natalie, limp and broken, trapped inside the trunk would haunt him forever. He hadn't protected her when she'd needed him most.

"Your sister is not to be moved. The doctor has forbidden it until he is satisfied she is recovering properly. I will have a room prepared for you. Forgive the rudimentary accommodations, but you see, my beloved father burned the manor to smithereens a few weeks ago." With that, he tugged at the bell pull to summon Mrs. Hampden. Hopefully, there were enough clean linens to have another room readied. He'd not expected to entertain guests so soon, and one oughtn't to put a viscount on an uncovered mattress.

Unable to remain in Darlington's company any longer, Garrett excused himself to seek out the housekeeper himself. Upon locating her, he requested a meal be served to the viscount while he waited for his room.

He wasn't sure how long he'd slept, but it could have been hours. He rushed upstairs, once again, to check on Natalie.

Mrs. Hampden had sent for a young maid from the village to look after Natalie while she dealt with other household duties. Sitting beside Natalie's bed now, the girl looked to be perhaps sixteen, dressed in an apron and mop cap. Garrett dismissed her, and she curtsied and hurried away. After entering the darkened room, he closed the door behind him. A small fire burned in the grate, casting the room in shadows. The drapes were pulled closed. The doctor had suggested that harsh lights might cause Natalie undue pain.

Shock swept through Garrett. Listless and pale, Natalie's delicate face lacked her normal rosy hue. He set a hand upon her forehead. She was cool to touch. His heart nearly breaking, he smoothed a few tendrils of hair away from her face. Her eyelashes fluttered before opening slowly.

"Ah," he said softly, "you are returned from

dreamland."

"Where am I? I thought you were leaving," she said in a hoarse voice.

Garrett spotted a glass of water sitting on the bureau and brought it to her. "We are at Maple Hall—the dower house, that is." And then, propping her up, he put the glass to her lips. "Drink slowly," he cautioned. "Tell me if you feel ill again. That's a good girl." She lay back against the pillow while he returned the glass to the table.

She closed her eyes and didn't speak for a moment. Was she sleeping again?

"Maple Hall?" She absorbed the information. "But why?"

Garrett put one foot on the bed frame and leaned over to peer down at her. "I hoped you could tell me."

She opened her eyes again and attempted to look about as though the answer were somewhere in the room. But that was too much for her. She flinched and let her head fall back into the pillow, closing her eyes yet again.

"You took a violent blow to the head, love. The doctor said we could give you some laudanum for the pain, but you've been unconscious since we found you. Are you in pain now?"

"My brain feels scrambled," she said. "It hurts when I think. Good gracious, now I'll be the perfect English maiden."

Garrett laughed despite himself. What a relief to see a spark of her spirit break through. He bent forward and placed his lips on her forehead.

"You've been perfect since the day I first laid eyes upon you." The words were meant to be lighthearted, but there was truth in them. In all his dealings with her, she'd proven to be his ideal. He only wished he could be the same for her.

She gasped suddenly and covered her mouth. "Garrett," she whispered, looking very distraught.

"What is it?" Had she remembered something? Was she in pain? He should get the laudanum.

"Did I…" She cringed. "Did I vomit when you were here earlier?"

He grinned down at her. "Well, a gentleman perhaps ought not to remember such a thing."

"Oh, I did, didn't I? And now I must look a fright. And how the devil did I get here?" Her brows furrowed as she again seemed to be searching her memory. She was still muddled.

"You did, but you look beautiful, and we do not know what happened but can sort that all out when you are feeling better." He brought her hand to his lips and pressed a kiss there. "But for now, you will rest." If she could not sleep again, he would have the medication brought up.

She seemed to relax but clutched his hand still. "You would tell me if something terrible had happened, wouldn't you? You aren't keeping anything from me?" Her lips were pinched. She *was* in pain.

"I would tell you." Would he? "Lie still. You don't want to be ill again. Your head is giving you all kinds of fits, isn't it?" At her slight nod, he retrieved the wet cloth he'd used earlier and placed it upon her forehead. He felt helpless to see her in pain. Unable to bear it, he patted her and left to locate the medicine.

****

"Do Mama and Papa know I am here?" Natalie

whispered. She'd been tempted to feign sleep when she realized who sat beside her bed, but Darly was not going to go away. Surely he would lecture her. She'd almost rather have woken to found her father beside her bed.

At her question, her brother glanced away from the window he'd been staring out and pinned her with his stare. He leaned forward quietly. He didn't say a word, but his expression spoke volumes.

Natalie wished she could sit up. Speaking with Darlington intimidated her under the very best of circumstances. Doing so from a supine position promised to be unbearable.

And then to add to her disadvantage, he rose and stood to his full height. "Do you think I would keep something like this from them?"

"Oh, Darly!" She knew what was coming. This situation could very well turn up worse than her broken engagement.

"Mrs. Tinsdale worried when you failed to return to your chamber. I've never seen our mother so distraught." He went on to explain how they'd searched the large house from the attics to the cellars. Experiencing no luck there, they'd then turned apart the stable block and every vehicle on the estate. Adding to her guilt, he then told her that the woods had been walked numerous times. House party guests and villagers had desperately scoured the property after hearing of her disappearance. Natalie wished she could duck her head beneath the covers and never come out again. How utterly mortifying! In her entire life, she would never live this down.

"We were on the verge of dragging the canals.

Mother was beside herself."

As Darlington continued speaking, Natalie's eyes filled with tears. Oh, what a bother she was! She'd caused her mother such grief! And her father, well, he would banish her to Scotland for certain this time!

"They have been informed of your safety—and your injuries." Darlington went on. And then he began pacing. "How on earth did you come to be in that trunk? And in your nightclothes? Were you attacked? Was it Farley? Or Trident? Don't you remember anything? Or did you think such a wicked prank might be entertaining?"

But she did not know. She did not!

Seeing that he'd made her cry, he frowned. "I cannot fathom what you might have been doing out of doors in your night clothes. Have you nothing to say for yourself? Nothing at all?"

She would not have put herself inside of the trunk! Of course, she would not! And yet…

Darlington's words teased her memory. She'd left her chamber to find something urgent…to look at something…And the trunk. In her mind's eye, she could picture herself climbing into it, *looking for something*. But what? Why? "I was not attacked, Darly. I'm almost certain of it. I believe I chose to go outside on my own." As she spoke, a fog seemed to settle on her. She attempted to see through it in order to discover the answers he wanted but…words stopped making sense as she listened to her own voice. There were little dark-haired boys running about…her dream. What had she dreamt and what was real? But Darlington wanted answers. He did not wish to hear about her dreams. "I'm sorry! I don't know, Darly. I can't think." She cried out in frustration and then lifted her hand to her head when pain stabbed behind her eyes. "I feel as though I remember…and then…" More tears escaped. Nobody liked disappointing Darlington.

Her most reticent brother, then, looking uncomfortable, reached out and soothed her head. Although his hand felt cool on her skin, it did not impart the same comfort as Garrett's had. *Had she followed Garrett in some lame attempt to win his love?* That would be mortifying! She would not have! Of course, she wouldn't have done something so foolish…so needy!

She admitted to herself that she loved Garrett, and he was drawn to her, but he'd been crystal clear in the meadow. Under no circumstances did he wish to marry her. He'd left her no room for doubt. Was it just yesterday he'd offered her that dreadful proposal? Oh, yes, and the *petite mort*. Natalie pushed her brother's hand away when the latter thought came into her mind.

Darlington shoved his hands into his pockets, obviously still unhappy with her answers. "Best not tire yourself, Nat. The doctor said it is important you are not fatigued." He spoke grudgingly.

"I'm not." Natalie licked her lips. "I'm thirsty."

Her brother took this as an excuse to leave. "I'll send for the maid." He patted her hand once and then strode out the door. Natalie knew the maid would be here within moments. Few people failed to jump into action when Darlington issued orders.

Glancing around the room, she was reminded that she lay in Garrett's bed. She, Lady Natalie Spencer, daughter of the Earl of Ravensdale, lay in Garrett Castleton's bedchamber in the Dower House at Maple

Hall. Garrett's bedchamber! Oh, lord!

Again, confusion clouded her thoughts. The furnishings were shabby, but the chamber otherwise appeared neat and tidy. Embers in the hearth provided the only light within the room as the curtains were drawn. She tried to sit up, but doing so caused a new wave of nausea to sweep through her. Best to stay lying down. How could she feel so ghastly and yet so agitated at the same time? *There is something...* She would not have gone outside alone in her night clothes if it hadn't been important. For heaven's sake, she'd even donned one of her day dresses when she'd taken Baby Bear outside in the middle of the night to do his business. What had been so very urgent?

As she suspected, the maid rushed into the room breathlessly. "His Lordship said you needed assistance, my lady." She looked harried and sleep-tousled. Good lord, leave it to Darlington to awaken the poor girl to fetch her *a sip of water*!

"My mouth feels like it's full of sand." Natalie attempted to make her need sound more urgent than it really was. She didn't want the maid to feel as though she'd been awoken for no reason. "And perhaps some willow bark?" All she'd managed to do by worrying was provoke her headache. But something else bothered her dreadfully. She touched her hair self-consciously before asking, "Tomorrow, do you think you could do something about this mess?"

Chapter Twenty-Five

It was in his best interest to avoid her. She'd done something different with her hair, now, and appeared to be regaining her health quickly. Which was a good thing, a wonderful thing. But nothing taunted him more than the sight of Lady Natalie Spencer in his bed, dressed in only a thin cotton gown.

As her health improved, her cheerful spirits returned as well. She sang the praises of the young girl presently acting as her lady's maid. It seemed she might have found a replacement for Mrs. Tinsdale after all.

During one visit, she confided to Garrett that she'd given the care of Baby Bear over to her old nurse. Before knowing her, he might have assumed she had merely grown tired of the pup and was shirking her responsibility. But he knew differently. She'd realized the elderly woman was lonely. No, it had not been an easy decision for her.

Lord Darlington's company, on the other hand, was becoming something of a nuisance.

He continued to press for Garrett to obtain a special license. As each day passed, Darlington's insistence that Garrett marry his sister increased. As did Garrett's resolve. Only as the last possible option, he'd finally conceded one night, would he marry her. For otherwise, Natalie's brother might have demanded a meeting at dawn. Natalie would hate them both if matters devolved to that.

It wasn't that Garrett did not yearn with his entire being to make Natalie his. Of course, he wanted to marry her! If he were any other man, with any other father, living any other life.

Having her in his home was almost more than he could bear. He longed for the day she would leave but also dreaded it.

Garrett escaped the dower house as often as possible, focusing on the immediate needs of this broken-down estate he'd inherited. In his busyness, trudging from one tenant's holding to another, he sought to regain equilibrium and clarity. But removing himself from her presence was easier than removing her from his thoughts. He often found himself wishing to tell her about this or that little incident but then stifled such notions before they took root.

And then there were the nights.

His memories of pleasuring her in the meadow the afternoon he'd left Raven's Park plagued him with images and feelings he struggled to deny. Knowing she lay steps away mocked his unmet needs. His lust for her was almost as powerful as his feelings of tenderness and regard.

He loved her, dammit.

Which made it imperative he not act selfishly. When he'd thought her life in danger, he'd been devastated. Her safety, her well-being, and ultimately her happiness must be assured at all costs. Even if the price was to live his life without her.

She might think him cruel now, but she was young and unable to consider the ramifications of rash decisions. She believed herself in love with him. To such an innocent, he must seem exciting and unpredictable, the antithesis of her former betrothed.

She would believe it romantic to consider herself in love with a rake, a man of mystery to the *ton*. She'd sought him out for adventure—for passion. She'd been on the rebound, so to speak. Tossed over by her fiancé, certain of her needs had gone unfulfilled. She'd wanted to know what it felt like to succumb to desire. She'd sought it out unilaterally. He'd made the mistake of getting caught up in her acts of rebellion.

She'd also wanted, God preserve them all, to help him! She wanted to *save him* from himself. On the very day of his arrival, she'd taken steps to redeem him so he could return to society. She'd even found him a valet, for God's sake. She'd taken to him as though he were a stray pup, much as she'd taken to Baby Bear. She wished to soothe his wounds and wash away his past with her love.

How long could such feelings last? How much pain and hurt could her pitying love endure?

For pain and hurt would be her lot if she married him.

Her infatuation would not endure being tied to a husband who could not—would not—give her a child. An even worse scenario would be the birth of a child who was not of sound mind.

For he knew himself. Caught up in the throes of passion, he could easily release his seed too quickly. All it would take would be one time. God, what a mess that would be.

And what of her life in society? That would be over. As his wife, she would be painted with the same taint of scandal that had followed him throughout all

England. For what woman in her right mind would knowingly marry a man with insanity in his blood? There would be no invitations to attend the various balls and parties she'd presided over throughout the previous two years. She would no longer be welcome in the drawing rooms of persons she considered to be her friends. They could not stroll through Hyde Park during the fashionable hour, for it would be too painful to feel the cut direct as face after face turned away from her. Garrett could not bear to see her scorned.

****

Five days into her recovery, both Lord and Lady Ravensdale arrived at Maple Hall. They arrived with outriders in full livery and a battalion of personal servants. The countess brought her lady's maid, and Mr. Whipple attended the earl.

Garrett had known the party would be arriving and had just managed to set up lodgings for the entire entourage. The bedchamber beside Garrett's, where Lady Natalie slept, had been cleaned, aired, and the bed fitted with new linen. Garrett hoped the couple would not have misgivings about sharing a bed. There simply wasn't another available.

Wasting no time after alighting from their conveyance, the countess excused herself to check on her daughter.

Lord Ravensdale requested a private word with Garrett.

Ah, another inquisition. The screws were to be tightened even further. Garrett steeled himself.

The earl was forthright. "Darlington tells me you do not wish to marry my daughter, in defiance of the fact that you have compromised her."

Good God! Must he rehearse this conversation again? Of course. And he must be most convincing of all today.

"It is not a matter of what I wish," Garrett began. "There are other avenues that can and should be explored before forcing her into an unsuitable marriage." Garrett spoke with conviction. "I am surprised you are not in full agreement with me. You, more than anyone, know that an alliance with the Earl of Hawthorne places your daughter in an altogether different public scorn. One which will never be forgiven." Looking at the man directly, Garrett was forced to reveal he'd overheard the man's words to his daughter just a short time ago. "You allowed my presence in your home as a concession to the assistance I've given you in business. You said you would not want a degenerate such as myself to be anywhere near your daughter." Garrett looked down at his hands. "You were right in such an opinion."

"Natalie told you this?" Ravensdale's brows lowered into a stern frown. "I cannot believe my daughter would share this information with you."

Garrett sighed. "She did not, my lord." Looking up wearily, he confessed to eavesdropping. "I came to see you before I left Raven's Park. The door to your study was open, and I overheard you scolding Natalie, Lady Natalie, that is, to keep away from me." When the earl went to interrupt him, Garrett held up a hand and continued. "I did not then, nor do I now, find fault in your judgment. That is why I am surprised you persist with this notion of a betrothal. You could send her on holiday to the Continent. Hell, she could go to America. It would just have to be for a year or two. The *ton* will forget this. They are fickle about these matters, and you know it as well as I."

The earl stared down at his boots. "I did not mean you to hear those words, my boy."

"Nonetheless, they were words of wisdom." And then Garrett felt the need to add, "It is not that I wouldn't treasure your daughter as my countess, as my wife, but she would come out the worse for it." He paused, swallowing the lump in his throat. "If your family decides marriage is the only thing to save her, you have my word I will meet her at the altar and give her my name. But first I insist you take her home, allow her a measure of peace before forcing her into a decision. Marriage is not to be entered into hastily. It is for life."

The earl studied Garrett closely. "And if she insists on marriage, you will abide by her decision?"

She wouldn't. He would not allow it. "I will. The doctor has said she may travel in a day or so. I apologize for the rudimentary accommodations here, but you and the countess are welcome to stay as long as you wish." *But take your daughter with you soon, please.* He could only endure so much.

Chapter Twenty-Six

Natalie remembered almost everything leading to her arrival at Maple Hall. Everything that is, except for why she climbed into the trunk. She'd not been following Lord Hawthorne. She'd acted most inappropriately with Garrett, she admitted to herself, but she was not such a hoyden as to stow away in his trunk. Good heavens! She hoped not anyhow.

Her headaches had subsided to a dull annoying pinch now and then. The bouts of nausea were gone, and she could think more clearly.

And her new maid, Sissy, whom Natalie would never relinquish willingly, had proven quite capable at creating the latest styles in "her ladyship's" hair. Sissy insisted the designs were fresh from Paris. A cousin of hers worked as lady's maid to a very modern French lady, and she'd shared many of her secrets with Sissy.

Unfortunately, Natalie was still restricted to bed rest and forced to remain in nothing more colorful or inspiring than the housekeeper's borrowed nightclothes. Her mother had brought day clothing for her to wear, but in the rush, Tinsdale had failed to pack any of her nightgowns. Nonetheless, she was grateful to Sissy for keeping her hair stylish and presentable. It lifted her spirits considerably.

As could a certain handsome gentleman visitor.

When he chose to grace her with his presence, that

was.

She had been certain, upon reflecting on his treatment of her during the first few days following her injury, that he loved her. He'd been tender and sweet, treating her as though she were the most important person in the world. His voice had whispered soothing reassurances into her ear, and his hands had been gentle as they caressed her hair and face. And when she'd begun to show signs of mending, he'd ordered her not to overtax herself. He'd been quite protective, in fact.

But his demeanor had changed. As she recovered, his visits grew farther and farther apart.

Which disturbed her, to say the least. Especially in light of the fact that she loved him.

Yes, she'd remembered that. Fat lot of good it did her. The rest of the world only cared about saving her reputation.

Every person within her midst had voiced their opinion that the earl *absolutely must* marry her. She'd been carried away overnight, without her parents' permission or knowledge, without a chaperone to the earl's home. *They must marry*.

Darlington demanded it, most persistently.

Mrs. Hampden expected it, while clucking her tongue.

Sissy encouraged it, with a romantic sigh.

And even her mother would have it, quite matter-of-factly, at that! Everyone whose opinion could be heard was in accord upon the matter. Everybody, that is, except the prospective groom.

And of course, nobody thought to ask Natalie for *her* opinion. If anyone had bothered, they would have gotten an earful.

Because under no circumstances, ever again, would she allow herself to be forced into a marriage with a reluctant groom. Especially when she loved the idiot!

A knock on the door interrupted her frustrated musings.

Upon being given permission to enter, Garrett himself pushed it open. It was as though her aching heart had summoned him.

Despite looking tired, he'd dressed in form-fitting breeches, waistcoat, jacket, and an expertly tied cravat. Marcus would have dressed him for this occasion. Oh, her father must be forcing him to propose to her now. He'd given in, the poor man. Ah, well, she'd put him out of his misery.

He looked fidgety, nervous. His hair was mussed, and his eyes more sunken than usual. None of this detracted from his looks, however. She still felt drawn to him. A physical pull exerted itself whenever he was near.

He, the addlepated male, seemed oblivious to her yearning.

"Sit down," she invited. "I imagine you've been talking with Papa."

Garrett nodded. "I have." And then he sat on the side of her bed, well, his bed really. "You and I must talk."

Not the most romantic choice of words with which to begin his proposal...

"You remember our last afternoon together at Raven's Park—in the meadow?" At her blush, he rushed onward. "No, not that part—later, when we talked—when I told you why I could never marry and have a family."

271

Natalie tilted her head, confused. "Yes."

Appearing even more agitated, Garrett left the bed and strode to the window where the curtain had been pulled halfway open. "Well, it still stands."

It took a moment for Natalie to absorb his blunt words. They were not at all what she expected. She could not see his face. It was in shadow. Not fair!

"Look at me," she demanded. "What are you saying?"

Shoving his hands into his pockets, Garrett did not turn away from the window. "Your father and I have come to an agreement. Only as a last resort will you and I marry. There are other ways to ward off this scandal, and every one of them must be explored first. I do not wish to marry you." He refused to look at her.

And then he did.

Behind his harsh words and feigned calm, sadness shadowed his eyes. His lips were tight and thin. He held himself rigidly.

"So"—Natalie needed to be certain she understood exactly what he was saying—"as the very last, the absolute last antidote to repair my reputation, you will then marry me—under duress—so to speak. Because...?" Natalie twirled her hands in the air as though summoning his reasoning. "This is all because of your father?"

"And the mud you would be dragged through as my wife. I won't have it."

Natalie took a deep breath. A part of her wanted to weep and beg, but she would not give into it. Another part was trying to remind her of something. There was something...

"Perhaps it would be *I* who would be dragging *you*

through the mud," she suggested calmly.

"It would not."

Ah, so he would not be moved. He had been badgered by both her oldest brother and her father and refused to yield his position. Admirable, really, in any other situation.

"Only in the direst of circumstances?" she confirmed.

He nodded.

"You give me your word? You will not hide from me if my reputation cannot be repaired? You will not change your mind if the *ton* cannot forgive me this time?"

"You have my word."

This was the Garrett who had refused to allow her to compromise herself with him. The one who had halted her passion when she'd abandoned all sense of propriety. She loved him all the more for it, and yet she would strangle him for his stubbornness. Again, he would not look directly at her.

"And this is open-ended? Is there a timeline attached to your promise?"

He did not answer right away. And then finally, "No. Well, within reason, I suppose."

"A year? Two?" She paused, goading him. "Ten?"

His demeanor remained stoic and impersonal. "Two seems reasonable enough, if that is acceptable to you?"

She memorized his features. He must become a memory to her then? Was she to live her life with heartbreak? Lost to her one true love? Surely there must be some way…

And then she could not help herself. "Please don't

do this, Garrett. I do not mind about the children."

Ah, so she would allow this pathetic part of herself to have a voice. "I...would find other ways to have a meaningful life. I...care so much for you. You must know that?" Oh, what an utter fool she was! She might as well declare her undying love for him. And then he could pat her on the head and tell her to be a good girl and go find another beau...Her confidence in his affections flagged. Perhaps he saw her as a child.

In a rush of motion, Garrett covered the steps between the two of them and pulled her into his arms. For a full minute, he didn't say a word. His breathing sounded harsh, and he held her tightly, so tight that it almost hurt.

Finally, his embrace slackened, and he pulled back to look at her. "You are so very precious to me," he rasped. "But you are also so...damn naïve!" Releasing her shoulders, he grasped her hands in his. "You have your entire life ahead of you. A life as a wife, a life as a mother, and then a grandmother." Raising her hands to his lips, he implored her with the intensity of his gaze. "Allow me to do this for you. I could not live with myself if I ensnared you in my world. I won't do it."

She searched his eyes. So black. When she'd first known him, she'd seen them as dangerous, practically evil. She knew better now. Warm, dark and sensual, they aroused all the emotions she'd lacked in her engagement. She sat back. There was time. She had all the time in the world. She would think of something. She would find a way to convince him of his right to happiness, and she would lay claim to it for both of them.

She just wished she knew how.

"You will kiss me?"

Garrett groaned. But then dropped her hands and placed his hands on the sides of her face.

Although he held her tenderly, his mouth demanded everything. His lips urged hers apart and swept beyond all inhibitions. Natalie took hold of his wrists for balance. Despite her weak condition, she found the strength to push into him and demand this connection with equal urgency. He tasted, oh, he tasted of Garrett. Hot, spicy, familiar. Garrett's hands gripped her tighter.

The other times he'd kissed her, he'd kept a part of himself under tight rein. This kiss was different. It conveyed desperation, imparting both love and agony. He kissed her as though it would be their last. It could not. It would not! She would fight for him, for them, if only she knew how.

She whimpered when he drew away and pulled a mask of distance back over his features. "I will not bother you alone again." He meant this to be their goodbye.

****

Upon completing his examination of Natalie, the doctor announced she was as well as she might ever be. Her parents could safely travel with her back to Raven's Park. He told her she might never regain her full memory of the accident and then advised her against any rigorous physical or mental activity. Natalie wondered what he meant by rigorous mental activity.

For she was frantically trying to concoct a scheme to bring Garrett around to her way of thinking. Thus far, however, her rigorous mental activity had been lamentably unproductive.

She was going to have to return to Raven's Park without extracting his passionate declaration of love—without hearing the romantic proposal she desired.

It was time to retreat. She must devise a new strategy. What that would be, she still did not know. She clung to his promise of marriage (as a last option) for the tenuous connection it provided.

And so, with a melancholy heart, she allowed him to escort her to her father's carriage the next morning. Out of bed for the first time in a week, she dressed in a pale rose cotton gown. She knew it flattered her complexion and enhanced the color of her eyes. It was important that she leave Garrett with a flattering image of herself. When he remembered her, when he conjured her in his imagination, she would have him forget the image of her lying in bed with her hair sticking everywhere.

She wanted to laugh but nearly choked on a sob instead.

As he assisted her up the step, she glanced down at his dear, familiar hand. The hand that had soothed her and touched her intimately. Her gaze moved to his, and she was encouraged to see his emotions revealed again. They were intense. They practically devoured her.

"Thank you again, my lord, for your hospitality. I am sorry for giving you such a fright with my arrival." Her mother sat behind her on the bench, facing front.

Garrett released her as she found her seat beside Mama. He leaned into the cabin of the carriage to speak. "I am grateful you are recovering. And I am again so very sorry for my part in all of this…Please, if it occurs to you, I would be obliged if you would send me word when you have recovered your memory." His words were formal, but his eyes shown with love.

"And the other matter, my lord," she added. "I will contact you regarding it as well."

Her words had the immediate effect of extinguishing all ardor from his eyes. With a shudder, it was quickly replaced with that grim determination he'd embraced ever since making his non-proposal to her. Could she be wrong about his feelings? This was not the last memory she wished to take with her. Nor for her to leave with him.

"Of course," he said. And then he backed out of the coach so that the maid could climb in.

Sissy Girard had accepted the position as Natalie's new lady's maid and was handed into the carriage lastly. Natalie's father and Darlington would ride outside on their mounts. After Sissy took her seat facing backward, Garrett pounded on the side of the carriage, and the driver signaled the horses to move out.

Natalie could not help herself but to peer out her window and watch Garrett as they drove off. He did not smile but lifted one hand in a slight wave. Natalie raised her fingers to the window and gave him a sad smile. She watched his lean figure disappear as they drove off the fire-ravaged estate. And then she could contain her tears no longer.

Her mama wrapped her arms around her soothingly. "There, there, my love. All will be well. We shall make a grand plan, and you needn't be reminded of this episode again."

With these words, Natalie's sobs grew louder. "But, Mama, I lo-o-ove him," she wailed.

Lady Ravensdale's hand, which was rubbing her daughter's back, stilled at Natalie's declaration. "Oh, well," she said softly, "why, that changes everything." She pulled out a handkerchief and handed it to her daughter. "And his feelings? What do you suspect of his feelings for you?"

Natalie sat back in the plush leather. The carriage bounced despite being well sprung. How on earth had she slept through an entire journey in a trunk, for heaven's sake? She was thankful indeed, that she *had* slept. Being conscious while trapped would have been unendurable! "I *believe* he loves me. I think he is being selfless. He keeps nattering on about my reputation and society and…children." Could she discuss this with her *mother?*

"And he believes these obstacles are insurmountable?" her mother asked calmly.

"Oh, Mama, he is adamant about it. But I disagree." She dabbed at a few fresh tears, which were threatening to fall. "And I would forgo children if necessary. What matters is that I am with him. Do you understand?" Of course her mother would not understand.

"Of course, I do, my darling." Her mother surprised her.

Both women sat without speaking for a moment.

And then Sissy's voice pierced the quiet. "He's a good man, if you don't mind my saying so, Lady Natalie, my lady," she ventured shyly. "It'd be worth it if you could think up some scheme to bring him 'round."

Her mama's eyes took on a gleam. "I've an idea, Natalie, but I don't wish to discuss it until you are fully recovered. When the time comes, we shall enlist the aid of Eleanor and perhaps a few of my other acquaintances. But these things take time." She patted Natalie's knee comfortingly. "Try to rest for now. That is our first order of business. You must recover your health completely. We'll address your...situation with Lord Hawthorne later."

Natalie wanted to question her mother but knew it was best to do as she said. She leaned her head back and closed her eyes. Let this journey not go on forever. She longed for the comfort of her own room, her own bed. She longed to feel like her old self again, although she thought perhaps her old self no longer existed.

By the time they turned into the drive to her father's manor, the sky had turned dark and several stars twinkled from above. This was her home, and yet, it felt so very different. After the footman pulled out the step and handed her down, Natalie looked around her childhood home with new eyes. The restless energy she'd experienced earlier in the summer was replaced with a steely determination. She was not so naïve as to believe she would get everything she wanted, but she would put forth her best effort. She would do her utmost to change Garrett's mind.

And if that did not work, then, well, she would go on. But she would go on knowing that she'd done all in her power to at least try. She would have no regrets.

Mrs. Winston greeted Sissy with more than a little suspicion and then led the young girl upstairs. Natalie found herself caught behind in the foyer, gruffly embraced by Peter and then Stone. They were not to lecture her tonight then. Thank God for that. She'd had enough from Darlington in the past week to account for them all.

Mr. Winston informed them all the guests had

departed except for Lady Sheffield. Mrs. Tinsdale, holding Baby Bear in her arms, stepped forward so Natalie could greet the pup properly. Only after receiving puppy-breath licks for a full two minutes could Natalie hand off her gloves and bonnet. Cooler temperatures had set in with the darkness, but the day had been warm. Natalie expressed her desire for a nice warm bath, and Tinsdale assured her the water was already heating.

Ah, sweet, familiar Tinsdale. Natalie and her mother would have to speak to her about relinquishing her position to Sissy. She must be assured she was still needed in the household. After all, who would care for Baby Bear?

And so, she was home again. Once again in the bosom of her beloved family. What had Garrett said about them that night in his room? *You have a father and a mother who would do anything to ensure your happiness. They love you deeply. Good God, they smile at you.*

And she loved them deeply, too. She did.

Turning to her father, she impulsively hugged him. "I am sorry, Papa, for scaring you so. Thank you for coming to Maple Hall with Mama to be with me." Her voice sounded muffled as she pressed her face into the comfort of her father's chest. *He would do anything for my happiness.* She was so very lucky.

Strong arms embraced her. "That's what papas are for, little one." His voice sounded garbled. "Now you be off to bed. It's been a long day, and you are not to be overtired. Tomorrow, you will rest some more. And after that—" He set her away from him. "Well, after that we begin to solve some problems." He tipped at her chin with one finger, forcing her to look at him. "I don't want you worrying. That is a direct order."

She smiled tremulously. "Yes, Papa." She wished she could do as he said. She was tired, yes, but how could she rest? How did one keep herself from worrying?

"Come along, my lady." Tinsdale beckoned to her. "Supper is being brought up to your room, and then a bath and bed. Things will look brighter in the morning."

"Thank you, Tinny." She cradled Baby Bear once again. Being home felt more than a little comforting, after all.

Chapter Twenty-Seven

Garrett stood outside for several minutes after Ravensdale's entourage disappeared. Watching the coach grow smaller, he mused that doing the right thing was not gratifying in the least. She'd looked ravishing this morning. He'd wanted to pull her from the carriage and announce their betrothal after all. It required all his resolve not to do so.

So very poised at times, had she experienced the same tumult as he? Or was her love already cooling? An impractical impulse within him hoped not, but the practical side knew this would be best. For if she still considered herself in love with him, then perhaps this was not finished at all. For Lady Natalie Spencer, with a notion in her head, could be like a dog with a bone. It would be unlike her to concede so easily.

A smile tipped up the sides of his mouth. Although delicate and genteel, she possessed the tenacity of her father. Hell, she was the perfect woman for him.

He hoped her family would pounce upon a quick resolution to right her social situation. Struggling to be free of her went against the urges of his heart...and other urges. He'd nearly changed his mind about everything this morning. She was just so...damn it, if he allowed his mind to continue in this vein, he'd be saddling Rumble and chasing her to ground within the hour.

Garrett pivoted on his heel and returned to the house. He'd just received some drawings from an architect he'd met with before leaving London. Best look them over now. He needed to move forward. And if Natalie continued to be a thorn in his side, then so be it. He would deal with that problem when the time came. If the time came. Best for all if the earl sent her off to America. He swallowed hard at the thought.

****

Natalie spent the next couple days in a solitary mood, her inability to remember why she had climbed into the trunk clawing at her. For she did remember doing just that. But why? What on God's earth had compelled her to embark on such a foolish errand?

At first, she rested.

And when she'd had enough of that, she prowled.

She retraced the walks she'd taken with Garrett, the wilderness path around the lake, the forest where Baby Bear liked to go, and the meadow where they'd been together that last afternoon. She even rowed herself around the lake a few times. She did *not* jump into the water. Much like a fatal disease, Garrett had taken hold of her. She lurked about the estate just as he lurked within her thoughts.

She told her parents she was not willing to travel to the Continent nor America. They discussed forgoing the Little Season in London that fall, but her father retained obligations in Parliament and felt he had little choice in the matter. He did not relish the thought of leaving his wife and daughter in the country without him for several weeks. Many thought it fashionable to spend time apart from one's spouse, but in this matter, he chose to forgo fashion. He would have his wife with him, if possible. And leaving Natalie alone was not an option.

If they were to leave, it would be in a few short weeks, as the entertainments were to begin in early September.

But would Natalie be shunned? Had she pushed too hard against the rules of society? There was as yet, no solution to her problem. So very un-Spencerish to ignore the situation, but her parents still had concerns for her health. Nobody wanted to cause her undue stress. Even her mother avoided the subject of the Earl of Hawthorne.

Nearly a fortnight after her return, late in the afternoon, Natalie found herself wandering around the manor on the third floor. She'd done much of this as of late, wandering, like an aimless ghost. She'd lost both her appetite and her ability to laugh, or so it seemed. Upon reaching the end of the corridor, she realized she'd arrived at the threshold to the room where she, Garrett, and Aunt Eleanor had unveiled his mother's paintings. She pushed the door open and entered the room. It smelled of lemon oil, having been recently dusted and cleaned. The sheets had been replaced on the chair, and an emptiness met her where the crates once sat. Natalie relaxed into one of the covered chairs and took a few deep breaths. Closing her eyes, she remembered that day.

She remembered the vivid colors of the paintings and Garrett's reaction to seeing his mother's work. He had been moved emotionally, she was certain of it. She also remembered Aunt Eleanor recalling the sad time when her brother had been killed. And the scandalous portraits of him.

The portraits!

The dimple!

She sprung to her feet.

Garrett's dimple had been drawn on the face of…what was his name?…Arthur. Yes! She'd climbed into the trunk to look at the portraits again! She'd needed to discover if she had merely imagined it.

And she had not! When she'd climbed into the trunk, she'd verified that Lady Sheffield's brother and Garrett Castleton shared a dimple in precisely the exact corner of each of their respective mouths. Could it be a coincidence? It could not. It was too uncanny.

Hurrying into the hallway, she felt a spurt of energy she'd not experienced for days. She must find Lady Sheffield. She must ask her. Aunt Eleanor would know the truth. Surely she would have the answers.

Where would she be now? What time was it? Glancing at the large clock at the end of the corridor—half past three—Natalie considered her mother's schedule. Lady Sheffield and Mama would be in the drawing room. Taking tea most likely.

Natalie dashed down the stairs, not willing to waste a moment. Upon throwing open the doors of the drawing room, Natalie faced two sets of eyes. Both her mother and Lady Sheffield seemed quite taken aback at her abrupt entrance.

"What's is the matter, my dear?" her mother enquired, setting her teacup and saucer to the side. "Are you unwell?"

Natalie could not hold back her excitement. "I have remembered! I have remembered how I ended up in the trunk! Oh, Mama, I was not being foolish." And then she looked over at Aunt Eleanor. "I needed to view the portraits again, the portraits of your brother." Seeing the woman's brows rise, Natalie made her way into the room and took the empty seat beside her on the settee. "Arthur was Garrett's father, was he not? Your brother fathered a son before the old earl killed him." Natalie held her breath as she awaited the older lady's response.

Her godmother sat the teacup aside and let out a long, deep breath. "He is." And then as though in agony, she turned to her dear friend, Natalie's mama, and said, "He did. Perhaps it is time for the truth."

Natalie, experiencing great relief, thought she would have fainted if she had a more delicate constitution. Garrett was *not* the biological son of the Earl of Hawthorne. But did it affect his inheritance? Surely not, for legally, he was the son of the earl. He had been born to the earl's wife. The earl never denied paternity.

"It is your truth to tell, Eleanor," Lady Ravensdale said. "You lived through the scandal once. It is your choice if it is to be unearthed and bandied about again."

"Please." Natalie implored the woman beside her. "Garrett has decided he will not sire any children, ever, because of the old earl's mental deficiencies. He refuses to marry because of this...well, in part because of this."

"Oh, you poor child." Aunt Eleanor turned and took Natalie's hands in hers. "It is true, then? You have developed a *tendre* for Garrett? For my...nephew?" Tears glistened in the woman's eyes.

"I love him. I do not want to go through life without him."

Her aunt stood and paced the room slowly, her hands steepled in front of her lips. After a few tension-filled moments, she announced her decision. "Well, goddaughter of mine"—she smiled—"I will do whatever I can to assist you. I cannot bear to see you unhappy, especially after what you did for Lilly." She dabbed at the corner of her eye and took her seat once again. "Now explain to me how things were left between the two of you when you last spoke."

And so, Natalie poured out everything—well, not *quite* everything—to her godmother and her mama. "He has promised, given me his word, he would marry me if I insist. I would never insist he do such a thing for my own sake, but I believe now that I might do so for *his*, *for our sake*. For I do believe he loves me—I think so anyhow." She said this bravely, for there were a few niggling doubts. "If I demand the marriage, and he comes to terms with the fact that he is not predisposed to sire an unhealthy child, then he maybe—well, perhaps then, he will allow himself to love me." The last words were nearly a whisper. It terrified her to speak the possibility out loud.

"But there is more to it than that." Lady Ravensdale spoke in a cautioning tone. "He does not wish to expose you to more scandal. And you, my dear, must admit your reputation cannot absorb much more if you ever expect to return to society again."

Snapping her fingers, Natalie's dismissed such a notion. "I could care this much about the *ton*, Mama."

"But," her mama said, "it is, and you must respect this, one of *his* reasons. It concerns the earl greatly."

The room fell quiet as the three women pondered this new obstacle.

It was Aunt Eleanor who finally broke the silence. "A large wedding," she declared with no uncertainty whatsoever. "At Saint George's on Hanover Square, at the peak of the Little Season, in mid-October."

Both Natalie and her mama turned toward Lady Sheffield, Mama with dawning understanding and Natalie with horror.

"But nobody will come!" Natalie said.

Lady Ravensdale nodded. "We must take measures to assure the church is full to bursting. Of course, Lord Hawthorne will be in town for the same special Parliamentary session Broderick must attend. We must do everything in our power to assure he is received. For if he is not a social pariah, then neither shall you be, when you marry."

"It's awfully risky." Natalie was stunned, but then as she considered it, she knew it must be done.

"You must write to Lord Hawthorne to notify him of your decision to marry, along with when and where, and also inform him of the true identity of his father." Natalie's mama had been addressing her but then turned toward Aunt Eleanor. "You are quite certain, Eleanor, this is what you wish?" At a nod from her friend, Natalie's mama then forged ahead. "He will need some time to absorb it. And by the time the Season starts, the campaign to restore him to society will be well underway."

"I think," Aunt Eleanor added, "the best tactic is to inform the world he was not sired by the Earl of Hawthorne as soon as possible. For his greatest sin, according to the *ton*, is having a madman for a father."

Natalie felt hopeful but not entirely convinced. "But would he not be shunned then, for being a bastard?" And Garrett would most likely not appreciate having such personal information about him aired for all and sundry. But if it worked…

Lady Ravensdale mused, "Technically, he is not a bastard. In addition to that, he is a very wealthy man who, as luck would have it, holds one of the oldest titles in England. With enough support, he *will* be received. As your godmother says, his circumstances will have become the lesser of two evils." She waited a moment and then with a gleam of anticipation added, "It's all a matter of execution, my dear."

Allowing no room for further argument, Lady Ravensdale rang the bell pull and requested her lap desk. "Eleanor, for all of London to hear the news, we need only send letters to a few select acquaintances, particularly those who are patronesses at Almack's. I'm certain we won't be disappointed." And with that, she began listing names, stopping only for a moment to address Natalie. "You had best inform the groom of your plans to marry, my dear. He'll need to arrange for the church and the banns." Then turning back to Aunt Eleanor. "Now how ought we to word this...?"

Natalie took a piece of parchment from her mother and rose slowly, her hands shaking. Oh, God, if this didn't work, her entire life would be ruined. And Garrett would never speak to her again.

Even if he *was* her husband!

Chapter Twenty-Eight

Oh, hell.

Garrett held the envelope in his hands as though it contained a bomb. For it must. Raven's Park had been printed in small letters on the envelope, and his own directions were written in very feminine writing. It was not seemly for a single woman to correspond with a single gentleman, but they had already done numerous things that would not have been considered seemly. Why not exchange some correspondence in addition to all their other sins?

Would the letter inform him of her intent to leave the country? The thought of this caused a stabbing pain in the organ that pumped blood through his body. Would she be telling him goodbye? Was she to release him from the promise he'd made?

Or was her news worse?

Forcing his fingertips to open the envelope, Garrett pulled back the flap and removed the folded sheets of paper. Her curling handwriting nearly covered them both completely.

Her news was much worse.

It read:

Lord Hawthorne,

I wish to marry and am holding you to your promise.

In all his life, he'd not thought it possible to feel

explosive anger, relief, and utter joy at the same time. Leave it to Natalie to evoke exactly that.

They had an understanding!

The idea of traveling abroad to escape society's measure and returning to an unresolved scandal is untenable. For I would be forced to be without my family and away from all that is familiar to me with no promise whatsoever of having my reputation restored. And without a restored reputation, I shall never find a suitable husband. I shall find myself upon the shelf, a brittle old maid, and I cannot tolerate this.

Another matter has been resolved as well. I have remembered everything! The reason I climbed into the trunk was to have another look at the portraits of Lady Sheffield's deceased brother. For I had begun to suspect something, which I have upon further investigation discovered to be true. I do hope you are sitting down for this news. Are you sitting? Well do so!

Feeling a little silly, he dropped onto the nearest chair. She would laugh at him if she were here. What was she rambling on about? He added amusement to the list of emotions that now engulfed him. Merely reading her words unraveled the apathetic haze he'd been in for nearly a month now.

Your mother carried you before she married the Earl of Hawthorne. Your biological father is Lady Sheffield's brother, Mr. Arthur Winters. There is a great deal of resemblance between the two of you. I observed it upon examining the portraits closely. But even more importantly, Lady Sheffield, who is indeed your aunt, has confirmed the fact.

What? Wait, what? He went back and read the words a second and then third time before continuing onto the next paragraph.

So you needn't worry about having any children with the same afflictions as the late Lord Hawthorne, any more than any other man, presumably. Therefore, we can lie together freely, as man and wife. I do so look forward to this aspect of marriage!

Yours faithfully,

Natalie

Post Script: Please contact St. George's on Hanover Square and schedule the wedding for the morning of the 23rd of October (of this year, of course) and arrange to have the banns read. Mama and I shall attend to the other details. You will, of course, speak with Papa about contracts when we are all in London for the Little Season.

He was being punished, for what, he knew not. He just knew he was being punished. And she would feel the sting of it as well. For they would say their vows before an empty church and then face a crowd of hecklers as they exited onto the street.

Throughout her life, she would suffer for her association with him. Didn't she realize this information could only provoke more scandal?

What was he to do? When he'd made this promise, he'd not in a million years have believed she would lay claim to it. She abhorred the notion of a coerced betrothal! She'd admitted this to him more than once!

And yet, he had, in fact, made this promise. Was she really going to claim him for her husband this way? That did not sound at all like Natalie Spencer.

And then it dawned on him. Oh, Hell, she believed, still, that she could save him! He did not want her to save him! He wished to save *her!*

And then as the significance of her other news struck him, he bolted out of his chair.

William Castleton was not his father.

Finding himself at the liquor cabinet, Garrett poured himself a generous amount of scotch, sloshing some onto the floor in the process.

William Castleton is not my father.

What of the earldom? He would not accept the title under false pretense. But who else could claim it? He needed to notify the regent.

Did he even want it? Hell, he'd not wanted it to begin with, but now…after working with the tenants, making them promises…

In a fit of frustration, he swept the piles of paper covering his desk onto the floor.

Seizing the scotch again, he ignored his glass and drank directly from the bottle. As the alcohol warmed his insides, the thought reverberated, once again, in his head.

William Castleton is not my father.

This time the words were a balm to his soul.

But he could not rely upon an old woman's memory. He would write a letter of his own. This one to the Earl of Ravensdale, and then later, he would write to his solicitors. If this new information voided his inheritance, then so be it. He was wealthy in his own right. But a part of him would be saddened. The estate was the only home he'd ever known. And he'd already launched extensive plans to rebuild it. The tenants were just now coming around to accept him. They were coming to trust his words and assurances. Where would they be without an earl to see to their prosperity?

And what of Natalie and this apparent betrothal she demanded? If he was not the earl, then what was he? Who was he?

Good God, what a Pandora's box this was. Leave it to Natalie to throw it open with gleeful abandon.

Garrett threw his head back and closed his eyes. And then, unbidden, long suppressed memories wedged their way into his racing thoughts. Memories of the childhood he'd suffered at the hands of the man he'd believed to be his father. As though they'd occurred only yesterday, the insults, the beatings, the long hours he'd been forced to spend memorizing scriptures, jolted him into the past. Garrett wondered if the earl had suspected his son was fathered by another man.

He must have!

But who was this other man? He wished he'd listened more closely when Lady Sheffield had reminisced about him, the man she claimed to be his father. He wished he'd looked closer at the drawings.

But they were still in the trunk—here, at Maple Hall. He wanted to see them. Standing, he strode purposefully to the kitchen. Mrs. Hampden directed him to the attic, where the items now rested.

Taking the steps two at a time, his sense of urgency grew. He needed answers. Would examining the drawings give him any?

Throwing back the drapes at one end of the room, he allowed the sunlight to illuminate the clean and tidy space. His gaze found the trunk easily, and a shudder passed through him as he remembered the last time he'd opened it.

He'd nearly lost her forever. Shaking his head, he pushed back the morbid thought and lifted the lid.

Natalie's blood tore at him as he gazed down at the stained and torn wedding gown. He pushed it aside and then scratched around the bottom of the container to collect the papers. As he pulled them together forming a stack, an envelope fell to the floor at his feet.

On the envelope, no name had been written, only the words *My Dearest Child* in feminine, flowing letters. It was the same handwriting his mother used to sign her name on her paintings.

My Dearest Child. That was him. Another letter!

Garrett closed the trunk and sat down upon its lid. Reaching down, he discarded the drawings for the moment and lifted the second ominous letter he'd held in his hands within the past hour. He broke the seal and took a deep breath.

To my child,

I do not know you yet. You are still in my womb. If you are reading this now, then you have reached your majority and are either a strapping young man or a lovely young woman, possibly married by now. I hope to watch you grow but am doubtful I will survive childbirth. I am focusing all my strength upon bringing you into this world, but I despair of having enough for both of us.

Nonetheless, I cannot go to the grave without making the truth of your parentage known to you. God help me, Lord Hawthorne is not your father. I do not believe he suspects this fact, and I am hopeful he treats you as he would a child of his own.

Please do not hate me. Your real papa, Mr. Arthur Winters, and I had every intention of marrying, even before we knew of your existence. Your father was charming, tender of heart, well-read, and clever, but alas, he lacked ruthlessness and was killed in a duel. I was forced to marry Lord Hawthorne a few days afterward.

I hope this information is not a burden, but I have concerns that Lord Hawthorne is not of sound mind. He frightens me, and I want you to be able to face your life without believing you are blood relations with one such as he. I am so very sorry I have not been with you for your childhood. I pray protection over you.

But above all else, I want you to know that you are loved. Please know of my love for you and that of your papa's so you may have something of us with you forever.

Find happiness, my dear,

Your mama,

Lady Cordelia Castleton

It was true, then.

Garrett folded the letter, replaced it in the envelope, and gathered the drawings together. He didn't waste any more time in the stifling room. He needed to get outside. This was too much. He felt as though ghosts were speaking to him from the past—ghosts he'd believed to be long gone.

Upon reaching the main floor, Garrett stashed the papers in his desk and, almost without thinking, struck out for the stables. There, he breathed in the familiar smells of hay and animal as he strode to Rumble. His faithful mount welcomed him with a bob of his head. Seeking comfort for himself, Garrett stroked the coarse black hair of his horse's neck and back. Rumble reached around his head to nuzzle him. Burying his face against Rumble, Garrett absorbed the horse's calm. After a few moments, he finally saddled up. They would ride. He didn't know where or for how long, but together they would ride.

And then later, he would deal with it all.

Chapter Twenty-Nine

After ten days, Garrett had not written to Natalie with any sort of personal response. He had contacted her father, however, with legal questions and to obtain further verification of his parentage. He'd also promised her father to discuss marriage contracts once in London. It was her father who informed her that Garrett had scheduled the wedding and the banns were set to be read.

But she had no idea as to what Garrett was feeling, what he was thinking. And the not-knowing was killing her! Did he hate her for this? Would he follow through with the wedding? Of course, he would, but really, *would he*? She and her mother had addressed and sent hundreds of invitations, ordered masses of flowers, a fashionable gown, and planned a lavish wedding breakfast. The gown would be altered after a final fitting once they arrived in London.

All the planning in the world couldn't ensure a happy marriage if he resented her now.

Did he miss her, even the tiniest little bit?

She missed *him.*

How had she come to rely upon his friendship, his nearness, in so short a time as they'd had together? How had it occurred that his presence in her life gave it new meaning? She wished he would write to her. She wished even more that he would visit her at Raven's

Park before summer's end.

He did neither.

Was he punishing her? That must be his reason. He must be very angry with her. She'd taken away his choices—his choices and his freedom. Oh, but she hoped she was doing the right thing, for both of their sakes.

When the time came to leave for London, Natalie's emotions were as brittle as a dried rose. Climbing into the carriage with her mother, she glanced down to see her hand shaking. She could barely untie her bonnet. And they had not even left Raven's Park yet.

They could have completed the journey in one day but had decided to travel at a leisurely pace and stop for the night at an inn. It was an unnecessary delay, but Natalie had been unable to convince her mother to forgo it.

Darlington and Stone were already in London, having left the week before, but Father and Peter rode mounts alongside the carriage. Natalie suspected Peter would become impatient and ride ahead before they passed through the local village. The large entourage of coaches carrying baggage and servants followed at an even slower pace. Oh, if only one could fly!

Over the past few weeks, she had became more and more anxious to speak with Garrett, her fiancé. Good Lord, with over three hundred invitations having been sent out, she hoped to goodness that she did, in fact, have a fiancé!

****

A week in London, and still, Natalie hadn't heard one word from her betrothed. She knew he'd signed the marriage contracts with her father, but he had not bothered yet to wait upon her. And a lady could not call upon a gentleman. She wasn't a harridan, for goodness sake! And she most certainly would not go to his home in search of the proposal she'd hoped he'd make officially, once and for all.

The first event of the Little Season was nearing, and as each day passed, Natalie's anxiety grew into nothing short of terror. She hoped it would all be worth it.

She could do nothing but wait.

****

As had become her daily ritual, after taking breakfast, Natalie expelled some of her restlessness by pacing the length of the room while her mother perused the gossip columns. Since arriving, she'd been unable to sit still long enough to read a book, or attempt any sewing projects, or focus on anything else, really, except for her tenuous situation.

On this particular morning, she'd twisted her handkerchief into a nearly unrecognizable knot, when Mr. Thomas, the butler, stepped in to announce an unscheduled caller. Her mother glanced up, startled, when Natalie squealed in delight. The familiar face she saw behind the butler was a person she'd not expected to see so soon.

She had missed Lilly, now the Duchess of Cortland, more than she'd realized. Dressed in an impeccable morning gown of mint green and sky blue, her dear friend wore a jaunty hat atop her elegantly coiled platinum hair.

"Lilly!" Natalie rushed over to her friend, holding both hands out to grasp hers.

Lilly smiled and held Natalie's hands in hers. "I

have missed you so much! When Aunt Eleanor told me you were in town, I came right over!" She squeezed Natalie's hands warmly. "The duke and I have just arrived back from our honeymoon, but my thoughts have been with you since the day we left."

"Please, sit down, Your Grace," Natalie's mother invited, using the title that ought to have been bestowed upon her own daughter. Nonetheless, she spoke in polite and welcoming tones. "Your wedding travels were pleasant and uneventful then?"

Lilly nodded and then went on to tell of some of the places she and Cortland had traveled to. She appeared to be so very happy. She moved with a lightness that hadn't been there before. In fact, she glowed.

"But that is not why I have imposed upon you this morning. I have come because my aunt informed me of your, er…situation." And then looking at Natalie with a gleam in her eye, she added, "It is true, then? You are to marry Lord Hawthorne, and I am to have *two* new cousins?"

Natalie hadn't considered the familial connection between Lilly and Garrett. But of course, if Lady Sheffield was Garrett's aunt and Lilly's aunt, then the two of them would be cousins. "You are not related to Lady Eleanor through Lord Sheffield?"

Lilly smiled warmly. "Lady Sheffield is my late mother's older sister. Lord Hawthorne's father was their brother. He was the middle child. So, yes, we are first cousins! You can imagine my astonishment when I read my aunt's letter."

"Are you acquainted with Lord Hawthorne, with Garrett?" Natalie asked the question cautiously. For the older earl had attempted to *kill* Lilly. He'd kidnapped Lilly, but she'd managed to get away. She'd knocked over a lantern filled with fuel while climbing out of a second-story window at Maple Hall. She'd been lucky to escape unharmed. It was why the estate came to be in ruins.

Natalie placed her hand on Lilly's arm. Lilly had been so very brave! She'd been so strong! Natalie felt ashamed for her own self-pitying thoughts of late, considering.

Lilly's smile disappeared for a moment. "Despite all that occurred with his father, with the old earl and myself, I have never spoken with his heir. I never thought there would be any reason to. But he had nothing to do with what Hawthorne tried to do to Michael and me. He is his own person, and unless I discover anything to contradict this, I am happy to meet him, to welcome him into our lives—if he wishes it."

Natalie tilted her head sideways. "Does it upset you greatly? Knowing your cousin was raised by…a murderer? Because I must tell you Garrett is a most honorable gentleman. He has proven this to me on numerous occasions."

"It did, initially, but my aunt has convinced me of his good character. My sister and parents have passed on, and I believed Glenda and Aunt Sheffield were my only living relations. I am pleased to have found more family."

"So with Glenda being married to Joseph, you are not only to be my sister-in-law, but my cousin-in-law as well. Would you think me a dolt for not having considered this connection before this morning?"

Natalie's mother tugged at the bell pull. "It is

nearing nuncheon, Your Grace. Will you stay for sandwiches and tea?"

Lilly turned her attention to include Lady Ravensdale. "I'd be delighted. But what I wish to ask you is what Michael—*His Grace*"—Lilly corrected herself with a blush—"and I can do to help." Looking back to Natalie, she explained. "I understand there was something of a situation earlier this summer? It sounds harrowing, but you look to be well. Are you completely recovered then?"

Natalie summoned a faint smile, as her nerves, which had disappeared for the last few minutes, made a clamoring return. "I am fine now, Lilly, but Lord Hawthorne faces a few social hurdles. And if he cannot manage to clear them, I'm not certain my groom will show up for our wedding.

"Tell me what I can do. I am a *duchess* now, ladies, as you well know! And that must be good for something!"

At these words, Natalie's mother leaned forward. "As a matter of fact…"

****

Through the post, Lord Ravensdale had confirmed to Garrett that his father was Mr. Arthur Winters. He and Lady Ravensdale, having a close relationship with Lady Sheffield, had suspected this for years. The events surrounding his birth and then later, the uncanny resemblance between Garrett and the late Mr. Arthur Winters validated their suspicions. Natalie's father wrote to him that Mr. Winters had been a man of gentle birth, with no claims to any title or nobility. This information served as confirmation of that which Garrett had already come to believe as truth.

Garrett himself had examined more closely the drawings stored in the trunk. And yes, he saw a strong resemblance. He was surprised he'd not noticed it initially. He was coming to terms with the reality that William Castleton had not fathered him. His own chances of siring a healthy child, as far as he was aware, were the same as any other man. He could partake of his marriage bed with no concerns in that area.

Garrett also received word from both his solicitors and the crown, with their determination regarding Garrett's claim to the title. Both assured him that his position as the Earl of Hawthorne was secure. They based the declaration upon "marital paternity presumption." The letter from the crown explained that "a child born during a marriage is to be considered the offspring of the husband." Even a child born of a wife's adulterous affair would be recognized as a legitimate child of the marriage. His solicitor explained in the letter that this rule recognized a husband could rebut the marital presumption only by proving his impotence or his absence from the country. Since the late Lord Hawthorne had never rebutted Garrett's claim as his son, then no one could question his inheritance. Even if the fact became common knowledge, the law would continue to recognize Garrett as the legal heir. At this point, there was no long-lost relative willing to step forward and challenge his ascendency.

Garrett presumed it would not be convenient to find somebody else willing to take on the rebuilding of Maple Hall. Might as well be himself as anyone else.

And so he would retain the title about which he'd grown to have very mixed feelings.

Upon arriving in London, Garrett went directly to Burtis Hall, one of the more imposing manors in Mayfield. He'd visited Ravensdale before, but only on business, and with much less at stake. He and the earl were to sort out the marriage contracts.

Unless of course, Natalie had come to her senses and decided to call the entire thing off.

Each time he expressed his concerns, they fell on deaf ears. When he sat down with Ravensdale that morning, the earl merely lit a cigar and shrugged. "Nothing to do but wait and see." His future father-in-law showed a surprising lack of concern.

Garrett felt as though he were falling off a cliff.

In drawing up the marriage contract, Lord Ravensdale insisted on including the same dowry he'd promised the Duke of Cortland. Garrett agreed, only so long as the majority was put into trust for Natalie and their children. He would not take her property. The earl did not argue this point. The dowry encompassed considerable wealth, and Garrett refused to benefit in any way, monetarily, from this marriage.

After agreeing upon, and signing the contracts, Garrett had no legitimate reason to wait around. The ladies had gone out that morning. They had left earlier for some fittings on Bond Street and whatnot. Lord Ravensdale jovially slapped Garrett on the back and told him that with women, there was no telling how long they would be out. "Get used to it, my boy," he said, walking Garrett to the door.

Garrett had hoped to spend a few moments alone, in Natalie's company. He'd not spoken with her for over a month. He wanted to behold her smile, hear her laugh. And then he would give her a tongue-lashing for planning their very public farce of a wedding, which promised to be the social debacle of the decade. He still wasn't sure what to think of it all. What the hell were the Spencers thinking allowing Natalie to go forward with such plans? Would it not have been better for them to tie the knot in some obscure church in the country?

He was going to marry her.

It still seemed unreal.

Since arriving in London, Garrett had spent as little time in public as possible. He attended his duties at Parliament and then usually returned to his townhouse. He did not attempt to visit White's, Brooks', or any other club. On the three occasions he'd endeavored to visit his betrothed, she had been away from home. Apparently, wedding apparel required a lady to make several visits to her *modiste*. As usual, he turned to work for a distraction.

He'd contracted construction of a new manor to begin as soon as possible. There were a few months of warm weather left, and he did not wish to delay. He was also considering some new investment possibilities. Turning his attention to such details and decisions created a convenient, albeit temporary diversion. It allowed him a sense of control over his business affairs, at least. He'd long abandoned any semblance of control over his personal affairs.

Just as he was putting away some reports, his butler entered the room to announce a guest.

The Duchess of Cortland?

Garrett directed the butler to escort Her Grace into the drawing room where he would attend to her shortly. What could possibly be the reason for such a visit? In a vague memory, he recalled she had been a friend of

Natalie's and then married Natalie's betrothed. Whatever the reason, Garrett found himself both annoyed and intrigued. Was she to give him a piece of her mind for daring to marry such a lady as Lady Natalie Spencer? Pinching the bridge of his nose, Garrett prepared himself for an unpleasant encounter.

He donned his jacket and checked his cravat. Inspecting himself in a conveniently placed looking glass, he then stepped into the front drawing room. He'd had no cause to use it before today. Glancing around, he was pleased to find the room tidy and fresh. The servants who'd chosen to stay on after his father's death cared for the townhouse impeccably.

A woman, presumably the Duchess of Cortland, sat primly on a brocaded love seat. She was not tight-lipped, and she did not appear to be full of reprimand. She was, in fact, very pretty. She looked quite pleased with the world and herself. Of course, Cortland would not have married a homely woman.

"Cousin Garrett?" she asked tentatively, "If I may be so bold?" She smiled and actually appeared a little nervous. The duchess, nervous? And then he registered her words.

Cousin?

Garrett bowed formally. "I am Garrett Castleton. As to the other, perhaps. Stranger things have happened lately."

"Please do sit down," the duchess implored him. "Lady Sheffield is my aunt."

Her aunt…?

Befuddled initially, it took a moment for him to recall that, although Natalie referred to Lady Sheffield as her aunt, the woman was, in fact, her godmother.

But Lady Sheffield was the duchess's aunt, in truth.

Her Grace went on to explain, in detail, the family connection. Although a beautiful woman, the duchess aroused not even a stirring of attraction in him. She was his cousin?

She was his cousin.

"And so we are family," Garrett said. Ah, hell, but this was awkward. He'd not made enough small talk in his lifetime for this sort of thing. Should he discuss the weather? What was the social etiquette for conversing with a lost relation? But then he realized he need not worry. His newfound female relation had no such qualms and went about insisting he attend an event she and the duke were hosting. A water party to launch the Little Season. He *must* attend with the Spencers. She would accept no excuses. It seemed he had no choice.

Feeling as though this just might be the beginning of the end, he agreed. Natalie would see the impossibility of his social position when the guests at Cortland's party openly shunned him. He hoped she would not receive the same treatment.

And then, as Garrett escorted the duchess out the front entrance, she placed her hand over his.

"I am so pleased for Natalie—and for you." She spoke softly, but then her voice took on greater conviction. "I will not allow the two of you to be anything but *ecstatically* happy. You see, I attribute Natalie's intrepidity to my own happiness. She is a courageous and generous lady. And now she is to marry my very own cousin. Thank you so much for your promise to attend. I am most eager to see the two of you, together, at the party." And with that, she turned and a footman handed her onto a very elegant crested carriage. A duchess indeed, and his cousin at that!

Chapter Thirty

Two days later, Garrett arrived at Burtis Hall braced for an uncomfortable and humbling afternoon. He followed the butler like a man headed for the gallows, into the drawing room, where Lord Ravensdale and his four sons awaited the womenfolk.

Joseph, recently returned from his wedding journey, looked utterly pleased with himself in his newfound connubial bliss. Garrett reached out a hand and offered his congratulations. The fresh-faced husband was relaxed and happy whereas the remaining men were gripped in a slow hum of tension. Of course, they were aware of the unpleasantness that lay ahead of them this evening.

Most likely they were bracing themselves for Natalie's reintroduction as well. All the troops had been rallied, and the Spencer boys were prepared for battle. Lord Ravensdale offered Garrett a brandy, which he refused. He would go through this afternoon sober.

"Beautiful weather we're having." Stone broke the silence and grinned. "One would think if the sky were falling, there would at least be a few clouds hanging about."

Peter and Joseph Spencer laughed out loud. Darlington scowled.

Garrett merely shook his head at his friend and tugged at his cravat.

"Nothing to worry about." The earl didn't look nearly as concerned as his sons. "I'm considering investing in a few ships, Hawthorne. Tomorrow, perhaps you'd come down to the docks with me to look one of them over. I always appreciate your sound opinion."

"Of course." How could the man be thinking about business today? Perhaps it was a clever excuse to lure him down to the docks and throw him into the river.

The gentlemen made stilted conversation until they heard a rustling of silk and taffeta in the foyer.

Along with a hint of feminine perfume, the women brought with them smiles and laughter, carefully descending the stairs in their afternoon finery. Behind Lady Ravensdale, a young girl immediately attached herself to the arm of Mr. Joseph Spencer. He'd been informed this was the duchess's niece or stepdaughter? Was she, too, then some relation to him? Before Garrett could turn his attention to Natalie, introductions were made. Ah, yes, Mrs. Joseph Spencer was a second cousin of his.

Finally, finally, he could turn to Natalie. Although beautiful, as always, she looked pale and drawn. Not exactly the blushing bride, Garrett thought, feeling his heart drop slightly. Oh, but she did look lovely. He took her hand and raised it to his lips. He could not take his eyes off her. It had been too long. Emotions he'd denied for several weeks came roaring to life.

Dear God, for but a moment he could pretend they had a future! He would spend his life loving her and society could hang!

"Good afternoon, my lady."

She smiled and curtsied prettily. "My lord." Her

smile was shy, but holding her hand in his, he watched as the sparkle he loved appeared in her eyes.

As the two of them gazed longingly at each other, he realized the room had become awkward and quiet.

Lady Ravensdale saved the moment. "Are we ready to depart then?"

Three carriages waited outside. Garrett had brought his own and led his betrothed and her parents toward it. After handing his future mother-in-law, and then Natalie in, he waited for Lord Ravensdale to board before climbing in himself. Ah, Natalie sat facing the back of the carriage. Alone. He was to be allowed to sit beside her then.

A vision in a cream-colored dress with a lace overlay of gold and light blue threads, she looked stunning. Everything looked beautiful on her, even that pink confection she'd worn the day she fell in the lake.

Her hair, twisted and braided, was tucked under a tiny hat which matched the lace perfectly. A few escaping curls invited him to caress the soft skin of her neck and shoulders—with his eyes, of course. When he took his seat on the leather bench, he allowed his hand to rest alongside his leg. Her own hand was hidden, lost in the folds of her dress. Until it wasn't.

She wrapped cold fingers around his.

He squeezed them lightly.

Lady Ravensdale spoke, piercing the clanging silence. "The duke has hired a steam-powered yacht for this party. I understand it's one of the largest of its kind, all very modern. Everyone in town will be in attendance." Eyeing Garrett, she added, "Should be quite a squeeze."

Garrett nodded. "Yes, I have considered this

possibility." Natalie's hand took on some of his warmth.

"Lilly looked so happy when she visited," Natalie spoke up. With a wicked smile, she added, "True love apparently."

Garrett knew Lord Ravensdale would not wish to hear of this. He wondered that the relationship between the two men was not strained.

Lady Ravensdale smoothed the moment by taking her husband's hand. "True love has its benefits." She smiled over at the earl. Garrett allowed himself a glance at Natalie. Her gaze caught his, and she blushed prettily. He would enjoy the time he could spend with her now. For he'd no idea how long, or short, a time they would have before she put a halt to everything. Or if they did go through with the wedding, how long it would be before she began to resent being tied to him.

He needed to speak with her alone but not today. Well, perhaps afterward. Perhaps everything would have revealed itself then.

A long line of phaetons and open barouches inched their way toward the end of the dock. It was crowded, both with other vehicles and mingling guests waiting to board the yacht. Several partygoers, holding flutes of champagne in their hands, had already stepped onto the vessel and lined the rails.

Arriving at the cordoned off entrance, they pulled to a halt, and the coach bounced as the outriders and drivers jumped off.

It was then that Garrett felt a tremor run through the lady beside him. She was not so confident as she'd like him to believe. She was simply being brave.

Knowing he would do whatever necessary to

protect her, he squeezed her hand one more time but was then forced to release it. The footmen put down the step and the four of them climbed out.

The earl and countess would lead the way to the entrance. Behind them were all of Natalie's brothers and young Spencer's wife. Feeling as though they were going into a battle of sorts, Garrett tucked Natalie's hand around his sleeve and escorted her toward the throng of invitees.

She held her chin high and met the eyes of several ladies and gentlemen as they edged forward. Fearlessly clutching Garrett's arm, she ought to have instead removed herself from his side for her own self-preservation. Not Natalie, though. She made polite conversation and smiled brightly at everybody they met. Garrett nodded and added his own greetings.

Although a few eyes looked past him coldly, most, surprisingly, met his gaze. And then as they stepped on board, Garrett recognized the petite platinum-haired lady who'd visited him two days before. Her husband, the Duke of Cortland, stood beside her protectively as they greeted each of their guests. When Garrett stepped forward, the duchess introduced him to her husband as her long-lost cousin. Although the duke seemed to size him up critically, the couple's welcome seemed genuine.

"Welcome to the family, Hawthorne." The clean-cut elegantly attired gentleman shook Garrett's hand. "My wife speaks highly of you. Felicitations on your engagement." With a glance at Natalie, his eyes twinkled a bit. "My compliments on your choice of fiancée."

Garrett placed a possessive hand over Natalie's.

Natalie smiled and laughed at the duke's comment. "This one shall not get off as easily as you did, Your Grace," she said fondly. A few nearby onlookers looked shocked at her reference to her own broken engagement.

The duke laughed and winked at Garrett. "I should hope not," was all he said.

Garrett and Natalie moved on so as not to hold up the reception line. "That wasn't so bad, now, was it?" Natalie whispered.

He tilted his head to hear her and let a smile play about his mouth.

He didn't answer as they worked their way through the crowd to an open section of the railing. They stood together in an odd sort of silence until the engines roared to life, propelling the vessel away from shore. Vibrant scenery rolled past them as they picked up speed. Trees and shrubs blazed a myriad of colors, ranging from greens to golds to bright reds. The lawns spread out like a giant carpet, and autumn flowers bloomed, mostly chrysanthemums. Several mansions backed up to the river along this section. A slight breeze kept the sunshine from being overly warm.

The two of them stood alone, together, watching the passing landscape quietly, until Natalie broke the silence. "Are you so very, terribly angry with me then?"

But he was! He had been. Where was his anger now? Had he completely forgotten it after spending a few moments in her presence? He turned his back on the passing scenery and faced her fully. She looked sheepish and yet pleased with herself. How had the duchess described Natalie to him? Intrepid. That was the word she'd used. It fitted the minx perfectly.

"Would it do any good?" he asked. She opened her eyes in feigned innocence, and so he changed the subject. "I have been by your father's house several times to wait upon you, but you have been away each time. I was beginning to think you might be avoiding me…"

Natalie didn't take his bait. Appearing contrite, she bit her lip and then looked into his eyes. "I know you did not want any of this."

Garrett shrugged. In that moment, he found her stubbornness and manipulation not so very problematic after all. In fact, if not for her willfulness, he would not now be standing beside her, floating along on a beautiful day with a glass of champagne in his hand. Ignoring the somber nature of their conversation, he grinned. "You look lovelier than ever today." His gaze fell upon her lips. "It seems you must be getting on well with Sissy, your new maid."

Natalie touched her hair in a self-conscious motion. Tilting her head, she laughed. "Oh, we are." With that, she launched into a rush of words as to how Tinsdale was managing as sole guardian of Baby Bear and how delighted she'd been to see Lilly again. Garrett enjoyed listening. She glowed with warmth and sunshine after a lifetime of weighted darkness. It would be dark again when this was all over. Perhaps not forever, but for a long time. He did not anticipate it.

He was yet to believe they did not have insurmountable impediments in their path. But he pushed these thoughts away.

He informed her of Marcus's progress, of his plans to rebuild Maple Hall, and even a few bills he was considering that were to be presented in Parliament.

Her questions showed keen intelligence. When a chime rang, signifying a toast, Garrett was surprised at how much he'd been talking. Their absorption in each other was scandalous, really. Not what they needed, but he had missed her.

He'd yearned just to be with her.

They both paused and turned to listen to the duke as he commanded his guests' attention. Natalie's hand found his own, hidden again by the folds of her gown. Unexpected warmth filled his heart at the connection.

"My dear friends." The duke's voice rang out clearly. All eyes focused on him. The man possessed a very strong presence. "My duchess and I, first and foremost, would like to thank all of you for joining us in celebration." The duke paused and looked around at the now-curious onlookers. "For, yes, celebrations are in order. You see, my lovely duchess, her aunt, Lady Sheffield, and our niece, now Mrs. Joseph Spencer, have been reunited with a relation who until recently was unknown to them. They are delighted to have discovered their cousin and nephew, Garrett Castleton, the Earl of Hawthorne."

All eyes swung toward Garrett and Natalie.

"My duchess wished to celebrate the occasion by bringing our dearest friends together to join us in welcoming him to our family. Join us," he commanded, "in welcoming Lord Hawthorne and his lovely fiancée, Lady Natalie Spencer. For a cousin of my wife's is a cousin of mine." This last, the duke said almost threateningly. "And so I propose, as the summer season comes to an end, a toast to new connections, be it by marriage or be it by blood." He lifted his glass toward Natalie and Garrett with a martial gleam in his eyes.

"New connections," several of the guests repeated with raised glasses. The duke did not lift the glass to his lips until all other glasses were raised. It seemed a line had been drawn. Watching Natalie from behind the rim of his own, Garrett raised one eyebrow questioningly at his fiancée.

What have you done?

Taking a sip of the sparkling drink, the corners of her lips tilted upwards.

It seemed they had more support than he'd realized.

Chapter Thirty-One

Throughout the next few weeks, Natalie and Garrett endured the diligent eyes of the ton, watching them, everywhere they went. The high sticklers of society, it seemed, were holding their breath, waiting for Natalie or Garrett to step out of line and give them full right to rain down their judgment upon the couple. But until then, no one dared censure the earl and his flighty fiancée. For some reason, London's most disgraceful pair had been warmly embraced by a few of the *ton's* most powerful members. It was difficult to understand how the Duke of Cortland could act so kindly toward her. She'd jilted him, after all, had she not?

With mixed feelings of excitement and sheer terror, Natalie, her mother, and Aunt Eleanor whirled about from one event to another. On a few occasions, they were escorted by Lord Hawthorne and her father. But it would be unseemly to appear to be living in his pocket. It was best that she remain close to her chaperones. And although worse than her punishment last spring, she dared not take any missteps. This time she had everything to lose.

Natalie celebrated one happy event amidst it all. For one of the events they all attended was the wedding of Miss Abigail Wright to the Duke of Monfort, no less! Taking full credit for their courtship, she wished another duchess well and assumed she'd learn of that story another time, perhaps.

And all the while, like a storm on the horizon, her own nuptials loomed nearer and nearer.

What was Garrett thinking? What was he feeling? At the water party, he'd denied being angry with her. He'd also told her it didn't matter either way. She wished she could feel as certain of his love now as she had this summer. She *had* felt certain then, but only after they'd been alone together a great deal. Everything felt different now. They'd not talked, *really talked*, since she'd left Maple Hall with her parents.

And she was to marry him.

In one week.

In five days.

Tomorrow.

This morning.

Oh, Lord, the day was finally here. Her wedding day. God willing, Garrett would present himself at the church on time.

God willing, he would present himself, period.

She'd die if he abandoned her at the altar.

She'd rather undergo physical torture than for him to be late.

Hundreds of guests had RSVP'd, and a large wedding breakfast awaited at Burtis Hall. Natalie's parents had decided that, after spending the wedding night in town, the bride and groom would remove themselves for a few weeks to London Hills, Natalie's dower property. It was assumed they would return to Maple Hall for the winter. There was also some discussion of a Christmas house party at Summers Park, the Duke of Cortland's principal seat. It would be a family gathering. Yes, Garrett was family now.

Wedding day nerves attacked her with a vengeance. One moment, tearful sentimentality engulfed her, and the next, nausea-inducing terror. She would do well to make it down the aisle without shattering into a million pieces. She wished she could act with the same confidence she'd had when originally undertaking this plan.

Just as Sissy finished pinning a charming little bonnet into Natalie's hair, Lady Ravensdale entered the room. She'd visited Natalie the night before to reveal to her only daughter the details of the physical act that would be expected on her wedding night. Natalie had nodded and acted as though it was all new information, but in truth her mother's words were much less informative than her experiences with Garrett.

Natalie had no dread of her wedding night. She simply dreaded the wedding itself.

This morning, her mother was tearful yet happy.

"Oh, my darling," she said with a sigh, catching her daughter's eyes in the mirror. "You are going to be the most beautiful bride ever to marry at St. George's!"

With that Natalie scrunched her nose, marring the effect of serene beauty the veil on her bonnet helped to create. "Mama, I am terrified. What if I was wrong? What if he does not love me? He will hate me forever knowing I've trapped him. For that's what I did, Mama, I trapped him."

Her mother turned Natalie away from the mirror and took her hands between her own. "A man such as your fiancé would not allow himself to be trapped. Lord Hawthorne is marrying you because he wants to." She tilted her head and gave Natalie a watery smile. "I've seen how he looks at you, my darling. He loves you. You are the best thing that man has ever known, and he knows it. He is not a fool." Seeing her tears form, her mother moved Natalie's veil aside and with a handkerchief, dabbed at the corners of her eyes. "Now, we don't want to be late. I will see you at the church." With that, she kissed her on the cheek and then left Natalie alone with her thoughts.

And then her father appeared to escort her downstairs and out to the carriage. Everything was moving along as planned. With lightning speed.

****

Considering the events of the past several weeks, Garrett ought not to have been surprised when he stepped out of the vestibule near the altar to see the church bursting at the seams. There were, even, several guests left standing near the back. Garrett pulled at his cravat. Marcus had tied it much tighter today than usual. Ah, yes, Marcus took his job very seriously.

His dedicated valet, in fact, had insisted Garrett dress in the latest formal wedding attire, with white breeches, a silver waistcoat, and a silver and blue jacket. Garrett felt conspicuous. He would have been much more at ease in his normal black attire and a pair of riding boots.

When he went to tug at his cravat once again, Stone, his best man, leaned in and whispered, "You're going to ruin the knot." His friends voice rumbled with more than a hint of laughter.

Garrett suppressed a growl. "There will come a day when we trade places, my friend, and then you shall know the feeling."

Stone chuckled.

And then a murmur rose at the back of the church.

She was here. A hush fell over the sanctuary, and then the music trumpeted, signifying the beginning of the ceremony. The vision at the end of the aisle glowed. Carrying yellow roses, she wore a dress made up of golds and white.

His breath caught. Natalie was going through with it. His bride. She was beautiful, courageous, the light of his life, and it seemed that all would be well after all. The sky wasn't falling, and the earth had not collapsed upon itself. A warmth unlike anything he'd known blossomed inside him at the stunning epiphany.

Everything was going to be all right.

He was in love and marrying the woman of his dreams. How had this happened? When had everything fallen into place so perfectly? And how was it he was only just now realizing this?

His eyes caught hers as she drew nearer to the front of the large cathedral on her father's arm. She appeared a little pale, more delicate than usual. Her cornflower blue eyes were large in her face. They looked uncertain as she met his gaze.

Until Garrett smiled at her.

In that smile, he allowed all the love he felt at that moment to overflow from his heart. Watching him, she stumbled slightly. Her father caught her so that it was hardly noticeable. Garrett loved her. He loved her.

Ah, yes. I love her.

The bishop began speaking, and all Garrett managed to think of was how very lucky he was to have been saved by Lady Natalie Spencer. He would spend his life doing all he could to bring her happiness. He would take her abroad, on the travels she'd missed out on this summer. While the manor was rebuilt, he would show her some of the most beautiful places in England and on the continent. He would take her to Italy, to Spain, hell, even to India. He would show her the world! And then when the construction and furnishing at Maple Hall were all completed, they would return, and they would begin a family. And he would cherish her.

He felt like a groom.

****

Stepping into the church, Natalie nearly collapsed in relief at the sight of her fiancé standing at the end of the aisle.

She was also glad to see her brothers were not lined up behind him with pistols pointed at his head.

If he showed, she had half expected he would be attired in his normal unrelieved blacks. And although he looked handsome enough in those, she was oh, so pleased to see him dressed for this occasion. He looked more handsome than any man she'd ever known.

His chiseled features were strong and sturdy, his eyes honest and true. As she stepped toward him, holding onto her father with one hand and her bouquet in the other, her doubts returned, for he looked grim.

Her feet felt leaden as she approached the altar.

And then he smiled at her.

Not a wry smile, or a condescending smile, or even a smile of laughter. She'd seen all of those over the past few weeks as they'd attended balls and parties and all sorts of *ton* events together. This smile was different.

This smile spread a warmth from the top of her head, through her breasts, her abdomen, and down to her toes. This smile was one she'd not experienced before.

It was love.

The power of it nearly sent her toppling to the floor. Her father grasped her tightly, however, and kept her from making a fool of herself. She looked again into Garrett's eyes and marveled at what she saw. He looked as though the weight of the world had been lifted from him.

Leaving her father, she allowed Garrett to take her hand in his, and together they turned to face the bishop. Her senses hummed as she inhaled the scent of his masculine cologne and felt the warmth of him beside her. Her knees weakened in relief. She'd not been mistaken after all!

The priest spoke of how the two would become one. And she felt at one with him. The distance she'd felt before was gone. She felt as though she was in a dream, a wonderful dream, as he slipped the wedding band on her third finger. When he'd slid it all the way on, he lifted her hand to his lips and placed a kiss there as well. The congregation sighed, seeing such a sign of what was surely a love match.

And in the blink of an eye, they were man and wife.

Chapter Thirty-Two

By the time the newlyweds departed the large formal wedding breakfast, with kisses and hugs all around, the sun was high in the sky. The weather held all the promises of an Indian summer day.

Garrett helped Natalie into his elegant town coach, and they waved together as the driver signaled the horses. Natalie sat beside her husband with his arm draped behind her. They were alone.

Finally.

As the carriage drove away from the throngs of well-wishers, Garrett reached across her and closed the curtains.

And then his lips were on hers, and his arms clasped about her fiercely. Pausing only to whisper endearments, he gasped her name in between kisses. "Natalie," he said, "my dearest, my love."

She could not hold back tears of happiness. With each drop that fell, Garrett kissed away the pain. He seemed to understand that she'd not been certain of anything. "You knew all along, didn't you?" But it wasn't really a question. Taking a few deep breaths and placing a hand upon her hair, he pressed her head into his chest. "You knew."

She pulled her head back and tilted it to gaze into his eyes. "Knew what?" she asked, knowing the answer. Knowing what he was going to say, but needing to hear it nonetheless.

"You knew that I loved you," he said. "You knew that I needed you...And you were courageous enough to face the world for both of us." His hands cradled her face as he looked at her in awe. "I have been such a fool, thinking all along that I was protecting you." He kissed her eyes, her forehead, her nose. "But in the future, dearest wife, will you allow me to do the protecting?"

With both hands in his hair, Natalie pulled his face down to resume where his kisses had left off. She inhaled the fragrance of his skin before flicking her tongue out to taste it. "Of course," she said. But she could not help herself. "My lord."

Garrett growled.

****

Upon arriving at his townhouse, Garrett informed the servants no formal dinner would be required that evening. He would ring for them when necessary. Without delay, he led his countess upstairs to the suite they were to share. He'd had the furnishings and wall covering in the main suites completely done over in the past month. It was not that they were outdated or worn, but they'd belonged to a history he would not claim.

He'd ordered her chamber made up of periwinkle blue, gold, and yellow. The brocaded walls were a subtle golden hue in an intricate floral design. The curtains at the windows and over the bed were light blue and yellow with a matching counterpane. The carpeting a darker blue. He'd done it especially for her.

Natalie's young maid awaited her, having arrived earlier with her mistress's trunks and clothing. Garrett bowed formally to his wife and told her he would return in half an hour's time. He could wait no longer.

Exiting through the adjoining sitting rooms, he entered into the chamber he'd made his own as well. With darker blue tones, it was luxuriously appointed, but simple, less opulent. William Castleton had decorated it far too ornately for his tastes, and Garrett felt pleased with the change. For the first time since inheriting, as he stepped into the room, he did not feel a clenching in his gut. He felt satisfaction that he'd taken control of what was now his.

Garrett heard Marcus in the bathing room drawing a bath. He welcomed the modern plumbing. Such a convenient luxury, he was sure Natalie would appreciate as well. Wasting no time, Garrett washed and changed into his dressing gown. The sun was still high in the sky, but he and Natalie were not going to wait.

Exactly thirty minutes from the time he'd left her, Garrett knocked twice on the door to Natalie's bedchamber before pushing it open. When he peeked around, he caught sight of her standing timidly before a mirror.

She was an angel—*his angel.*

His breath caught as he took in the silhouette of her long slim legs, rounded hips, trim waist, and sweet perfect breasts. Her unbound hair fell to her waist. Some of the strands matched the gold in the room perfectly. *She is mine.* When his eyes finally met hers, he was amused to see her all-too-familiar blush.

Looking over at Sissy, she said, "You may go."

Sissy smiled impishly and then, curtseying, disappeared from the room. Garrett closed the door to the sitting room behind him and walked barefoot across to her. At last.

As dismissive as she'd been with her mother, in regard to her wedding night, Natalie was surprised at the butterflies that attacked her when Garrett returned to the beautiful room he'd had prepared for her. Good heavens, but she felt nervous—a little frightened even. Garrett wore a black dressing gown of silk, tied at his waist. It reminded her of the night she'd gone to his room to apologize. Her eyes fell to his feet. He was barefoot. He did not wear any slippers.

Was he naked beneath his robe?

Most likely.

She swallowed hard and then met his gaze.

It burned with a combination of tenderness and passion. Ah, this must be how a husband looked at his wife. A tremor of satisfaction shot through her.

"Does it bother you?" she asked. "Living in this house, the house where he lived?" She gestured around her. They hadn't yet discussed her discovery of earlier this summer. And despite having decided to forgo dinner and retire to their bedchambers, she would stall him with some conversation.

Garrett glanced around the room and shrugged elegantly. "It did, at first." He looked so beautiful. He was newly shaved and his hair appeared to be freshly washed. When she caught a hint of his fragrance, her breath hitched and an ache settled in her breasts.

The warm look in his eyes told her he understood exactly what she was doing and was going to be patient. "I notified the crown that I am not the true son of William Castleton. My lawyer even searched the records for another heir." He grimaced. "There is no one. If I do not retain the title, it goes into escheat. The crown declared me the heir based on the fact that I was born while Hawthorne and my mother were legally married. With nobody to contest"—he shrugged—"it is mine if I wish to keep it."

Natalie moved away from the bed and then sat on the loveseat near the window. Patting the spot beside her, she gestured for him to sit with her. "And do you? Wish to keep it, that is?"

Joining her, he took one of her hands in both of his. "I had not thought that I would." He massaged her palm with his thumbs. "I'd thought to divest myself of everything that reminded me of him...but I have changed. Living at Maple Hall this summer, I have come to recognize a connection I have with it—a sense of responsibility for it. God knows it will cost a fortune to rebuild, but perhaps that is why I have been allowed to prosper. Perhaps I was destined to take over the land and add value to the estate, to my legacy." He smiled sheepishly at her. "For the families who have worked the land for generations. For the people of the village who depend upon it for their livelihood...For our children."

Natalie blushed. "You spent most of your childhood there," she said. "You have some good memories then?"

"I suppose I do." He lifted her hand to his lips and kissed it. "And this summer, I have had some success in obtaining the goodwill of the tenants. The tides appear to be turning. The estate can be prosperous. It *will* be prosperous again." He looked into her eyes. "I have you to thank for a great deal, my love. You believed in me, when I didn't believe in myself. You were so brave. You fought me. You fought *for me*."

"And I," she said, "am grateful to you as well." She lifted her free hand and placed it over his. "You loved me enough to set me free. You gave me something to fight for. You were not chosen by my father or my brothers. You were not handed to me on a silver platter. You gave me choices." She laughed shakily. "I have missed you so much, though."

He watched her with the intensity she relished. "I have realized something," he said. He had an odd look on his face as he dropped down on one knee before her.

"Oh, Garrett," she said. She would not cry. She would not.

His hands still grasping hers, Garret's gaze never wavered as he stared up at her. "Will you, my dearest Natalie…What is your middle name?" he asked with a frown. "How is it I do not know your middle name?"

"The bishop said it during the ceremony," Natalie teased.

Garrett became serious again. "I did not hear a word he said. I could only look at you in amazement. Amazement that you were marrying me, that you would take such a risk to be with me."

"Josephine," she said. "It is Josephine."

He paused, seemingly content to gaze into her eyes. And then, "Natalie Josephine Spencer, will you make me the happiest of men and consent to be my wife, the mother of my children, my countess?"

She released his hands and placed both of hers on the sides of his face. "Oh, Garrett, yes," she whispered. "And I have wanted to tell you something." It had bothered her for some time now. "When I met you in the park last spring, when I failed to speak to you and then ran away, do you remember?"

331

Furrowing his brows, Garrett nodded. "It is no matter, love, I understand. I understood then—"

"But no, you didn't. You thought I did not wish to speak with you. In fact, I did. But I was nearly late returning home, and my father had threatened to send me to Scotland if I didn't follow his rules. If you can imagine! He would not have, really, but I was in so much trouble already. I just wanted you to know that." Her eyes were earnest now. "I *wanted* to know you. Even then. I truly did."

"I was a brute," Garrett said with a tender smile.

Touching his lips, she nodded. "You were. But I just wanted you to know…"

"I do," he said against her fingertips. "And now…"

The next thing she knew, he placed one arm under her knees, another around her back, and lifted her into the air. He spun her around twice before laying her on the bed and climbing in next to her. And then his mouth covered hers.

The hunger that had gnawed at them both for so long unleashed itself at last.

The belt on his dressing gown loosened, and Natalie took advantage to let her hands roam over his chest freely. His skin felt warm and smooth and muscled. She combed her fingers through the black hairs on his chest as his hands caressed her, slowly, leisurely. Her arms, her waist, her thighs. He covered her with his body. She arched her back to be closer to him and he groaned.

Pushing himself up, he sat back on his knees and watched her. Why had he stopped?

Without looking away from her face, one of his hands trailed down her leg and then grasped the hem of her nightgown. He slid it up, past her knees, her hips, her shoulders. She raised her arms and allowed him to pull it over her head.

Completely naked, she ought to feel embarrassed. She ought to move her hands to cover the place between her legs, to cover her breasts. But she did not.

Instead, she removed *his* dressing gown.

He was hard contours where she was soft. As he moved to lie atop her, the muscles under his skin rippled. He urged her legs apart and settled himself between them. She was acutely aware of the rigidity of his manhood pressing against her. Ah, yes. His hands explored her while she arched and twisted in approval. His mouth trailed along her skin with as much enthusiasm as his hands. Her trust in him complete, she joyfully surrendered her person to his onslaught.

This was her husband. This was Garrett. Yes.

Letting her knees fall apart further, she set her heels upon the mattress. Finally, Garrett reached between their bodies to touch her, there. Yes, there. His fingers explored and drew lazy circles around her opening. This caused her to want to draw him inside. She was all too aware of an emptiness that only he could fill.

And then he shifted so his sex poised to enter. Reaching down, she wrapped her hand around him and squeezed very lightly. He was all silken hardness. Holding himself above her with his arms, Garrett gazed down at her with half-closed eyes. "If you keep touching me like that, this isn't going to last very long," he said hoarsely.

She gave him one more gentle squeeze and then removed her hand.

And then he pressed himself inside her.

She let out a whimper. For she'd experienced a flash of pain when he'd pushed through her barrier. Hearing her startled cry, Garrett stopped moving and kissed her eyes and temples gently. He would wait. "Oh," Natalie said softly.

He pulled himself back out and before she could move, pushed himself in again, this time deeper. But he still hadn't entered fully.

"Oh," she breathed again.

Once more, he withdrew and then entered her completely with one firm stroke.

"Do you want me to stop?" he asked softly. "Tell me if we need to stop, sweetheart."

"Oh," Natalie replied, feeling an overwhelming tenderness. "No." And she pushed up with her hips, as though she could bring him deeper. He required no further encouragement.

His movements were long, and deep, and oh, so satisfying. She allowed his rhythm to guide her own. It was the ultimate surrender. She would have permitted him to do whatever he wished while she clung to him wantonly. *Garrett, my husband*. Her head fell back as he pressed his face into the side of her neck, both of them nearly panting.

The waves of pleasure building inside her were not so unfamiliar this time. She knew what was coming, and she welcomed it. She focused on his movements, how he seemed to have become an actual part of her physical person. He moved himself *inside of her*!

"Oh," she cried out as the sensations engulfed her. "Garrett, please." She clenched her inner muscles around him as his thrusts grew more powerful and more intense. The raggedness of his breathing increased as did the pace of his strokes. Her entire being overflowed with his passion. It was as though he would touch the innermost core of her body. A place only she and God knew existed.

And just as Garrett pressed forward with one last thrust, a surge of ecstasy pulsed from her loins to every inch of her skin. Good heavens. Garrett! Good heavens!

Garrett let out a guttural moan and held himself rigid. As awareness returned, she felt a heat deep inside. Awestruck, she absorbed the sensation. That must be his seed.

"My God, Natalie." His entire body relaxed now. He felt heavy upon her, but she welcomed his weight. They were still joined. His face was buried in her neck, her legs loosely wrapped around his thighs and waist. She felt his hot breath against her skin.

He pressed a soft open-mouthed kiss onto her shoulder. "How have I come to be so lucky? You are amazing—so brave, so beautiful—my angel." She felt boneless as he trailed more kisses around her ear. "I love you," he said softly. And then he lay still as well.

"Thank god I didn't marry Cortland," she said in wonder and felt Garrett chuckle. His face lay on the pillow beside her. She turned and studied him.

He was delightfully mussed. A droplet of sweat trickled down his brow. She could not resist and leaned forward to taste it with a flick of her tongue.

"You are quite pleased with yourself, then? For changing your mind?" His eyes danced with merriment as he watched her response.

Natalie narrowed her eyes as though in deep consideration. Finally, she stifled a yawn and answered,

Annabelle Anders

"Well, it is…a lady's prerogative…"

Garrett leaned over and kissed her. She could feel the smile stretch across his lips as he murmured into her mouth, "Minx."

SURPRISE BONUS CHAPTER!

To read a surprise bonus chapter of *A Lady's Prerogative*, sign up for my newsletter and you'll automatically get an e-mail back with the link to read.

Sign up at:
www.annabelleanders.com

A word from the author...

I've been a writer all my life but never actually completed a manuscript until autumn of 2014. I've worked in numerous fields, even owned businesses, but nothing ever panned out for me. My default job was bartending. With my days free, something finally clicked and I figured out that I could write books.

With my husband and kids cheering me on, I've been writing nonstop ever since. Ironically, bartending is the perfect complement to writing. It requires me to get dressed, go outside of my home, and interact with other human beings.

Writing romance novels is a dream come true. I hope my books can provide a fraction of the comfort Mary Balogh's books have brought me.

~*~

Follow me on Facebook at
https://www.facebook.com/HappyWritingGirl

~*~

Sign up for my newsletter at www.annabelleanders.com

Thank you for purchasing
this publication of The Wild Rose Press, Inc.

If you enjoyed the story, we would appreciate your
letting others know by leaving a review.

For other wonderful stories,
please visit our on-line bookstore at
www.thewildrosepress.com.

For questions or more information
contact us at
info@thewildrosepress.com.

The Wild Rose Press, Inc.
www.thewildrosepress.com

Stay current with The Wild Rose Press, Inc.

Like us on Facebook

https://www.facebook.com/TheWildRosePress

And Follow us on Twitter
https://twitter.com/WildRosePress